ACT OF MURDER

JOHN BISHOP
2019

For information about this title, contact:
Attention: Permissions Department
legalquestions@codedenver.com

ISBN: 978-1-7968559-6-8

Printed in the United States of America

To my wife, Joan Bishop, for her superb editing and dogged persistence in getting this project completed, and to our son, Jim Bishop, for his miraculous novel restoration skills.

CONTENTS

CHAPTER 1

STEVIE

W hat I remember most about that day was the sound of a sickening thud. It was blended almost imperceptibly with the familiar screeching, both before and after the thud, of tires. I had been in the back yard watering our cherished potted plants and flowering shrubs. There were numerous clay pots of varying sizes filled with Mexican heather, geraniums, climbing ivy, and scattered white and purple pansies struggling to maintain themselves in the warming, spring weather. I dropped the plastic watering bucket and tore down the driveway toward the front yard, thanking God that the electric, wrought-iron gate was open, and praying that Mary Louise was not the source of the street sounds.

Although it wasn't but 150 feet or so from the backyard to the street, it seemed that I was moving in slow motion through a much longer distance. Our neighbor to the right, as we faced the street, was kneeling down over a small, blue lump. I remember initially thinking it was a neighborhood cat or dog with a sweater or something, but as I neared the scene, I saw that the blue lump was Bobbie's son, Stevie.

Bobbie was screaming, "OH, GOD! Oh, God! Jim Bob, is he all right? OH, GOD, JIM BOB, PLEASE LET HIM BE ALL

RIGHT!"

Stevie was not all right. I felt his tiny, ten-year-old wrist for a pulse. Nothing. I felt his left carotid artery. Nothing. I considered rolling him over on his back but was afraid that if he were in shock and not dead, I could paralyze him if his spine were fractured. Some of the other neighbors had arrived by then. I yelled for someone to call 911.

"Can't you give him mouth-to-mouth or something?" Bobbie had yelled. "You're a doctor for God's sake! DO something! Oh, please, do SOMETHING!" I felt helpless, and wished I could do something. Anything. A mother was losing her child, and all my years of medical training were, at that particular moment, useless. I waited with her and tried to keep her from moving Stevie. But how can you keep a mother from trying to shelter, protect, hide, and heal her child? Mostly, I waited with her and Stevie, feeling for his carotid pulse repeatedly, but my touch would not restore it.

It seemed like an eternity before the Houston Fire Department arrived, although later my neighbors would tell me it was only four or five minutes. The paramedics were affected as much as I was by the slight, crushed bundle. Although there was, thankfully, little external bleeding, they sensed the lifelessness as they gently moved him onto the stretcher and into the ambulance. He seemed so tiny to me as the paramedics deftly, and in a matter of moments, intubated Stevie and started an IV running. It appeared they injected his heart, probably with epinephrine, before they electro-shocked him. A heartbeat did not register on the monitor.

As I rode in the ambulance with Bobbie and the paramedics, I thanked God that Mary Louise was not the one being resuscitated. I remembered vaguely, her running outside during the commotion. Knowing her, and her composure and intelligence, she probably had called 911 before I had time to give those instructions. Her gentle hand had rested briefly on my shoulder as we loaded little Stevie into the ambulance. A great woman, that one. I was glad our only son, J.J., was away at college. At least he couldn't get run over in front of our house.

"You're a doc?" asked the least busy paramedic in the ambulance.

I nodded. "Jim Bob Brady."

All three continued to work on Stevie, attaching monitors, pushing IV drugs, and occasionally using the paddles to try to stimulate his heart into beating.

"What kind?" one of the other paramedics asked.

I thought that was a helluva time to be making small talk. Dead child, or presumably dead child. Mother, semi-hysterical, clinging to me. Ambulance speeding down Kirby, sirens blaring. Who cared what kind of doctor I was! Obviously, not a very good one. I had done nothing to help save that child. At that moment, I felt I should be anything but a doctor.

"Orthopedic surgeon, although this doesn't seem the time to discuss my career," I had snapped, in a semi-tactful way. The comment insured a silent journey the remaining five or six minutes to Children's Hospital.

Poor guys. We all become too calloused in the medical and surgical business, seeing murder, mayhem, and tragedy the way we do. But this was my neighbor's child, and I felt for her. And him. And me.

Fortunately, the traffic was light that Saturday afternoon. Normally, Fannin Street was stop-and-go in the several blocks known as the Texas Medical Center. As the ambulance pulled into the Emergency Center, people seemed to be everywhere. An injured child draws considerable attention, not that adults don't, but the Children's Hospital staff was impressively organized, showing efficiency, compassion, and skill. Within the next thirty minutes or so, they had, in fact, examined little Stevie and pronounced him dead. Apparently, the trauma team was composed of not only medical personnel, but of social workers, ministers, and counselors. Bobbie was, by then, shattered, requiring sedation. She was attended to, and I was left to give details of the accident. I fended questions regarding arrangements for the body and all the usual accompanying inquiries in such a situation.

I begged off from the full, frontal assault, explaining that I was a neighbor and had come along for the ride because I was a doctor, in case I could help. No, I didn't know anything, but if I could make a few calls, I could find some people to answer their questions.

I left the holding area in the back of the emergency room and returned to the lobby through the electric double doors. I assumed the personnel on duty had allowed me to remain in the NO VISITORS area, because they had heard from the paramedics that I was a physician. I was surprised, dressed as I was, in baggy shorts and a not-so-clean T-shirt. I had been dressed for gardening, not doctoring and death. The lobby was fairly empty except for a few sick children and their over-wrought parents. Not wanting to search for a physician's lounge and the privacy it would afford, I used a pay phone to call home. I had to borrow a quarter from a phone neighbor.

"Hello?"

"It's me."

"How are you holding up?" Mary Louise asked.

"I'm all right, other than feeling useless. Stevie's dead. Seems he was killed instantly. The chief pediatric surgeon thinks his chest was crushed. Ruptured heart. They'll have to do an autopsy to know for sure. Bobbie collapsed. They have her on a stretcher in one of the exam rooms, sedated. They've been incredibly kind and attentive."

"I feel so sorry for her. Is anyone else there yet?"

"Well, that's one reason I called. The hospital staff is asking all kinds of questions. The police will want to talk to witnesses. Someone needs to be here who knows more about their personal lives and preferences than I do. Do you know where Pete is?"

"He's on his way. He was working at the office. He's involved in some big trial that starts Monday. At least that's what the Mullens told me. I called a few of the neighbors, and they called a few more people, and so on. You know how the network is around here. Bobbie's sister should be there soon, and Pete, God help him, should be there any minute." She paused. "Do you want me to come and get you?"

Great, Brady, I thought, you even forgot you have no car.

"No, that's all right. I'm going to hang out here until I see Pete,

4

or someone else I recognize, and see if I can help out with anything. I'll see you as soon as I can. Oh,...one more thing. I love you. For a long five seconds or so, I thought it might have been you out in the street."

"I'm still here, sweetie. I love you, too."

As Pete, Stevie's dad, and the other's arrived, I basically directed traffic and answered their questions as best I could. When I felt that I had done enough, I walked outside. The paramedics were still hanging around the Emergency entrance. I apologized for my rudeness in the ambulance, but they seemed to understand. They kindly offered me a ride home.

On the way, two of the men sat in the back with me and made small talk. About doctor stuff. I asked if either of them smoked. They looked at each other, laughed, then individually brought out their own packs of carcinogens. As we all lit up, I hoped that the oxygen had been turned off.

CHAPTER 2

DETECTIVE SUSAN BEESON

After a tender moment with Mary Louise, I found myself sitting in my favorite place of repose. I enjoyed my quiet times in the back-yard, under the ceiling fan, in the white cane rocker on the back porch. I relished an ice-cold beer and treated myself to a Marlboro Light. I had quit smoking three years before, but still enjoyed one or two, or occasionally three, after work. On the weekend, I timed them like a symphony's production of a Beethoven concerto...I lit up at just the right time.

Ours was normally a peaceful neighborhood, composed of old-er homes, all two or three story, with reasonably wide streets sur-rounded by aging, massive oaks. It was a distinct pleasure to be able to live in that type of area in Houston, Texas, considering we were the largest city in the country without a district zoning ordinance. While there were many beautiful areas in which to live, most folks didn't par-ticularly enjoy having a convenience store and a service station (de-emphasizing the "service") across the street from where kids played.

The area known as Avalon was bounded on the east by Shep-herd Drive and on the west by Kirby Boulevard. Just north of Wes-theimer, it extended north five or six streets to San Felipe. West of Kirby was the priciest section known as River Oaks. That entire subdi-vision of Houston was developed years ago as an exclusive retreat from the hustle and bustle of daily life in a city made wealthy by oil and gas production. Most of the homes in River Oaks were built or owned by petrochemical producers, dealers, and "wildcatters," or by the descendants of the same. Other owners predominant in the area included those men, and occasionally women, who were instrumental in oil and gas deal-making, such as insurance magnates, bankers, and attorneys.

When the 1980's brought oil and gas prices plummeting, the complexion of River Oaks changed. While there still resided scions of family fortunes in old or new mansions, new entrepreneurs emerged as well: software inventors, computer-chip manufacturers, real estate developers, athletes, owners and player representatives of sports teams, and (my personal favorite) the many plaintiff's attorneys, who had profited from the "Great American Injury Giveaway." While a handful of successful doctors also lived there, that number was steadily diminishing with all the changing medical environment.

Those of us living in Avalon tended to be the same people who lived in River Oaks, only not quite as successful. The neighborhoods looked similar, although in Avalon mansions were few and far between. In River Oaks, there was at least one per block.

Avalon was comfortable, understated, and usually, very safe. One could work in the yard without designer overalls and, usually, could be assumed to be the homeowner. Unlike River Oaks. There, if you were lost and needed to ask directions, you were out of luck unless you spoke fluent Spanish or one of the Oriental languages.

On that particular day, I was unwinding in my modest, bricked backyard, complete with a small lap pool surrounded by our many flowers and pots, when the back door opened.

"There's someone to see you, Jim Bob," Mary Louise said. "Can I get you anything to drink?" she asked the young woman.

Our visitor looked at me and my beer. I finished it in one or two swallows. At least she couldn't have mine, I figured.

"No ma'am.

I'm on duty. I'd just like to ask your husband a few questions about the events of this morning," was the polite reply.

She appeared to be about thirty years old, dressed in tan slacks, matching jacket, a print blouse, and comfortable walking shoes. Her hair was blonde, cut short in a casual style.

"Dr. Brady, I'm Detective Susan Beeson, and I'm investigating the death of the Huntley boy."

I stood. "Have a seat, please. If you don't mind, I'd like to talk outside. The weather is just too good to miss."

"That's fine, sir. Can you tell me what happened this morning?" she asked.

I couldn't help but wonder what this nice, attractive woman was doing as a police officer. A detective, even, I thought, to myself of course. I almost felt a little sorry for her. Why would she be risking her life in a city like Houston. Was there a husband...and kids?

She sat. I talked. When I finished, she asked me what I thought to be a strange inquiry.

"Did you see the car? Or was it a car? Or some other kind of vehicle?" Detective Beeson asked.

"Well, I don't know that I remember a car. I was so caught up with worrying whether Mary Louise had been run over, and then worrying that Stevie was dead, and then worrying about Bobbie, and then worrying that I wasn't doing anything, that I don't think I noticed anything! Pretty stupid, huh?"

"No sir, not at all. In fact, in the blur of traumatic events, many surrounding objects or even people may not be consciously remembered," Officer Beeson kindly retorted.

This new, socially-aware and educated police force was a treat. I appreciated the fact that she did not make me feel ignorant or unobservant. After all, as an orthopedic surgeon, I should be attentive to details. At least, my patients would expect me to be so.

"Perhaps," she continued, "if you try to relive the events of the morning, you will remember something that is hidden in your psyche. It may reveal itself if you repeatedly render aloud everything you remember, to yourself only."

"I'll do my best and let you know. Did anyone else see anything?"

"Doctor, we've found over the years when studying profiles of witnesses, it's best not to confuse their natural memory banks with extraneous data from other witnesses. If you would, simply try to remember all that you can. Write it down, and when you feel that you have further information that would be helpful to our investigation, let me know."

"All right. I'll do just that."

I felt totally inadequate next to Susan Beeson. Had she ever heard of Steven Seagal? Bruce Willis? I knew about those law enforcement officers. They were movie cops. But this one? She was something else. I was grateful, and pleasantly surprised. Of course, I had operated on the police chief. I wondered if she knew that, or if she was this way with all potential witnesses.

"I'll be leaving now, sir. Thank you for your time. Good afternoon," she said, shaking my hand.

After she was shown out the front door by my darling wife, Mary Louise joined me on the porch. She brought me another iced beer, and herself, a glass of chardonnay. We sat in silence for a moment.

"Beautiful day, except for poor Stevie," Mary Louise said. "You know, we have to go over there tonight. Pay our respects. See if we can do anything."

"Yes, but I hate it. I hate death and dying," I said. "That's why I went into orthopedics and not some other field full of sick people."

"I know, Jim Bob, but they're our neighbors. You'll just have to get through it. Put on your doctor face. Oh, never mind that. I know your doctor face. You act crazy up there at the hospital. My friends tell me all the time what a nut you are. They say it's a good thing you're a great surgeon, or you wouldn't have much business."

"All right. I'll go." I paused. "Did you see a car today?"

"Susan told me the same thing as she told you. My lips are sealed."

CHAPTER 3

VISITATION

As we dressed for the trip next door, I admired my wife of 22 years. Or was it 23? She was still quite the looker. Tall, five feet ten inches or so, buxom, with blonde hair that still looked as it did when we met. If she colored it, I couldn't tell. And, as it was with most women, or at least I assumed it was, she wouldn't say otherwise. Hazel eyes that penetrated to the soul. A woman you couldn't shock or even surprise. It was as though she always knew what you were thinking. Probably that, and maybe the buxom part, was what had attracted me to her most. I could say anything to her, as could my friends. Nothing bothered her. She wasn't judgmental at all, a good thing, with my history.

We shared a bathroom. It was her idea to remain close, thinking that sharing a bathroom was an intimate pleasure. It had always been my feeling that a bathroom should afford privacy, but she insisted that one could get the privacy one needed by simply closing the door when appropriate. She felt that the intimacy of the bathroom afforded pleasures not attainable spontaneously with separate bathrooms. And, as usual, she was correct. Especially on that particular evening. For some strange reason, the gravity of the events of the day had left me feeling amorous. Maybe it was my attempt to distract her sufficiently to avoid the sadness of tending to the Huntley disaster.

There was something special about watching the woman whom I cared for deeply get dressed, especially before she actually put on her clothes. With my sink to the left, hers to my right, razor in my hand, and not a stitch on either of us, I felt incredibly aroused--a situation one does not become distracted from easily. Perhaps a nuclear attack. With shaving cream on the half of my remaining unshaven face, I dropped the razor into the sink, and sauntered to my right with that "look."

"What do you think you're doing?" she asked lightly.

"I think I saw a mole on your back. I'm worried it might be melanoma. It needs attention. You don't mind, do you? After all, I'm a doctor. A surgeon even."

"Oh. I see you brought your, uh, scalpel along. Is it primed and ready for an operation?"

"Yes, ma'am, I'm ready for surgery," I stated matter of factly.

As I approached her from behind, she deftly reached around her thin waist, handled me with skill, and demurely leaned forward at just the right angle and brought me to her. May hands cupped her generous chest, and in a matter of minutes, although it was probably really seconds, it was over.

As she refreshed us both with a warm towel, she asked, "Feel better?"

"Yes, thank you. Except I don't have enough strength left to shave. Guess I can't go, huh?"

"I'll finish shaving you if you like, or you can start your beard again on just that side of your face."

"No way out of this, I guess. No matter what I say or do?"

"That's right, Jim Bob. We have to go, boy."

I finished shaving, we dressed and headed next door. I felt much better, though, and thought I could face the situation with maturity.

The street was full of cars. As we stepped off our front porch, we noticed the people coming up the Huntley sidewalk.

"Mary Louise, the house will be crazy. They won't even know we were there. Let's come back tomorrow. There will be less people, and they will appreciate it much more."

"Get your butt up there and through that door, and quit moaning about it. They will remember everything everyone said or did today, because their son died, and they will want to relish every detail, good or bad." She stated this with some authority.

As we walked in, several neighbors greeted us. Quite a few people must have been relatives, or friends unknown to us, but nonetheless, it was definitely a houseful. It was a sad situation, but with that many people, even quiet talking became loud. Pete Huntley greeted us shortly after our arrival.

"Jim Bob. Mary Louise. Thanks for coming." He hugged us both.

Men in Texas hug each other. Just friendship. Italians and Greeks have done it for thousands of years, why not us. He had the ruddy complexion brought on by crying and an alcohol flush.

"Can I get you all something? There's food everywhere, and you know where the bar is. I've been there a lot today," he said. "Bobbie's in the bedroom. She's not dealing with this well, as you might think. She keeps talking about how nobody did anything to save Stevie. I think she mentioned you, Jim Bob, and the paramedics. We've all told her he was probably dead instantly, and even the docs at Children's told her that. But, you know, she just wants to have that few seconds back when she took her eyes off him and he got hit. Jesus, how could anybody not stop, Jim Bob. I cannot..." With that, he broke down. Mary Louise held him for a while. He apologized, went to the bar, and wandered outside.

"You know you have to face her. It's time."

Mary Louise's message rang clear as to why she had insisted on our visiting that night. To bring it out in the open. To clear the air. I had to convince Bobbie that no one, not even the neighbor doctor, who was on the scene, could have saved him. It was important to her, and also to me. How had she known that when I hadn't?

"Bobbie?" I called as I entered the bedroom. An older woman, possibly her mother, was sitting by her in a chair. Bobbie was curled up on the bed. She was a mess. Normally, she was attractive. Auburn hair, a little short, five foot two inches or so, but vivacious and funny.

"Jim Bob, just leave me alone. You let Stevie die." Just the words I wanted to hear.

"No, I didn't, Bobbie. He was gone when I knelt down beside you and felt his pulse for the first time. Nothing anybody could have done at that point would have saved him. I want you to believe that. I would have done anything to have helped him if I could have. Do you know that?"

She sobbed. After a while, she reached out and squeezed my neck until I thought I couldn't breathe. I confess, I cried.

"Thanks, J.B., for coming and telling me that. I know you hate wakes. Mary Louise must have made you." Her face was expression-less, and I suspected it would be a long time before she smiled again.

About that time, Mary Louise came in. They hugged, they cried, they shared grief.

"We're going now," Mary Louise softly said. "Call if you need us."

"Bye. Thanks. And Jim Bob, thanks for being there. You did all you could. I know that. I just wanted you to tell me," she waved weakly, then lay back down in the fetal position. As we left, the older woman patted her.

On the way out, we paid our respects to family members, who we either knew or to whom we were introduced. As we walked out their door, down the sidewalk, and into our yard, I said, I thought gal-lantly, "I'm sure glad we went. It was the right thing to do."

"Sure was, sweetie. A good idea. Better always to get things out in the open, especially unpleasant things. Don't you think?"

I mumbled about how right she was, knowing that she was most always right and that she was wonderful. Without Mary Louise I would have been a bull in a china closet, maybe good-intentioned, but ineffective in my delivery. I put my arm around her, and kissed her cheek. We gazed up at the new moon. A beautiful night, and an incredibly sad night. Contrasts always puzzled me.

We went to bed and fell asleep in each other's arms. Once again, I appreciated the comfort and depth of our relationship.

CHAPTER 4

PONDERING

Sunday morning I awoke fairly early. Normally rising at 5 a.m. during the week, it was difficult for me to "sleep in" on the weekend. Mary Louise was sleeping soundly, so I got up, pulled on my robe, and stumbled down to make coffee. As it was brewing, I strolled outside to get the paper. The Houston Chronicle was on the sidewalk, fairly close to the house; the New York Times was on the grass, nearly at the street. As I retrieved the Times, I pondered the street scene from the day before. Thoughts of the tragedy, and Officer Beeson asking me to try to remember details lost in my subconscious, caused me to stop and do exactly what she had suggested.

As I was standing there, gazing into space, a car stopped in front of me. I noticed the tinted window of the fairly new BMW dropping. A familiar face appeared.

"Petit mal, Brady?"

"What?"

"You look like you're having a petit mal seizure. What are you doing?"

It was Bill Russell, a pediatrician with presumably the largest practice in the medical center, maybe the world. Maybe even the universe, if there were pediatricians on other planets. But then maybe other planets had conquered childhood diseases.

"Hey, Bill. I was just thinking about yesterday."

"The Huntley kid? Yeah, too bad. Better dead than a head injury, though. I've got too many of them now! Stay out of the street. You may be next! Gotta run. Early church. We're going sailing this afternoon."

With that, he accelerated, gunning his five-speed, seven or eight hundred something, with tires squealing. It was then that I realized what I had seen, or maybe heard, or maybe both. The squealing of tires! What was there? I pictured the street, Bobbie next to her son, a few neighbors running from the right, or east, the direction of Shepherd Drive. To my left, the Kirby side, there had been a car. No, a truck. Small truck. Red. Could that be right? A reduced-size pick-up, I thought. Not the regular, cowboy pick-up truck with gun racks on the rear window of the cab. Could be American or Japanese made. Everybody made them these days, and I didn't have the foggiest idea about truck brands and sizes any more. I hadn't owned one for fifteen years, at least. Not since I could afford something that didn't knock your teeth out when you went over the railroad tracks that intersected all over Houston.

I went back inside, poured myself a cup of coffee, and sat in one of the kitchen chairs that faced the backyard. After a few sips, I couldn't help but notice the birds gathered around the empty feeder and the cat hovering around the empty cat food bowl. I got up, prepared the cat food, and gathered the bird seed sack from the garage. I wondered if birds knew they were eating grass seed, a fact I had learned after I installed their bird feeder on the backyard berry tree in front of the kitchen window. Any bird seed left by the birds, and not scavenged by the squirrels, grew a patch of thick grass under the feeder. As I pondered this weighty subject, I reached down to pet the cat good morning and give her breakfast. I received her customary look...don't touch me, stupid.

Birds were grateful. Cats were...cats.

As I sat outside in my "spot," Mary Louise came out with her coffee, looking gorgeous as usual. When I arise, my hair sticks straight out of my head, my beard is grizzly, and I know my paunch has tripled overnight. Mary Louise looked like she stepped out of the makeover studio with her robe on. No shoes, but bright red toe nails.

"Morning, cutie," she said. "Already fed the troops?"

"Yes. The usual chirping from our winged friends, the usual rejection from Cat."

With those words hardly out of my mouth, the ungrateful cat demurely leaped into her owner's lap, laid down, and purred. Females. They all stuck together.

"Want me to get the papers, Jim Bob?"

"I got them already. They're on the cabinet."

"I really didn't notice. I'm still half asleep."

"As I was out in front, Bill Russell zoomed by on his way to church. I was staring into the street thinking about yesterday. He asked me if I was having a seizure."

"Cute. You weren't, were you?"

"No, I was trying to remember the events like the police officers suggested. I think I remember a small, red truck. Did you see anything, Mary Louise?"

"I'm not supposed to tell you, but no. I came outside after I called 911. By then, I don't think there was any street traffic. Are you sure about that truck? Which direction was it headed?"

"I'm pretty sure it was heading west toward Kirby. I remember the squealing. It's all pretty blurry, though."

"You'd better call Susan and tell her what you remember. Maybe some other people remember things as well. You never know what can come of small bits of information like that. Jim Bob? Are you listening?"

"Yes, but I don't want to be. It's Sunday. Day of rest and all that. I want to relax, read the paper, go for a walk, maybe go to a movie, eat sushi. You know, enjoy Sunday."

"It won't take that long. It's important. For Bobbie and Pete, and for Stevie's memory. And for you. You were the first one there after Bobbie. It's something you must do...today. Okay? I'll wait around for you, and we'll do everything you want to do, and maybe some things you want to do that you haven't thought about yet. Comprendé, señor?"

How could I refuse that offer?

"Okay, I'll make the call. Want some more coffee?"

"You buyin', big boy?"

"Yeah, buddy."

CHAPTER 5

A WALK

W e compromised. After drinking our coffee and reading the newspapers, I called the Houston Police Department. I asked for Detective Beeson, but was told that she was off duty. However, the duty officer informed me that the detective carried a beeper, and, from time to time, she did check in with headquarters. One way or the other, she would probably get back to me today. If not today, then tomorrow. Not wanting to limit my Sunday activities, I gave him our home number, my beeper number, and the cellular phone number--tools of the nineties. I could remember when no one wanted to be reached on their day off.

Mary Louise and I decided to take a walk. I decided to shave before we left, but my casual and often laid-back wife allowed as how that was silly. I allowed as how that if I ran into a patient, or got called in on an emergency, I needed to look presentable.

"You're sexier with a day's growth. Two is better," she said. "It turns me on. In fact, I may not be able to walk unless you...light my fire, so to speak."

Sometimes shaving and looking your best are not all that important. I lit her fire. Then I shaved, after we showered... together.

"I'm looking old, girl," I said afterward. "You're holding up much better than I am." I noted my receding hair line, with much more gray than brown. My sideburns, although short, were pure gray, as was the hair around my ears. I wore bifocals, even to shave. My mustache was mostly gray, and my beard, when allowed a few days growth, as on our ski trip in January, was also gray.

"You're still tall, Jim Bob, and your chest is great. I love that dimple in your chin, and your charming smile is irresistible."

"If you remember, I used to be six foot one. Now I'm more like five feet eleven and a half inches. My dad experienced the same thing. The older he got, the shorter he got. Even his chest got narrow. And he lost his teeth. You can't smile without teeth!"

"He died at seventy-six. His chest was still fabulous, just like yours. You know I love everything about you. Didn't I just prove that to you, you silly boy? And as for other women, do you really care what they think?"

What a question. Of course a man cared how he appeared to other women. I wanted to be thought of as attractive, even though my only additional interest was in knowing that I looked good to the opposite sex.

"I care for no one but you. You know that." I left out the silent soliloquy.

We dressed and went for a neighborhood stroll. Mary Louise would have preferred to really walk. Exercise walk. With her long legs and physical stamina, she could outdistance me in a few minutes. But being the kind soul that she was, she strolled. I huffed and puffed. I wore a pair of older shorts with a size 38 waist. I wished I had worn a newer pair. They had a 40 waist.

We walked west from Avalon toward Kirby, crossed the especially busy street for a Sunday afternoon, and walked down Ella Lee Boulevard toward River Oaks Boulevard. I had to admit to myself that "The Boulevard" was my favorite street. Stately mansions, always freshly painted, incredibly landscaped lawns with lush flower gardens year round. Houston's tropical climate allowed for great yards and landscapes. Except for a little cool weather in January and February, with only a rare freeze, we had eight months of hot, humid weather, two months of miserably hot, humid weather, and two months of great weather. October and March. We were enjoying the latter.

We strolled up to the River Oaks Country Club, at the north end of the Boulevard, circled around and went back east on Del Monte, crossed back over Kirby, and headed south on Pine Valley back into Avalon. The walk lasted an hour and a half or so. I feigned heat exhaustion, able to be revived only by a Miller Genuine Draft to be enjoyed only in my rocker, under the outdoor fan. My spot, my drink. I was disturbed by the ringing of the cellular phone.

"Dr. Brady, this is Susan Beeson. The duty officer at HPD said you called?"

"Yes, ma'am. I thought of something this morning that I had seemingly forgotten. I tried your technique. My neighbor thought I was having a seizure, but it seemed to work. I remembered that when..."

"Stop right there, sir. I want to hear this in person and make some notes. We interviewed some of your neighbors. Perhaps I can corroborate your remembrances and theirs, piecing together information we could use to apprehend the perpetrator. Are you available now, sir?"

"Well, we're sitting in the backyard having a little refreshment. You're welcome to join us. We're planning on having an early dinner, so it would be better if you could come now."

"On my way," she said and disconnected.

CHAPTER 6

DISCOVERY

Mary Louise answered the door and escorted the young detective into the backyard. I was still sitting in my chair, but sipping on my second beer. On ice, with a lime. One of the great inventions of the bartenders in Puerta Vallarta, Mexico. Only they used Corona, "la cerveza mas fina," as the bottle said. When in Texas, though, I preferred MGD, a recent commercial acronym that I thought quite catchy.

"Afternoon, Officer Beeson," I said. "Can we get you something?"

"What are you having, doctor?" She was casually dressed, in khakis and a light sweater.

"MGD lite, lime, on ice."

"If it's not too much trouble, I'll have the same, except Diet Coke."

That was Mary Louise's drink. At least she had good taste.

We made small talk for a minute or two while my wife kindly made herself and the policewoman their refreshments. Mary Louise also brought out a large bowl of tortilla chips and salsa. She made the best salsa. A perfect blend of tomatoes, onions, jalapeno peppers, pico de gallo, and who knows what else. Chilled. A true delight. I sipped and munched.

"Does this conversation need to be confidential between my husband and you? If so, I can retire to do indoor pleasures."

"Well, ma'am, if you have anything to add, I would prefer..."

"Listen, Detective, Beeson...by the way, what was your first name again?" I had said a little impatiently.

"Susan."

"Well, if you don't mind, Susan, I'd like her to stay. We did discuss our rememberings of the day, against your advice, and my wife came outside after the, uh, event had occurred. She heard the tires screeching, came to the front door, saw that there had been an accident, and immediately called 911. She then came out to the street, but by then had missed what I remember seeing. I prefer to have her with me."

Mary Louise smiled. I couldn't tell if it was an appreciative smile, or an "I wish you wouldn't have said anything, so I could take a nap" smile. Nonetheless, she stayed put.

"That's fine, doctor. Tell me what you saw, or think you saw."

I related my recollections of the red truck. It seemed minuscule when I told her about it, compared to the revelation it seemed when I told Mary Louise.

"I see. Doctor, I'm going to share some information with you that must remain confidential. It is essential to our investigation that you and Mrs. Brady be as cooperative as possible, and part of that is to not share information I deem necessary to divulge to you with anyone. And I mean, anyone. The assailant fled the scene of the crime, a crime against a juvenile. There is nothing more serious under the law than that. With all the gang-related killings in our cities, it is a social issue. This could be just that. It could have been an accident, with the driver simply too terrified to stop. It could have been more sordid, such as a premeditated hit-and-run, for reasons that we do not understand at this time. Do you see how complicated it could become? Do I have...the cooperation of both of you in this investigation?"

This had become serious. We said yes, with an obviously changed manner. It was an act of murder. No way around that. Whatever the reason, the fact that the driver of the car left the scene made it murder. Was it aggravated murder, or felony murder? I couldn't remember but was afraid to ask young Susan Beeson. She was smart, and I wanted to hold my ground with her. I would refresh my memory on the legal terminology later.

"We, meaning one other detective and several of our investigators, interviewed everyone that, to our knowledge, was actually at the scene. We also interviewed all the neighbors on this block that were home at the time, but who were not allegedly present at the scene."

Every statement a police officer or lawyer makes is hedged by the word allegedly. Imagine using that in the doctor business. I was the alleged surgeon who allegedly removed your appendix after the physical examination allegedly showed you had appendicitis.

She continued, "The information that we can substantiate is this. A small, red pick-up truck, short-wheel base, dark-tinted windows, with at least a 'C,' or 'E,' and a '7' on the license plate was seen on your street at about the time the Huntley boy was run down. It traveled west on Avalon from Shepherd Street to Kirby, then turned south. A thumping sound was determined to be associated with the car. We think this was the bass volume of the stereo system, turned up quite loud, since apparently, the windows were up. Essentially, that is all we have at this time.

"We have computers that can decipher all kinds of permutations and combinations based on registration information, but those parameters are not extremely helpful. Of course, what we have is better than nothing. We can gather a long list of potential vehicle owners with some combination or part of the data we have available, but in the length of time it would take to check all that out, the vehicle could be destroyed, repainted, or disguised with stolen tags. You see our problem?

"Also, in the course of the investigation, we have to delve into the background of the Huntleys, in the event that this is not a random gang killing, or an accident involving a panicked citizen, who may or may not come forward, depending on his conscience."

Ah. It came down to this. Investigating the Huntleys. It wasn't enough that their ten year old was dead, they had to be investigated. I was offended.

"What can you tell me about your neighbors that may be of help to us? I'm sure you're taking umbrage at my line of questioning, but I can assure you we want nothing more than to apprehend the offender and see him get his just reward. We will try to make this procedure as painless as possible to all involved, especially the Huntleys, but it is absolutely necessary."

Mary Louise and I eyed each other cautiously before I answered.

"Well, we bought this house in 1986. The Huntleys bought the house next door in 1991, I think. We thought at first that a developer was going to tear it down and build a spec house, but fortunately, the Huntleys spent about six months remodeling it before they moved in.

"It's customary for the folks on the block to have a party for new neighbors, so we met them...actually, we met them during the remodeling, but we came to know them after the block party. We knew them like most neighbors seem to know each other. You see them in the yard, make small talk, see each other at parties in the area. We occasionally went to dinner with them and the other couples that we know. That sort of thing.

"A couple of years ago, I guess, Bobbie called me one night and said that Stevie had fallen down in the backyard, and she thought his wrist was broken. I went next door, and in fact, he appeared to have done just that. She then told me that he had osteogenesis imperfecta, and that..."

"What was that again?" Officer Beeson asked.

"Osteogenesis imperfecta. It's a bone disease. There are five or six varieties, beginning with the most severe kind to the mildest kind.

The worst cases have bones so brittle that they break in the birth canal, and those babies are often stillborn. Other forms involve severely soft and brittle bones that require little or no trauma to break, but those kids are usually so severely crippled that they require custodial care. Some cases, like Stevie, have bones that may break easier than normal, but they can lead fairly normal lives, other than constantly worrying about being careful. Some of the kids seem to improve with age, and by the time they're adults, they are relatively normal, or at least, have the appearance of such.

"After that first time when I took care of him, he had probably two other wrist fractures, and one tibial fracture. The tibia is the shin bone."

"Do you normally take care of children, and specifically, children with this...bone problem?" she asked.

"No. I see some children, but mostly I have an adult practice. If Stevie had sustained a major fracture, or something that required surgery, I would have referred him to one of my associates who specializes in pediatric orthopedic surgery."

"I noticed, doctor, that the coroner's report stated that the child had on roller blades. Any comment about that?"

"Stevie, like all kids with an orthopedic problem, wanted very much to be normal. Pete and Bobbie had asked me what I thought about getting him roller blades for Christmas. I didn't really advise it, but I understood why they were asking me."

"What do you mean?"

"Well, they didn't want to create a problem for Stevie, but they wanted him to feel as normal as he could. I felt the blades added risk to his life, but told his parents that we, meaning us orthopedists, could fix just about anything we had to. I think they were acting as concerned parents. They loved that kid, best I could tell. He was an only child as far as I know."

"Anything to add, Mrs. Brady?"

"No." Mary Louise was painfully quiet.

"Well, I guess that's all for now. You've been very helpful. If you think of anything else, please call me. Thank you for your time." She handed me her card, and Mary Louise showed her out.

"You sure were quiet," I said to Mary Louise upon her return.

"You were doing just fine. And I really had nothing to add." She paused. "Everybody is a suspect until proven innocent these days. Whatever happened to 'innocent until proven guilty'? How did our society get so suspicious of everybody and everything?"

"I guess we've let ourselves down too many times, Mary Louise. Too many bad things have happened, and too many bad people have been allowed to get by with them."

She paused. "On the way to the car, Susan said you know her father. Stan Lombardo?"

"What? Police Chief Lombardo? My patient, Lombardo? Why didn't she say something to me?"

"I don't know. She told me, didn't she? I think she was being very professional. Let's change the subject. You hungry?" she asked.

"What time is it?"

"Jim Bob, I've known you for over 20 years, and every time I have asked you if you're hungry, you have always asked the time. Why is that?"

"Well, I ate a pound of your chips and salsa. Depending on the time, I want to know if I have one or two meals left to eat today. If I have two, I'll just have a sandwich. If it's say, after four o'clock or so, then there's only time for one, and I want sushi."

"Well, get dressed. We're having sushi." She went inside.

Oh boy, I thought. Miyako Restaurant. Lots of wasabi. I felt like having something spicy so I could set my tongue on fire. Maybe then I wouldn't have to talk to people about things I didn't want to talk to them about. Like children dying in the street, and parents immediately being suspects.

I labored over why Susan had not told me that Stan Lombardo was her father. Why Mary Louise, in private? Was I that difficult to talk to, or was she, as Mary Louise had said, just trying to be professional? My wife had the kind of face and spirit that people opened up to, so maybe it was simply natural for Susan to feel she could talk to her more intimately. I didn't know, and I decided I really didn't care. I was hungry.

CHAPTER 7

FRAN

T he sushi was cold and wonderful. Tekka maki, kappa maki, California roll, fresh tuna, and the best hamachi I had ever tasted. Miyako Restaurant was on Kirby almost at its intersection with the Southwest Freeway, also known as Highway 59. In a small five-story office building, it occupied the ground floor. With a black exterior and a pink marble facade, one had to look closely to notice the M-I-Y-A-K-O in foot-high brass letters. Once inside, after a taste of the food, it would be difficult to forget it.

As delectable as it was, however, the typical Sunday night blues set in almost immediately upon returning home. It was only a five-minute drive to the house, but in that short span of time, I began to think about Monday. I didn't so much mind work once I was there, I even enjoyed it most of the time, but Sunday nights were, for me, depressing. Stay home, rest up, get plenty of sleep, be ready for Monday. This schedule almost invariably resulted in insomnia, with its resultant sleepiness and lethargy the next morning. I assumed this to be a fairly common pattern, since most of the people I dealt with on Monday seemed to be in the same shape.

Mary Louise called the neighbors' home and spoke to a member of the Huntley family. The funeral service for Stevie was to be on Monday at ten o'clock, with the grave-site service to be held immediately afterward. The funeral was to be at George Lewis' Mortuary on Kirby, followed by the customary procession to Forest Lawn cemetery.

My sensitive wife informed me of the details and suggested I call my secretary to make arrangements with respect to my schedule. In other words, cancel all or part of the morning.

"You have to be there, Jim Bob," she had said.

Fran Makowski lived in Wharton, a small town about 50 miles southwest of Houston. As I fumbled in my Rolodex for her number, I realized that the only time I ever called her at home was in the event of a tragedy, the last time being two years previous when my father had passed away. Fran lived with her family outside of Houston, partly for the safety it afforded, and partly because it was far less expensive to live in an outlying community. I had never been to their house, but understood it to be very roomy. It sat on several acres of land that would have been impossible for her to afford in Houston, even with double or triple the salary she received working for our clinic.

She had worked for me ever since she graduated from high school, which would have been about twelve years. We had grown up only about ten miles from each other, in very small towns outside Waco, Texas. Waco is normally a peaceful family town and is best known as the home of Baylor University for most of us. For some, memories of the FBI business with David Koresh and the Branch Dividians tarnished that image.

Fran and her husband, who had been a police officer with HPD, moved to Houston after high school to get out of the small-town lifestyle and into the bright lights of the big city. I had done the same after college, except to go to medical school at the best, or at least one of the best, institutions in the country. We had both ended up in the Texas Medical Center in the University Orthopedic Group.

After completing medical school, internship, and residency in the University Hospital's Affiliated Program, I stayed on with the largest group of orthopedic surgeons in the city. I had been in practice for sixteen years, and Fran had been with me a large portion of that time.

She was what I called a "home-grown" girl, the kind that never goes beyond her raising in her attitude towards other people. She was great with patients, and they all loved her dearly. About five foot eleven, and skinny as a rail, she drank Dr. Pepper all day and, whenever possible, sneaked into the stairwell off the twenty-second floor to smoke her Salems.

Some years earlier, David Makowski, while on duty chasing a burglary suspect, was shot in the chest with a .357 magnum hollow-point shell and almost died. He retired from the force, and they moved to the country. Not that there wasn't crime in Texas country. But apprehending an occasional castle rustler was a bit different than battling the Uzi-armed gangs of Houston, or so David told me after he became an insurance salesman.

"Hey, girl. How was your weekend?"

"What's wrong?" That was the response I expected.

"Stevie Huntley was killed yesterday. Car ran him down in front of his house. Hit-and-run."

"You mean our Stevie Huntley? The OI?"

"That's him, Fran. Hard to believe. I was there when it happened."

"Tell me about it," she asked curiously, yet sympathetically.

I related my whole story, down to my visit with Officer Beeson.

"That's awful. I'm glad every day that we live out here in the sticks. Except on the way to the office, and on the way home."

That was a constant complaint and I didn't blame her. It was at least an hour drive each way, longer if traffic was bad, which seemed more often than not.

"Listen, Fran, I'm sorry to call you at home only when something bad has happened, but the funeral is tomorrow morning, and Mary Louise says I have to go. Do you have the book?"

"I always have the book, Pop!" I was only fifteen years older than Fran, but she called me "Pop" either out of affection, or because she thought I was getting old. It seemed that she had only called me that the last two or three years.

"You have three cases in the morning, and office booked to start at one o'clock. What time is the funeral?"

"Ten. Graveside to follow. I need to be out of the hospital by nine-thirty, and can probably be back by twelve-thirty, one at the latest. Can you fix it?"

"Sure, Pop. You first case is a total knee, then a bunion, and last you have to re-debride the tibia on Mr. Sanders."

"Well, I can do the knee. Reschedule the bunion ASAP, and I'll see how Mr. Sanders is on rounds in the morning. I might have to try to squeeze him in before I go, or do it after office. I'll let you know tomorrow. He's easier to move around, since he's in the hospital. God, I hope his wound gets better."

He had been wounded on the opening day of Spring Turkey Hunting Season, a big event in this part of the world. Mistaken somehow, by an over-zealous hunter, for a gobbler, he was shot in the lower leg just above the ankle with a .22 rifle. Nasty wound, nasty infection. Open fracture. Bad.

"I'll call the bunion at home and work her in this week. Not to worry. Let me know about Sanders. And get some sleep."

"Thanks. See you tomorrow, Fran."

"Bye-bye."

"Everything taken care of?" Mary Louise asked.

"I guess so. Fran always seems to have it together. I'm lucky to have her."

"And she's lucky to have you. I'm tired. Night, sweetie."

She leaned over and kissed my cheek, then rolled over, and, in less than a minute, she breathed deeply. I read for a while, felt sleepy, and turned out the light. And stared for a while, noting that each of the four posters of our very comfortable king-sized bed resembled church spires. I pondered people who could run down and kill a child, or who could mistake an adult male for a turkey gobbler.

CHAPTER 8

UNIVERSITY HOSPITAL

T he alarm went off at five. I must have been awakened from deep sleep, because I didn't know where I was. REM (Rapid Eye Movement) sleep is that deepest sleep required for normal mental functioning. Deprived of it, people in psychological studies have been shown to lose the ability to concentrate, become irritable, and even, on occasion, lose their minds. This state of deprivation of REM sleep is requisite training in a surgical residency program. Explains why most surgeons act the way they do.

I showered, dressed in my standard surgical greens, and went downstairs for coffee. Mary Louise came down and noted that I needed to take or wear a suit for the funeral. Such a creature of habit I was. Wearing greens like that. Not that I was trying to avoid the required events of the morning.

She brought me the appropriate attire, poured me a cup of coffee to go, patted my shrinking behind, and sent me on my way. I wondered why aging caused the firm, desirable fatty tissue in one's buttocks to move around to the waist. It seemed a universal phenomenon. A little humor from the anatomy gods.

I took the same route as always. South on Shepherd to University Boulevard, and straight into the Texas Medical Center. Taking up a full city block, the University Hospital was the cornerstone medical facility, with seven other facilities in the medical complex, which extended four blocks. With two medical schools, three nursing schools, a dental school, and a pharmacy school, it was the largest of its kind in the world.

The University Hospital complex was comprised of several different hospitals, including Children's Hospital, where Stevie Huntley had been taken, The Cardiovascular Institute of Texas, The Neurological Institute, Harris County Trauma Center, Orthopedic Hospital, The Cancer Institute, and University Hospital Central. Over 2,000 beds all under one roof.

There were four office towers connected to the various hospitals, where academic and private physicians had their offices. In the early morning March light, they cast an impressive glow in the eastern sky, especially the newest thirty-story tower. A small lighthouse capped that particular building, acting as a beacon to the world. And also to low-flying aircraft--especially helicopters landing at the University Hospital heliport. The heliport allowed quick and efficient transport of acutely ill and injured patients into the medical center, most of whom were directed into the University Hospital.

I entered the building, flashed my code card at the ever-changing security guard, and went up to the University Orthopedic Clinic. There were 33 orthopedic surgeons in the group, including subspecialists in every remote area of the human anatomy. The clinic now encompassed four floors of the newest tower of the University Towers complex. I struggled my way through the two key-code-card systems to get back to my private office area.

My desk, as usual, was jammed with undone paperwork. No matter how late I worked on Friday afternoon, the desk gremlins managed to re-cover my desk by Monday with paperwork that I had never seen. I had yet to determine how a surgeon could see patients, make rounds at the hospital, operate on folks who needed operating on, and be left with several feet of paperwork daily from insurance companies, all demanding completion of their all-important forms prior to fulfilling their own obligation to pay said patients' medical bills. It, the massive mound of word-processed material that was filtered and stacked on my desk daily, continued to grow and prosper.

I carefully lifted the various piles of debris, found my hospital patient list, and gently extracted it without disturbing any of the litter. Fran always tried to hide my list, so that I would have to dictate or sign forms before finding it. I was too smart for that. I then headed back down the elevator to the second floor, where all the crosswalks to the four office buildings met and connected to the various hospital sections comprising the massive University Hospital.

My patients were generally in the Orthopedic Hospital, with patient rooms on the fifth, sixth, seventh, and eighth floors. Physical therapy was a huge layout, accommodating both inpatient and outpatient services and taking up the fourth floor. Surgery covered the third floor, with a large central lounge, for physicians and operating room personnel, and a small cafeteria. I took an elevator to the eighth floor, intending to start there and work my way down to six via the stairs.

I strolled to the central desk of the nurses' station and said good morning to the 11 to 7 shift, ladies I had known for years and who, unlike the security guard, never seemed to change. As usual, they were stationed in various chairs, resting up after another busy night. It was six o'clock, and they all had about an hour to go.

"Morning, ladies. How was the night shift?"

"Morning." A more or less unison reply.

"Okay."

"Crappy."

"God-awful!"

"Hey, Doc Brady!"

An obviously varied response, relative to which patients one had to care for during the night.

Before I could ask how my patients were, especially

Mr. Sanders, one of the nurses asked what I thought about my picture in the paper.

"What did you say?"

"Doc, your picture is on the front page of the city section of the Chronicle. With that little kid that was run over. Didn't you see it?"

I never read the paper in the morning. If I drank coffee, sat at the kitchen counter, and read the paper, I'd never get to work.

"No. Do you have it?"

"Sure." With that she whipped out the morning paper, pulled out the city section, and pointed to a photograph, albeit grainy, of Bobbie, Stevie, and myself in the middle of the street just after the accident. I did not remember any reporters or photographers being there at the time. The quality of the picture was poor, so I assumed a neighbor had taken it. The age of home video and photography. Newspapers and magazines, I understood, paid a lot of money for grizzly scenes they had not had an opportunity to cover.

I was unnerved. I scanned the article, noting some quotes from neighbors who had apparently lingered after the ambulance had left. I was mentioned as the next-door neighbor and the child's physician. I hated publicity. Avoided it like the plague.

"Let's make rounds," I said, my mood changing after seeing my picture. There was no more discussion at the nurses' station.

The patients left in the hospital over the weekend were all doing well except for Mr. Harold Sanders. Sixty-four years old, and an adult-onset diabetic, he was not faring well after his gunshot wound to the leg. According to the chart, he was still spiking temperatures to 102° to 103° and had chills and a consistently increased heart rate.

"How's it goin', ol' boy?" I had asked, knowing the answer.

"Not good, Doc. I feel like shit, and my leg is killing me. Are you going to cut it off today?"

"No, sir. I'm going to clean it out again and try to get rid of the infection if I can. With your diabetes and decreased circulation, it's tough. We're all doing our best, though."

I had called in all the appropriate specialists. The chief of Infection Control was handling the antibiotics, and the chief of Endocrinology, Sanders' personal physician, was trying to keep his diabetes under control, a virtually impossible task considering the severity of his infection. Mr. Sanders was quickly developing osteomyelitis of the tibia, a bone infection that, in a diabetic with poor circulation, was next to impossible to cure. Maybe he was right. Maybe he needed an amputation.

"I won't lie to you. The leg is bad. It may need to be removed if the infection gets any worse, or if you go into what's called septic shock," I said.

"What the hell is that?"

"If the bacteria in your leg get into your bloodstream, you become septic. It makes you real sick. Sicker than you are now. Your heart and circulatory system may shut down, and you, well,..."

"Bite the bullet, huh, Doc?" He gave a short laugh. "Pun intended."

"Yes, sir. That's about it. So, I'm going to do my best, and you hang in there, and you and I will give it our best shot. Okay, Mr. Sanders?"

"I like that, Brady. Give it our best 'shot.' Pretty ironic. That's one for you." And with that, he weakly put out his hand. I shook it and left the room, his nurse charting yet another note.

Nurses, also, spent far too much of their valuable time fighting massive reams of paperwork, which left precious little time to do what they had chosen to do...take care of patients. They had always been my best allies. If they thought you weren't doing the right thing for the patient, it was not uncommon for one of them to get right in your face and tell you what they thought. If they liked you, thought you did a good job, and felt you had the patient's best interest at heart, they would literally fight for you. I decided long ago that if there was another war and I had to participate, I would only go with a platoon of nurses. At least I'd have an edge in survival. Against any enemy.

CHAPTER 9

ROUNDS

I completed rounds, noting that my first surgical patient, a hip replacement, had already been gurneyed down to the operating room, or so the nurses had said. Knowing Mrs. Barnes, she could be anywhere, I thought. By then, it was almost seven o'clock, so I headed down to surgery. Greeting various nurses, operating room technicians, and early-rising surgeons such as myself, I arrived at the pre-operative holding area to identify Mrs. Hattie Barnes. Although I knew her well, "identification" was necessary before she, or any patient, could be brought into the operating room and anesthetized. I found her sitting up on the stretcher. She gave me a stern look.

"Where have you been?" she demanded. "It's after seven o'clock, time for my surgery, and you just now show up? Are you awake enough to fix this bad hip, or do we need to make it a little later so Jim Bob can have his coffee?"

I couldn't help but laugh. Here was this crusty, 76-year-old grandmother sitting up with a silly paper hat, a requirement for all patients, and much more ridiculous than the one I wore, and wearing a surgical gown that would barely cover a chill.

"No, ma'am. I'm wide awake. Been here since six. I was delayed by another patient. Sorry, but I didn't get to your room until after the nursing assistant picked you up. Don't worry. I'll make it up to you. You'll get a Bo Jackson hip."

She was an avid baseball fan and continually amazed that Bo could pay ball with that "plastic and steel contraption," as she called it.

"That's more like it, young man. Now get this show on the road. I never miss 'As The World Turns.' I expect to be in my room, and awake and alert, by twelve-thirty. Understand?"

With those comments, she reached over with her aged, calloused hands, gently picked up my right hand, brought it to her cheek, and briefly hugged it. I patted her back with my left hand, and we shared a moment of tenderness between patient and surgeon. That demonstration, although brief, of the emotional bond we had, again reminded me of the best reason I could think of to get up every morning and go to work.

As the nurses wheeled her off to surgery, I was reminded of our first meeting. Five or so years before, she had been out in the brush with a mother cow who was having a difficult delivery. Hattie owned a large cattle ranch in Cat Springs, a farming and ranching community 80 miles west of Houston. She and her long-time vet struggled for an hour or so, and finally got the calf out intact. As she stood up from her crouched position, she joyously danced a little jig, promptly slipped in the slick afterbirth, and fell onto her right hip. The vet carried her to his truck and hauled her to the emergency room at University Hospital where yours truly happened to be.

Normally, a patient arriving at the ER with an orthopedic problem would be seen by the emergency room physician and referred to an orthopedic surgeon on a rotating "on-call" basis, unless the patient knew someone, or unless the treating family practice doctor had referred the case to a particular surgeon. That was an especially busy Saturday, and after the x rays had been taken, showing the hip fracture, the doctor grabbed me and asked me to take care of the problem for him. I did, and the Barnes-Brady relationship began.

Unfortunately, Hattie had broken her hip at the femoral neck, the thinned-out area just behind the femoral head, or ball portion of the hip joint. It fit into the socket formed from a depression in the pelvic bone. The femoral neck area has a tenuous blood supply, and when the fracture occurred at this level, the small vessels were disrupted. This caused a disease called avascular necrosis of the femoral head, which resulted in severe degeneration of the bone. It became chalky and disintegrated, causing severe arthritis of the hip joint.

Mrs. Barnes had endured this painful condition for over four years, since her hip started degenerating within six months after the fracture. She had used a cane, taken Advil by the handful, and intermittently used what she called "Hank's brew." That was her name for Jim Beam whiskey, named for a song that made Hank Williams, Jr. famous.

While the nurses and anesthesiologist prepared Hattie for surgery, I grabbed a quick breakfast in the lounge. Greetings were exchanged between myself, a few nurses, and quite a few doctors for a Monday morning. As I scarfed down Mexican scrambled eggs with picante, one the neurosurgeons sat down beside me.

"How's it going, Brady? Have an exciting weekend? I guess you did, what with your picture in the paper and all. Did you get to do a little 'mouth-to-mouth'?" he chuckled, a little too sarcastically for me.

"Too bad you weren't there. You probably could have saved him, since you've always seemed to think you could walk on water. This was a ten-year-old kid, for God's sake. My neighbor's kid. Have you lost your sensitivity completely, Paul?"

He looked at me without saying a word. I stared back. In a different setting, we would have come to blows.

"Sorry," he said. "I've got an astrocytoma to do. Malignant probably. A woman thirty-three years old, four kids. She's dead, but the family doesn't know it, or won't accept it. I'm supposed to be the big hero, take out the tumor, cure the girl. It's all bullshit. I'll go in, remove as much of the cancer as I can without totally destroying her brain cells. Her head will be shaved, she'll wear a stocking cap, and we'll poison her with chemotherapy. She'll actually get better for a few months, but then she'll go downhill and crash and burn in six months to a year. The family will want me to do something, but there will be nothing to do except watch her die. I'll get paid a small fortune by some insurance company for an eight or ten hour craniotomy, and all I'll have to show for it is a dead mother of four. Ain't it a bitch?"

That was a little too much for me at that time of the morning. Paul Gertzbein had been the smartest guy in our medical school class and always planned on being a brain surgeon. It was too much death for me. I hated that service.

"Good luck, Paul," I said, patted him on the back, and headed for the operating room.

CHAPTER 10

OPERATING ROOM

I wound my way through the circuitous green-tiled hallways of the Orthopedic Surgical Center toward my designated operating rooms, 35 and 36. There were at least 50 surgical suites of varying sizes and shapes, allowing the luxury of assigned operating times in specific operating rooms for every full-time staff surgeon. I was assigned those two rooms Monday through Friday, 7:30 to 12:00. I spent Monday through Thursday afternoons in the office seeing patients. Friday afternoons were spent catching up on the dreaded paper "monster," taking care of emergency problems, or seeing after my own mental health.

One of the advantages of using the same operating rooms was having the same crew. Nurses and nursing assistants who knew the routine procedures and required surgical instruments allowed a smooth flow during and between cases.

As I stood outside Room 35 and watch Hattie Barnes being prepped for surgery, I scrubbed my hands with Betadiene soap and mentally planned her hip replacement. I always practiced the operation I was about to do in my mind while I scrubbed. That saved time and improved my concentration and effectiveness once the case had begun.

"Mornin', Doc. What do you want to hear?" Loretta, the head nurse, stuck her head out the O.R. door and asked.

"We have that new Willie Nelson C.D., don't we? Moonlight something?"

"You bet. I'll get it started. Sorry about your weekend."

"You heard, huh?"

"Heard? Man, everybody's talkin' about it. Your picture was in the paper. Just what you need on the weekend after this business we're in...excitement. Get on in here!"

I walked into surgery, said good morning to all present, dried my hands, gowned and gloved, and started. I had replaced so many hip joints that I thought I could do it in my sleep. Once the wound was opened and bleeding was under control, I used an electric saw to cut through the diseased femoral head and neck and then removed it. Reamers were also used to prepare the socket, or acetabulum, in the pelvis for the new plastic cup that fit around the stainless steel, titanium, or ceramic ball. The procedure went as smooth as silk, and we all sang along to Willie while I closed the wound. I didn't make small talk during the actual "meat" of the operation. Everyone knew that and respected it. The music was always on, though.

About halfway through Hattie's hip replacement, Mr. Harold Sanders was sent for. When I finished her surgery, I stepped outside and went into Room 36 to identify him. He looked especially bad in the bright lights of the operating room.

"You ready, young man?" I asked him.

"Best compliment I've had today. Do whatever you have to do, Dr. Brady. I trust you."

I nodded, and the anesthesiologist put him under. Once I started the surgical debridement of his leg, it became apparent that the infection had spread during the last few days. I removed quite a lot of diseased and non-viable muscle and bone. He would probably lose his leg, I thought; and I didn't want to wait around too long to do it. There was precious little blood flow during the case.

Once I had packed the wound open and dressed it, I stepped outside, dictated the operative reports for the hospital record, called the families, and headed back over to my office to change into funeral attire. Mary Louise and I had arranged to meet at the funeral home. On the way, I used my cellular phone to call the Cardiovascular Institute.

I wanted Mr. Sanders seen by a blood vessel surgeon to determine if there was any way to improve the blood flow to the leg. I told the secretary I would talk to any surgeon who was available, since it seemed to me that those guys were always in surgery. I was surprised when Jack Harris came to the phone.

"Jim Bob. What can I do you for?"

"Hey, Jack. Did you boys shut down over there or something? I don't think I've ever talked to you during daylight hours."

"Hell, Brady, they've totally wiped out my day. The air filtration system went on the fritz this morning. Nothing's sterile. They got a crew in here trying to clean everything up, but it's a God-awful mess. Won't be able to cut for at least three more hours. What's up?"

I gave him a brief scenario of Mr. Sanders' problem, and told him what I wanted him to do.

"And while I'm at it," he said, "I'll take a flying leap over the sun! You want a miracle, Jim Bob. We can't run a graft through an open wound. He might get better with a sympathectomy, but in a diabetic, that's unpredictable. You know all this. We spent a year together in residency until you decided to become a carpenter."

"Look, Jack. Go see him. Do what you can do. He's a nice guy. Besides, I think he's on the board or something. I remember that you're interested in those politician-type patients, aren't you?"

Jack had, in fact, been president of the medical staff and of the Harris County Medical Society. An upwardly mobile surgeon, destined for national prominence.

"Oh, shit. Not that Sanders! Harold Sanders? That guy owned, or still owns, American General Life Insurance. He's chairman of the hospital board, Brady. Why didn't you say so?"

He hung up the phone. I suspected he was trotting over to the recovery room at that very moment. I didn't really care what button I had to push, I just wanted someone skilled to see Mr. Sanders. Jack was perfect; political, but an excellent surgeon. If there were any way to help the patient and make himself come out ahead, Jack would find it.

CHAPTER 11

FUNERAL

I arrived in the foyer of the George Lewis Funeral Home minutes before the ten o'clock service was due to start. Mary Louise was waiting patiently.

"I was starting to worry about you," she said. "We'd better find a seat."

She gently clasped my hand, and we found a seat in the rear of the chapel. After all these years, her touch still excited me, comforted me, consoled me. The aisles were filled to the point that an usher had to ask people to move down somewhat to accommodate us. I gazed at the crowd. I knew people here and there, but it was impossible to see the immediate family. They were sequestered in a small alcove to the right of the pulpit. The casket was closed, with flowers atop the lid. There were wreaths packed all along the front and sides of the chapel.

"Sorry I'm late. I had two cases to do."

"You're not late. I'm glad you spared the time. Pete and Bobbie will appreciate it."

"I doubt they'll know I'm here, or you for that matter, M.L."

"Sure they will. When all the dust settles, and everybody goes back to their own lives, thanking God that it was someone else's child that was killed and not their own, they'll read the registration book and see that we were here. I signed it before you arrived."

As the minister stood to begin the service, I heard a slight commotion behind the closed chapel door. Since we were in the back row, I could hear a woman arguing to be allowed in. An usher said something about the fact that the funeral had already begun, and that the family and friends should not be disrupted. That was funeral home policy.

He apparently lost the argument, because at that moment the door opened to admit a woman dressed in a short, black dress with hat and veil. She was very quickly shown to a seat in the second row from the back, opposite us. She looked familiar, but I couldn't see her face. I noticed she appeared to cry throughout the service, dabbing her eyes constantly. For some reason, she distracted me from the words of the minister. Maybe the situation was too sad to deal with, and I subconsciously shut him out and focused on her. Mary Louise, however, seemed to remain focused on the service, tightening her hold on my hand periodically.

It ended amidst a great deal of crying. The family passed by the casket on their way out through a side door, on the opposite side of the chapel from where they had been sitting. Pete was literally holding Bobbie up. I wondered about God, the universe, and innocent dead children. Questions unanswered from my childhood continued to plague me in adulthood. It seemed that every day, I witnessed a new trial, tribulation, or something that would shake the faith of a saint. Someday, I thought, I would have to deal with all that.

As we exited, I turned to see if I recognized the woman who had arrived late. The crowd, streaming to the front to line up for the procession to the burial service at the cemetery coalesced and blocked my view. I needed to get back to the office. Mary Louise agreed to go to the cemetery without me and assured me that it was all right. She was glad I made it to the service, and she gently kissed me good bye.

I walked the two blocks to my car, on a side street off Kirby.

The wonderful smell of Carrabba's Italian Ristorante filtering out into the street beckoned me. A little Penne Mary Raia, with a house salad and a glass of chianti. Hard to beat, even harder to pass up. My lawyer and banker friends routinely went to lunch. They called it "business." I hadn't been out to lunch on a weekday when I was working since I had started practice. Fifteen years without a proper lunch during the week. That alone could produce mental anguish.

While I pondered the weighty decision of penne or tagliarini, I noticed the woman in black walking behind me, on the sidewalk on the opposite side of the street. As I approached my car, she stepped into the street and unlocked a fairly new-looking, bright red Porsche. My friends who drove them called that color "arrest me red." Appropriately named for the attention it drew from the Houston Police Department. She dropped down into the car, started the characteristically rumbling engine, and spun out into the street. I feigned having trouble getting my car open in order to try to see her face, but with the dark, tinted window, there was no way.

I got into my car, an '84 diesel Mercedes, and headed back to the office. I wished I had seen the woman's face. At that moment, I also wished for her car, considering the way mine was sputtering. But most of all, I desperately wanted my penne pasta.

CHAPTER 12

OFFICE

It was a harried afternoon. Monday brought the usual weekend-warrior injuries and post-operative problems that always seemed to develop when I was off. In addition, I saw the typical array of orthopedic maladies that found their way to my office. Although the University Orthopedic Group was an association of orthopedic surgeons representing the various orthopedic subspecialties, we all routinely saw general orthopedic problems as well. While I spent most of my time treating arthritic problems involving the hip and knee, I, like my associates, also treated problems out of my specified area of expertise. The advantage of a large multi-specialty group is that one can refer a problem that he or she doesn't know how to treat, or want to treat for that matter, to a colleague.

Monday designated me primarily a triage doctor. I sent numerous operative cases to my associates, while I treated my arthritic patients with anti-inflammatory medication, since few were ready for a joint replacement. With the funeral interspersed between surgery and a busy office, the afternoon left me drained. I spent a traumatic hour or so trying to thin out the mass of paper on my desk. In the midst, Fran came in and gave me my patient list for hospital rounds and my surgery schedule for Tuesday.

"I had to add the bunion we cancelled for today to tomorrow's schedule. Sorry. I know that makes it busier than you like," she said.

She was right. Two hip replacements, one knee replacement, and the added bunion.

"And I'm supposed to see patients at 1:00?"

"You'll make it. You're good, aren't you?" With that, she waved and left for the drive home to Wharton.

At that moment, I didn't feel "good." I felt tired. I gave up on my desk work and went over to the hospital to see Hattie Barnes and Harold Sanders. Hattie was doing great. Said she watched her soap opera and then spent the afternoon napping.

"Now my hip hurts like hell! I need a shot, or some Hank's brew, but I guess that's out of the question?"

"Yes, ma'am, it is, but I'll get your nurse. Have a good evening."

I got her nurse as she had asked, then went to see Mr. Sanders. He looked sick, and he was somnolent. His wife and daughter were there, and we briefly discussed his condition and prognosis. They were very understanding, saying that they felt he was getting the best care possible. They made a point of telling me that they appreciated me and what I was trying to do. At least, my mood improved. His wife, also, mentioned that Dr. Harris was planning a sympathectomy for Tuesday or Wednesday if it was all right with me. Of course, it was, and the sooner the better.

"What do they actually do in that operation?" Mrs. Sanders asked.

"Well, the sympathetic nerves are responsible for opening and closing the blood vessels. If you cut the nerves, the vessels are open, or 'on' all the time, which will help increase Mr. Sander's circulation, which will help heal the infection. We need all the help we can get right now to save his leg."

I explained it in fairly simple terms to help them understand it, thinking that Harris should have done that himself. But the cardiovascular boys didn't have time for the small stuff, like informed consent. I understood that. Most of their cases were life or death. If one of their operations wasn't successful, the patient died. But if the patient was going to die without the operation and the patient survived, then, as far as the family was concerned, the surgeon walked on water.

If one of my operations did not go well, however, the patient was crippled. In that case, rather than being a water-walker, I became submerged pond algae, answering to the plaintiff's lawyers, who lived on the other side of Kirby.

I pondered which of the specialties was better as I meandered the hallways toward the parking garage and home. I called Mary Louise from the car.

"Hey! What's for dinner?"

"Well, I've got a roast in the oven. Thought I would make a fresh green salad. How does that sound?"

"Good, but I'm dying for Carrabba's pasta. Can we put the roast off? I've been lusting after pasta since the funeral."

"How did the funeral...oh. You smelled it from the street. Sure we can. Roast beef sandwiches are one of your favorites. Maybe if you're a good boy, I'll make you a lunch for tomorrow. By the way, how was the rest of your day?"

"I'll tell you at dinner. You want to meet me there?"

"Why don't you pick me up. I need to talk to you about something involving Stevie Huntley. I'll be ready when you get here. Sound okay?"

"Sure. What about Stevie?"

"Let's talk over dinner. Come get me!"

She disconnected. I wondered what that was all about.

CHAPTER 13

BEVERLY RICHARD

As always, the parking attendant greeted us enthusiastically and shook my hand after opening the car door for Mary Louise. He never gave me a parking stub. I thought that we must both be very trusting souls. Me, with no parking stub to claim the car I intended to drive home. Him, with no way to identify the car if he suddenly lost his memory or his job during dinner. Neither possibility was likely, or so I hoped each and every time I turned over the car. But each and every time, he was there, as was the car, when we finished eating.

Carrabba's faces a small side street off Kirby between Richmond and Alabama. Wonderful green and white awnings cover a rim of outdoor tables. Inside, dark mahogany tables are packed fairly close together across from an open kitchen, leaving the aroma free to permeate at will. The place was packed, as usual, with people milling about outside waiting for a table. I charged up to the hostess stand, greeting Valerie, my patient, and asked for a table for two.

"Hi, Dr. Brady. I'm sorry, but it's so crowded now that I can't seat you for a little while. If you and your wife don't mind sitting at the bar, though, I can seat you now. A table will be, well, a little while. Sorry."

I think she was, although I wouldn't have minded cutting in line and getting seated before the "waitees." We took the immediate seating. Mary Louise loved the bar seats, since they stood right next to the open kitchen. We ordered the usual. House salad, fried calamari, penne for me, tagliarini for her, and a glass of house chianti for each of us.

As we sipped our wine and munched on tentacles, we exchanged stories about the day. She had gone to the gravesite service. Sad, but not too much to tell. When I asked her about the woman in black, who caused the disturbance at the funeral, she looked at me somewhat puzzled.

"You remember, the one who came in late and cried through the whole service? She walked down the same side street as I did on the way out. Drove a red Porsche. Targa, I think."

"Hmm. I didn't pay that much attention to her at the funeral, but she was quite noticeable at the cemetery."

"What do you mean?"

"Well, I think she must have been drunk, because she drove her car up into the grass. She hit a tree! The funeral attendants helped her out. She seemed to be all right, came over to the gravesite, and stood by herself. I noticed she left right after it was over. She spoke to no one. Her car seemed to run fine, but had a noticeable dent in one of the fenders. I think the right one. Who do you think she was?"

"I have no idea. I'll ask Pete about it in a few days. By the way, speaking of the Huntleys, what did you want to talk to me about?"

"Well, I had two visitors today. One was the detective, Susan Beeson. The other was a reporter from the Chronicle wanting to do a human interest story on Stevie, you, and..."

"Wait a minute. Why would a reporter want to do a story about me? By the way, my picture was in the paper today in the city section. You know I don't like publicity, Mary Louise. It's never good, even when that's how it's intended. You surely can't forget that mess with Beverly Richard. That's been what, eight years? It seems like yesterday." I paused. "Did you see that picture?"

"Jim Bob, before you get crazy on me, I do truly believe that the woman is honest and simply wants to write a story about the horror of a child being run down in the street, with the child's own doctor kneeling down beside him. The picture with you, Stevie, and Bobbie was moving, I thought. Would you just think about it?"

"Yes, but I'm not deciding anything tonight. I'm too tired. What did the detective want?"

"More questions. Anything I might have remembered since Saturday. Anything helpful about the way Pete and Bobbie had acted before or after. You know, general questions."

"General questions, my butt. Before it's over, I'll bet she figures out some way to blame the parents, so they won't have another un-solved hit-and-run on the books."

"Jim Bob, let's go home. You're exhausted. You aren't all that logical and rational when you get this tired. Come on, pay the tab, and I'll take you home and put you to bed."

And she did just that.

Unfortunately, I awoke at four o'clock in the morning, a full hour before the alarm was due to blast what I always considered gross-ly irritating music. The same music any other time seemed very pleas-ant. My first thought was of the Beverly Richard incident.

Pronounced "Re-shard," she had roots from southern Louisi-ana. Unfortunately, she was the nursing supervisor of the entire Uni-versity Orthopedic Hospital. She had started as a nurse in the operating room years before and, through a graduate degree that she supposedly had earned on sabbatical, and through connections to the administra-tion that were not clear to me, she rose quickly through the ranks to her current position. She also carried the title of Vice-President of University Hospital. Though there were many administrators with this title, she used it to her advantage in order to achieve autonomy over the entire nursing staff.

Nicknamed "The Shard," which was certainly appropriate, she

had been a thorn in my side as long as I could remember. She was probably forty, but looked much younger. She would be called attractive by an unbiased man; but to me, she would always be a mean-spirited woman, whose only concern was herself.

She had worked in orthopedics for a few years as an operating room nurse when I was first in practice. She was, as a staff nurse, basically rude and insensitive. She went by the book, whatever that meant, even if it inconvenienced you and your patient. She left for two or three years, then returned with a graduate degree and in a supervisory role in the operating room.

She was quickly promoted into management, and after only a year or two, she was given her current title.

Although we had never gotten along very well, our relationship took a significant downward turn one night eight years earlier. She was the on-call supervisor, a rotating obligation for all nursing administrators, when I had a problem with a patient. A young boy had been in a motorcycle accident, had broken both forearm bones, and had been admitted that afternoon.

During the evening, the floor nurses noted that his hand had suddenly become numb, whitish, and relatively pulseless. They had beeped me on a STAT basis, and when I responded, we agreed he must have a compartment syndrome. The forearm had apparently swelled so much, due to continued bleeding, that the circulation had almost been cut off. Knowing that this was a surgical emergency, requiring immediate fasciotomy to relieve the pressure, the nurses prepared him for surgery as they called me. I then called the O.R. to tell them I was bringing a STAT case down. The head nurse informed me that they were already running three rooms, all they had staff for. She needed permission from the administrative supervisor to call in another crew.

When she told me it was Shard, I knew I was in trouble. Since it took me only about eight minutes to get to the hospital, Shard had just called as I arrived in the operating room. She told the head nurse the case could wait. I picked up another extension to plead my case. She told me the case could wait. I told her she could go fuck herself.

I went upstairs, and with the help of the night shift nurses, brought the young man down to surgery myself. I lost no time in finding an anesthesiologist, who was assigned to Labor and Delivery, but not busy, and took him and my patient into surgery. As he quickly put him to sleep, I opened the instruments myself, prepped the boy, then operated on him. Of course, this was totally against every rule in the book, and was certainly indicated in my opinion.

For weeks after that, every negative report that possibly could be written about a surgeon was submitted to the hospital administration and Dr. T. Edward Wilson, the chief of orthopedic surgery. Wilson also happened to be my mentor and managing partner of the University Orthopedic Group, of which I was a member. Although Shard fought a bitter fight to have me disciplined, if not removed from the staff, all she managed to achieve was humiliation for herself and an official reprimand for unbecoming conduct or something to that effect. I had won.

The conflict had not ended there. The patient, apparently high on whatever was fashionable at the time, had been involved in some sort of moving traffic violation and had been chased by the police. The story was that HPD ran him off the road, and he injured his arm. He had other injuries, bruises, and lacerations, but nothing serious except for the forearm fracture. Due to the fracture, he could not be taken to jail immediately. Thus, his admission to University Hospital.

Eventually, the socially prominent family's lawyer and the city's lawyer worked out some kind of deal, the family agreeing to modify their lawsuit against the city for injuring their son irreparably, and the city agreeing to modify their charges against him so as not to tarnish a fine, upstanding citizen's traffic record.

Meanwhile, the reporters learned of the hospital conflict between Shard and me. A story was published in the paper entitled, "Doctor Does Surgery Alone To Save Boy's Arm." Shard was made to be the culprit.

We had not spoken since. I was sure she hated me. And I hated publicity.

CHAPTER 14

SLEEPLESS

Abad mood settled in and permeated my psyche that Tuesday morning. Waking an hour early, hashing old mental trauma, was no way to start a busy day. My attempts to return to sleep were unsuccessful, but I waited until the alarm blasted before giving up. After carrying through with my morning ritual, I went downstairs, chugged hot coffee, and fed the ungrateful cat, who was sleeping in my favorite outdoor chair. I murmured obscenities at the she-beast. She responded with a carefree stretch, bounding off after a few bites of food to do whatever cats do at five-thirty in the morning.

I returned inside to get my briefcase and found Mary Louise preparing two roast beef sandwiches as promised. She poured me another cup of coffee, kissed me, and wished me luck on my battles of the day.

I blitzed through patient rounds, pleased that all but one were doing well, some even ready to go home. Except for Harold Sanders, who was still somnolent and febrile. The head nurse informed me that his sympathectomy had been rescheduled for that day instead of Wednesday. That was good, I thought. The sooner he had more blood flow to the leg, the sooner he could get better.

All four surgeries went well, even though I was quieter than usual. The nurses and anesthetists asked if I was all right several times. Just a busy day I had said. More than I can do in a day. They understood that and left me to my quiet concentration.

I had agreed to the interview with the newspaper reporter. It was to be on Wednesday night, since Tuesday was too hectic a day to deal with that sort of thing in the evening. I wanted a night to rest. That was my usual weekday pattern, anyway, working from a little before six in the morning to seven or so at night. Wednesday was not supposed to be as busy, so it seemed a better time to ruin my evening.

My office was hectic, but not quite as wild as Monday. I took a call from Jack Harris in the middle of patients. He told me all had gone well with Mr. Sanders, although he wasn't that optimistic about improving his blood flow enough to save the leg.

"By the way, we had a little trouble with his blood pressure during surgery," he said, "so we sent him to Surgical ICU for at least the night."

"That's fine, Jack, and thanks," I answered. And the day went on.

After finishing patients in the office, attempting to shuffle paperwork around to make Fran think I had done some of it, and checking on the post-op patients at the hospital, I finally headed home. I called from the car.

"Hey, girl. Your man is on the way."

"It's about time, Jim Bob. Killer day again?"

"Yep. I want sleep."

"Dinner first, young man. You need a good meal. How were my sandwiches?"

"Highlight of my day. How was yours?"

"Fine. Charity meetings, lunch at the Women's Center. Nothing too stressful. A luxury you allow me."

"Maybe, but it's not like you didn't pay your dues. Be there shortly." I hung up, thinking she had paid her dues.

Mary Louise had been in the retail business all her life, working her way up to general manager of one of the top women's fashion stores in Houston and then on to vice-president of the same chain. She had been retired for two years and seemed to be enjoying it. She was involved in so many fund-raising activities with the charity-oriented retail company, that she was in hot demand as a fund-raiser upon her retirement. She seemed to know everyone in town, and most everyone liked and respected her. Especially me.

We had a nice dinner, and watched a therapeutically-mindless television show or two. We discussed the interview I was to do on Wednesday, Mary Louise giving me pointers on what to say, and most importantly, what not to say. She was an expert in those areas.

We turned in about nine-thirty. I was looking forward to a good night's sleep. I had just that, until 2 a.m. That was when the ICU called. Harold Sanders had slipped into a coma. They had intubated him and placed him on a respirator. Would I mind coming in and making some decisions about what to do next. They had already called the family.

I was out of the house in five minutes.

CHAPTER 15

CODE BLUE

O ne of the many advantages of working in a teaching hospital was evident in Harold Sanders' room. Coverage. There were five or six doctors there, either interns, residents, and/or fellows. They were in training, so to speak, with various levels of experience in different fields of medicine, and they were part of what was called the "Code Blue" team. Representing various medical specialties and anesthesiology, this team rushed to the scene wherever they were needed to resuscitate someone in the hospital. Their job, in essence, was to try to bring a patient who had died "temporarily" back to life. Since Mr. Sanders had been put in the cardiovascular intensive care unit after his surgery, the fellow who worked under Dr. Jack Harris was there as well. While interns and residents were still in a "learning" mode, a fellow was usually a board-certified surgeon, gaining further specialty training in a particular area. In this case, young Dr. Sheely was gaining an extra two years of experience in heart surgery with Dr. Harris.

"Are you Dr. Brady, his orthopod?" he had asked.

"Yes. And you?"

"George Sheely, Dr. Harris' fellow. The Code Blue team got here pretty fast. I was already pumping his chest. He had been extubated this afternoon after the sympathectomy and was doing okay, but he cratered around one-thirty. Anesthesia re-intubated him. We got his heart going, but it's taking Dopamine and Levophed to keep his pressure up. The respirator is keeping his breathing going, but when I tried to back off on it, he had zero independent respirations. Since you're the treating M.D., I guess you'll have to make the decision whether to keep him going or not. Sorry to have to drag you in."

He seemed a competent and diligent young doctor.

"Thanks, George. You did a commendable job. I'll have to get with the family and see what they want to do. Any idea what prompted this arrest?"

"No, sir, not really. We operated on him late this morning. Yesterday morning, that is. He did all right during surgery, although his blood pressure was a little labile. He woke up fine, we took his endotracheal tube out when he was breathing, and we--Dr. Harris, that is-- thought it would be a good idea to keep him in ICU overnight. Good thing, huh?"

"Yes. I don't think the result would have been the same up on the Orthopedic ward. Not that the care isn't good there, but they're really not set up for a cardiac arrest. Were you here already? In the ICU?"

"Yes, sir. This is my three months in hell. Well, that's what we call it. As a fellow, or a first-year fellow anyway, we have to spend a three-month rotation in ICU. We live here. Harris...uh, Dr. Harris thinks it helps prepare us for the intensive practice in which we have chosen to spend our lives. I know one thing, though. You don't sleep much, or at least, I don't. All night long, you can hear the beeping and whistling of intravenous line monitors, cardiac monitors, and respirators. It really can drive you nuts. But I knew about it when I signed on, so what can I say? I did my general surgery here at University, so I was totally familiar with the schedule. Can't blame anybody but myself."

"Wife? Kids?" I asked.

"Yep. And three little ones. The kids think I'm in jail. I get to see them on Sunday afternoon. We have a four-hour break while one of the other fellows covers the ICU. I thought real hard about doing orthopedics for a while. Better hours, you know. But then, I see you here, so maybe it's all the same. Anyway, gotta run. Sick people everywhere. Sixty-bed ICU, and it's full. Good luck with your patient."

He shook my hand and went about his business. What an insane schedule. But, if it were my wife who was in the ICU and critical, I would be thankful he was there. Hell, I was thankful he was there for Harold Sanders.

Once the patient was stable, the house staff left to return to their duties or get some sleep. The interns and residents had a rotating "on call" schedule, meaning they had to stay in the hospital when they were on duty. This varied from every other night to every third night. It was grueling. I had done it, as all surgeons had. You could only do something like that when you were young. I already knew that I would be worthless on Wednesday with only four hours of sleep.

By then, the Sanders family had arrived. So had a representative of hospital administration. Board member arrests, administration arrives. Maybe as a courtesy, maybe to cover their respective butts. Maybe to represent the trustees in case he left a large portion of his estate to the hospital. At any rate, I apprised those in attendance of Mr. Sanders' condition. The family had called their parish priest, and the kindly, older man, dressed in civies, asked about giving him the last rights. I told him I thought that might be premature. He answered that it was never too soon to get ready to meet your Maker. If I would be so kind to take him to the beside, please.

How can one argue with a statement like that? I took Father McBride and Mrs. Sanders in. The ICU had a two-visitor rule, and a cardiac arrest was no exception. I became very emotional at the site of the brief homily in the presence of Mrs. Sanders and all those damn, beeping machines. The ICU was constructed for maximum efficiency, with four "open" beds per section. Two of the other patients were awake somewhat, tubes in every orifice. Nurses were scurrying about. It was truly a madhouse. And in the midst of all that, a tender moment with a dying man, his wife, his priest, and maybe his God. What did we really know? How conscious was Harold Sanders? No one knew, and no one on our side of the rainbow would ever know.

After the family had filtered through, and Mr. Sanders had been blessed, I asked them all what they wanted to do.

"Harold never wanted to be a vegetable. He would want us to pull the plug. If he dies, then it will be God's will," Mrs. Sanders lead the discussion.

His children were not so emphatic, but were in agreement. My suggestion was to give him a day or two and see what happened. Let the endocrinologist and the infectious disease doctor see him in the morning. I wondered, at that moment, where they were. Why was the orthopedic surgeon here and the medical doctor home in bed? Was this not a medical problem? I told the family that a consensus of opinion should be reached by the treating physicians as to his reasonable chances of survival, and then an intelligent decision could be made regarding what should be done.

That seemed logical to all present, so I said good night. It was four o'clock. The family remained to await the next official visiting time, which was six o'clock. I went home to try to get some sleep. I was due to get up at five.

I crawled into bed and snuggled up against Mary Louise for all of thirty minutes. As I was falling asleep, the alarm went off. A country station was playing "Blue Eyes Crying in the Rain." I figured they couldn't have picked a more appropriate song.

CHAPTER 16

AUNT MILDRED

The best thing I can say about Wednesday morning is that it passed. No problems with inpatients other than Harold Sanders, whose condition had not changed.

Hattie Barnes was up to the bathroom on her walker on the second post-operative day, demanding to know when she could be released. The ranch would fall apart without her, she claimed. Those cowboys who worked for her probably would be fine for at least a month, or until payday came. I felt sure that they really ran the place. But I could picture Hattie in her Jeep, which I'm sure was without its top most of the year, standing up and waving with her cane, barking instructions at the top of her voice.

People could say what they pleased about all the famous Texas men, and they were legion, from warriors at the Alamo, to Sam Houston at San Jacinto, to Judge Roy Bean, and so on. The list was endless. However, it is my suspicion that the women of Texas were the real heroes. Partly a modification of that old saying, "Behind every successful man is a woman pushing him like hell," and partly because of women like Hattie. Historians may disagree, and legend-passing writers may be offended, but most men, and all women, know I am right.

Two cases were scheduled that morning. One was to be a knee replacement on an aunt of mine, my mother's sister. The other was a complicated spine case, in which I was to first-assist my partner, Greg Mayfield. He and I had trained together, through medical school, internship, and residency. Except for a year or two of separation, off doing fellowship training, we had spent over twenty years together, the last fifteen or so in practice at University Orthopedic. Greg was a stellar spine surgeon, performing complicated spine operations that, to me, were harrowing at best. I didn't mind assisting him. In fact, I enjoyed it. But I had no desire to take responsibility for cases in which the back, or lumbar spine, was opened, the abdomen was opened and the front of the spine was exposed, and the whole five or six segment section was welded, or fused, together with plates and screws. All this work was done a gnat's hair away from the spinal cord.

As I greeted Aunt Mildred in the pre-operative area, I was reminded of my mother and her seven sisters. They had grown up in East Texas, Palestine being the place where her family finally settled in. Her parents, and their parents before them, had been itinerant Pentecostal preachers. With eight children, and The Great Depression in progress, everyone worked at something. So these sisters all were pretty hard-nosed, opinionated women, and singularly, tough as hell. Together, as a group, they were impenetrable. In another war, if they had been younger, I would have taken them over the nursing platoon. Just the eight of them. Ranging from sixty to seventy-five years old, they had, in their younger days, been a formidable force. Thank God they had all mellowed a little, except for the oldest sister, who happened to be my own dear mother.

My Dad, who had passed away two years before, had been a mellowing force in my mother's life. Growing up in the country around Austin, also in the Depression, and with eight older siblings, they were a stark contrast. Dad and his family were quiet Methodists. Mom and her family were loud Pentecostals. Dad liked to read and spend time by himself, thinking and planning new projects. Mom played the piano, sang, and needed to be with people all the time. All my life I have wondered how those two ever got together and then stayed together. Mother said she had fallen in love with the letters he sent her when he was in Europe during World War II, and later with his strength of character and his reliability. Dad said he wanted to settle down and have a family with a good Christian woman, and it seemed like a good idea at the time. We used to laugh to the point of crying over that line. He must have said it a thousand times when I was growing up. But he was smart enough to say it to me only, never in front of her.

It was always a surprise to me that I was an only child, considering that there were seventeen children in their two families. Mother attributed it to the fact that she was Rh-negative, and I was Rh-positive. That would mean she was carrying antibodies to the Rh-factor, and in those days, since there was no Rhogam to counteract a reaction, her system would cause a miscarriage of another non-compatible child. I have always meant to look that up, about Rhogam not being available in 1946. Dad said that maybe all that was true, but having grown up in a household with nine children and no money, he was interested in providing well for one child as best he could. I think he was also interested in some peace and quiet, and one child was all the disruption he could handle.

I mulled these thoughts over as I replaced Aunt Mildred's knee. Mom would be coming down that day or the next to check on her sister. She would stay with us, or another sister, who lived in Houston. I silently hoped for the sister.

By the time I finished the surgery, Greg was ready for me to help with his back-rebuilding operation. We always had a good time together, whether in surgery, out to dinner, or dove hunting in South Texas. As he and I had grown older, we both had become less angry at the "feared and dangerous" doves, preferring to sip cervezas and listen to Waylon and Willie from the tailgate of the pick-up truck. We occasionally had to shoot one, just to prove to fellow hunters that we could. But "getting our limit" was no longer the goal. Relaxing and enjoying the outdoors was the prime motive for our excursions.

The dove situation has worsened for me in the last two years, since an entire family of morning doves took up residence in the back-yard of our Avalon home. We had seen many new offspring grow and make their own families; and Mary Louise, pointing out that doves mated for life, was always horrified that I could possibly kill one of her little darlings.

Mulling over those ethereal concepts, I spent two hours with Greg, holding the intestines back with one retractor, and the spinal cord and nerve roots with the other. He had the most fun, doing all the mechanical work of fusing and plate and screw inserting. But then, he had the worry of the surgery not healing well, the patient complaints, the problems, and the headaches. I could simply walk away with a small first-assistant's fee and a clear head. Sometimes I thought I could do that for a living. But then, we surgeons were all masochistic, want-ing our own patients, our own surgery, our own headaches and prob-lems, and massive reams of paperwork. All of which rolled into what I liked to call the "Whip me, beat me, call me Edna" routine.

Greg and I finished the back surgery, had a small lunch, and wandered over to the clinic to see patients. Fortunately, I was antici-pating a light day, since I was scheduled to be home at five o'clock and ready for the interview with the newspaper reporter at six.

During the office, I took three phone calls from Harold Sand-ers' other doctors, including Jack Harris. All they could tell me was that his kidneys had shut down, and that he was being dialyzed. There was nothing any of them could do. Considering he had suffered a car-diac arrest, was on a respirator, and was in renal failure, I did not have much hope for his survival.

I turned my attention back to people who were just crippled, not dying. They seemed to have the better deal, although few of them appreciated it.

CHAPTER 17

INTERVIEW

I arrived home about five-thirty, showered, dressed, and prepared myself for the interview. I had a beer and some homemade nachos. Barbara Hoffman arrived a few minutes late, with a photographer that reminded me of Berkeley in the 1960s. Or Austin during that same, crazy period. Tall, rail thin, long hair in a braid, sweat band, purple-tinted rimless glasses.

"Hi, folks," she said as she entered the living room. "This is Todd, my almost constant companion. At work anyway. Say hi to the nice people, Todd."

"'lo." That Todd was a talker.

"Let me look around and find the ideal background." Barbara wandered through the downstairs, not that there was all that much to wander in. As you entered the front door, a hallway went straight through to the rear door leading to the backyard. We liked our set-up, front and rear doors only. Two doors had seemed safer to us when we built the house than French doors that, while they looked attractive, had to be sensitized with expensive alarm wiring and checked constantly to make sure they were locked.

As you entered the house, there was a dark-paneled study to the right and a smallish, but cozy, living room with a fireplace to the left. A half-bath, a den which Mary Louise preferred to call the "sun room," and an airy kitchen with an adjacent dining room completed the downstairs. The sun room also had a fireplace, several colorful oil paintings by native American artists, and a view, through fake French doors, into the backyard's colorful flowers and squeaky-clean lap pool.

"I like this room, y'all. This is the spot," Barbara announced.

She and Todd made themselves at home, setting up a camera, extra lighting, microphone, and recorder.

"Dr. Brady, let me start with you. I'm going to ask you some questions, and you respond the best way you can. Some of the questions will be simple, such as your background, and others will require, well, some thought on your part. We'll edit the whole thing, and end up with a three to five minute spot. We'll run it tonight at ten, and probably tomorrow at noon and six. Todd will keep the camera going. Ready?"

"Wait a minute. I thought this was for the newspaper. You're set up for television." I panicked.

Mary Louise looked at me somewhat apologetically. "Jim Bob, this interview is a little different than what you and I talked about. Originally, it was just a newspaper interview, but when Barbara called me...she's in our Women's Center Volunteer Corps...I thought it would be nice. It will be in the paper as well, in a somewhat different format, but Barbara and I thought, well, it would be a good human interest story. Also, Detective Beeson thought it might get her some leads."

"When did she get involved in all this? Man, this sounds like you all have plotted against me. I really don't like this, Mary Louise. I really don't!"

I hoped she had been a little coerced herself, and I suspected Susan Beeson had quite a lot to do with it.

"Dr. Brady, let me give you the straight poop." Barbara appeared serious. "The detective who visited you has come up with zip this week investigating the Huntley boy's murder. It is murder, you know. Your wife and I, along with Susan, decided, with a little prodding toward Mary Louise, that it might open a window for the investigation. The police need some help. You may be able to help them. Indirectly, anyway. See? It's for the good of the cause. The family has decided to offer a reward for information to anyone who has any clue whatsoever that will help HPD solve this crime. Now,..."

"Look, Barbara, I'm all in favor of helping find the driver of the car, or truck, or whatever ran over Stevie. What I don't want is to be targeted by whoever was in that damn car! Nor do I want any risk whatsoever to be placed on the safety of my wife!
I think you and the detective manipulated her into getting me to do this. What if my picture is splattered all over the TV, and the newspaper, and some low-life decides to take his revenge out on us. I mean, we don't know who he is, but whoever he is will sure as hell know who we are. I don't like it, at all." I was pissed. Big time.

"Dr. Brady. Your spot on the program will be strictly human interest only. We want to focus on you as his treating physician. You're there when he dies. It's a great story. I couldn't have scripted it any better. We'll follow the spot with a generic reward offering, with a number to call. In the event you or your wife have any suspicious activity at your house, or abject phone calls, or anything that worries you at all, the police will be at your disposal twenty-four hours a day. You have my assurance, and, more importantly, HPD's assurance. Not to worry."

I excused myself for a minute. Mary Louise followed. We had a very intense discussion. She felt strongly that it was the right thing to do for the Huntleys, and for us. She managed to calm me down. I hated publicity, especially the kind that could get either of us hurt. It wasn't worth it. She talked, I listened. I finally acquiesced. I smoked a cigarette while she returned inside.

When I re-entered the sun room, there were two more guests. Susan Beeson was there, as well as a reporter, introducing herself as Harriet Mills from the Houston Chronicle. She was to do the article for the paper. The HPD representative looked a little sheepish, as well she should, and simply greeted me with a nod.

"Well, the gang's all here," I said. "Let's get it over with. And one thing before we start. This will be your...and by that I mean all of you...your only chance to get to hear, or see, what I might think, or feel, about this whole business with Stevie Huntley. So whatever you think you need to know, or want to know, this is the only time you'll be able to find that out. Is that understood?"

They all nodded. Except Todd. He looked blank. It fit his face well. The interview started.

It was over in less than an hour. I felt guilty that I had been so upset, but not so much that I let them all know that. Barbara was an expert interviewer, easily getting me into the flow of questions and answers. Harriet Mills asked a few pertinent questions, such as background on Mary Louise and I, the sort of information that lent itself to reading in print rather than viewing on television. Over all, it went well. There was really nothing to incriminate me, or Mary Louise for that matter. As usual, she had been right.

We had dinner on TV trays and watched "Home Improvement." If anyone could make me laugh and improve my mood, it was Tim Allen. I was beat by 8:30, so we went upstairs to get ready for bed. I had wanted to stay up for the 10:00 news and catch the interview, but there was no way. As I was nodding off, Mary Louise exited the bathroom wearing something that was too risqué for Victoria's Secret.

"What are you wearing? Something left over from when you were twelve? It doesn't fit you any more." I started to get a little, shall I say, riled up?

"You don't like it?"

"Oh, no. I didn't say that. I was just about to fall asleep. I don't quite know what I'm saying."

"You've had a rough day and night. I really feel bad about that interview. I feel as though I conspired against you, and you know I would never do anything to hurt you, for any reason. Do you know that? That I truly love you?"

"Yes," I said. "You're not going to hurt me, are you?"

"Not exactly what I had in mind," she said as she laughed, lit a candle, and cut the lights.

CHAPTER 18

PROBATION

As I drove to work Thursday morning, the cellular phone rang. "Dr. Brady."

"I need a doctor, doctor. Can you help me?"

Mary Louise's sleepy voice almost pulled me back home.

"Good morning, sunshine. Thanks for my...massage last night. I feel fairly chipper this morning."

"Well, for a man who was exhausted from work and lack of sleep, you were quite, shall we say, energetic?"

"A man is only as good as the woman who loves him."

"That's an awesome thought. Who said it?"

"My dad. Wish I could take credit for it. He told me that the night before you and I married."

"You've never told me that."

"I was saving it for an appropriate time."

"Your dad was a great guy. I miss him."

"Me too." I still got emotional about Dad, even though it had been two years. "Did you stay up and watch the interview?"

"Yes. It was very tasteful. You're not allowed to do any more, though. You're much too cute. Some sweet, young thing might see you and make a play. Then I'd have to pull her head off with my bare hands and bury her in the backyard. Too messy. Might break a nail."

She had me laughing.

"Really, did I say or do anything that I should be embarrassed about? I'm sure I'll run into people today who saw it."

"You were great. Very touching, about seeing your patient die. That little explanation you gave about osteogenesis imperfecta was very informative. It was good, Jim Bob. I taped it for you. You can see it tonight."

"Okay. Thanks. I'm here now, so I gotta go. Love you."

"Bye." God, she had a great morning voice. Husky. Sultry. I was glad I got to go back to her at night.

After making morning rounds, I stopped by the ICU. The Sanders family was there, apparently to say good bye.
Mrs. Sanders told me that they, as a group, had decided to stop the respirator. Father McBride was there, as were the children and quite a few other people. They seemed to be a family of strong faith. I admired that. As a group, they thanked me for all I had done. Mrs. Sanders hugged me. Since I rarely had any patients sick enough to die, I didn't have much experience in handling such a situation. I guess I appeared upset, feeling perhaps that I had let them down, especially Harold. I hugged her back, but really couldn't say anything. She looked up at me, put her hands on my cheeks, and said, "God bless you."

During surgery, one of the ICU nurses called the operating room and told me that Mr. Sanders had expired. It was not a great message to get over the speaker phone while I worked, but I was glad he didn't linger.

I received several comments from the nursing staff, and from the occasional doctor, about the TV spot the preceding night. I was shocked when I was told that the news commentator mentioned a reward of $100,000 for information regarding the death of Stevie Huntley. I couldn't believe that Pete and Bobbie had put up that kind of money, but then, what value could one really put on the life of one's child?

During office hours, I took two phone calls. One was from the pathologist that was to perform an autopsy on Harold Sanders. The family had agreed to cooperate with the hospital policy of trying to get one on all deaths. University was, after all, a teaching hospital, and the purpose of an autopsy was to learn as much as possible about the disease. This necessitated learning why a particular patient had died.

Being the admitting physician, I was notified in case I wanted to attend. I was due to be off on Friday, since we had rented a beach house in Galveston for the weekend. The pathologist said they would start their procedure, as he called it, at 8:00 in the morning. I thought I might go. It was so rare to be in this situation, and, being a concerned physician, I wanted the assurance that I had done everything humanly possible to treat the man. In other words, I needed to be sure that his death was not my fault. Call it what you want, paranoia, responsibility, due diligence, or plain old cover-your-ass. I told him I would be there.

The other call came from Dr. T. Edward Wilson, the managing partner of our group and my mentor. He was as much of a friend to me as an aloof, wealthy, powerful man like him could be. His phone calls still made me nervous. He wanted to meet with me in his office at 5:30, and would I be so kind as to be on time, as he had a hospital board meeting at 6:00.

"Yes, sir," I said.

I worked hard to get through with the office on time. Since I would be off the next day, I had to see a few extra people who thought they might have a problem on Friday or over the weekend. Their way of making an appointment was to inform us they were on the way to my office. My nurse, Rae Harris, was always willing for us to find time for anyone who even thought they had a problem. That was standard policy. It made for far-too-busy patient days, but she was great at keeping things under control if at all possible.

A country girl from Baytown, she was the best nurse with people, at least as far as those I had ever worked with. Fran was the best everything else. Rae, too, lived about 50 miles from work. East, toward Liberty, Texas. I often wondered how, in a city of three million people, I had chosen two hard workers who lived in towns far outside the city limits. Why hadn't I found local people to work for me, I wondered. Maybe people who lived in Houston did not want to work as hard. Maybe I simply identified better with people who grew up in the country, they being kindred spirits and all that.

I was on time for Dr. Wilson.

"Afternoon, James." The only other person who called me by my given name was my mother.

"Hi, Ed. What's going on?"

"Oh, the usual. Keeping you 32 guys focused is a big job. Relations with the hospital board, the administration, the government, the insurance carriers. It's a tough time now, James. Our main goal is keeping our contracted payors happy. That way we still have patients for you men to treat. Used to be easy. A patient wanted to see me, they picked up the phone and made an appointment. Not any more. They have to be seen by the family practitioner, treated if possible, then referred to a specialty provider in the network. Then, if the patient needs surgery, the surgery has to be approved, the price agreed upon, and the hospital stay negotiated. Quite a business these days. But then, that's not why I called.

"I saw your interview last night. I'm very displeased about it. You and I had this same discussion some years ago over the Beverly Richard incident. My instructions to you at the time were to never, ever, appear on television, or grant an interview, regarding any subject that was the least bit controversial, or that might reflect negatively on University Hospital, or on the University Orthopedic Group, without prior approval. And, once again, you have created a problem for me. For all of us."

"Ed, I really didn't want to do that interview. It just kind of happened. Mary Louise..."

"James, I don't want to hear any excuses, or any explanations of what you thought was appropriate. Anything of that nature gets cleared by the group, and especially, by me. I brought you over here to tell you in person that I'm going to call a meeting of the executive committee and recommend to them that you be placed on probation immediately. I'm also going to suggest that your hospital privileges be suspended for at least one week to remind you, once again, that when you speak, you are representing a group, not just yourself."

"What? Have you lost your mind? You would think that I came to work drunk and operated on the wrong, damn leg. The group will never go for that. You're over-reacting, Ed, and you are way out of line!" I rose from my chair, red-faced, I'm sure.

"We'll see, James. We'll see. You are excused. The committee will meet Friday afternoon. That's tomorrow. You'll hear from one of us after the meeting. And I suggest you start making plans to cancel your surgery schedule for next week. I'm quite sure the committee will go along with me on this." And with that, he stood and stared at me.

I left. I slammed his door as hard as I could, hearing something behind the door fall and break. I heard some kind of expletive, but wasn't sure which one. Good. Served the old, fart right. Probation? Temporary suspension? Had he lost his mind?

CHAPTER 19

DR. T. EDWARD WATSON

The seething I was experiencing from the rebuke by Wilson caused me to forget to call Mary Louise and tell her I was headed home. When I barged through the door like a charging bull, she simply stepped out of my way and observed me. I headed straight for the bar and poured myself half a tumbler of unblended Scotch whiskey, no ice. I proceeded out to my sanctuary and lit a cigarette.

"Rough day?" she asked.

I gave a little half laugh and related the events of my meeting with Ed Wilson. She was speechless. Almost.

"Jim Bob, that man has been in our house for dinner I don't know how many times over the years. You've known each other twenty years. What on earth has gotten into him?"

"I'll tell you, Mary Louise. There he was, sitting in that fabulous corner office that looks south toward the Astrodome, dressed to the nines, giving me all that bullshit. His perfect head of silver hair, manicured nails, and a double-breasted suit that probably cost $1,000. And there I was, grubby, greens on, like a whipped dog being told to sleep outside. It was all I could do not to jump across that desk and pound his head against the window sill."

"Strange behavior for Ed. Is he still practicing?"

"A little. He sees VIPs. Board members, hospital administrators, trustees, and their families. He doesn't operate any more. Patients he sees, who need surgery, are referred to one of us. His 'boys'."

I thought about the Ed Wilson I had known for years. He had a huge practice and had systematically, over the years, recruited all his favorite residents in the orthopedic surgery program to join him. Adding a man or two every year, he ended up with the University Orthopedic Group, a well-respected and capable sub-specialty group of surgeons.

In his early seventies, he still seemed to have an excellent mind, or so I thought until that day. He was a member of all the right organizations, the right church, the right country club, the right social club. He even married the right woman, the daughter of an eccentric oil wildcatter, who, after discovering the Spindletop oil fields, which became part of the Humble Oil Company, which later became Exxon, gave his money away. After, of course, setting aside massive trusts for his children. Thus, Ed Wilson, in addition to having a good surgery practice, had married into money, his main calling card into the top levels of Houston society.

Ed's wife had died a few years earlier, and they had no children. All Ed had, really, was the business and his power structure.

"Are you all right, Jim Bob?" Mary Louise asked.

"Huh?"

"Are you all right?"

"Yeah. I was just thinking about Ed and his life. I guess all he has is the group. To him, power is everything. I'm just trying to understand it all."

"You need to go play with the boys tonight. Aren't you off tomorrow? We're going to Galveston this weekend, aren't we?"

"Yes, we're going. I don't have anything official scheduled for tomorrow, but..." I told her about the Sanders scenario and the autopsy.

"I could go play tonight. I'm sure they wouldn't mind. And if I wanted to stay late, I could. Good idea, girl. I think I need to pound the ivories. Good therapy, huh?"

"Yes. I don't think you'll be very good company, anyway. You'll just brood. The music will let you forget about Ed, at least for a while. Let's go eat first, though. You don't mind buying a girl dinner before she sends you on your way, do you?"

"Okay. I need to shower and change. What are you hungry for?"

"One thing, and one thing only. Mexican food and margaritas. You?"

"Teala's?"

"Uh-huh."

"You know, you may get me out of this bad mood yet."

"That's my job. Whatever it takes."

CHAPTER 20

JUKE JOINTERS

T he Juke Jointers. I thought about that name and what an unlikely
combination we made. Considering my Thursday so far, I was looking
forward to playing with their band that night. As Mary Louise sensed,
good therapy.

I had come across this rather motley crew of musicians some
years ago in the University Hospital Emergency Room. The E.R. doctor had called, said he had a man with what appeared to be a broken
hand, and asked how I wanted him to proceed. I recommended the
usual: an x-ray and a call for the orthopedic resident to come down and
take a look. The resident phoned back and confirmed that, yes, the
hand was broken. Three metacarpals and two fingers, proximal pha-
langes, and surgery was needed.

That was three o'clock in the morning on a Saturday, which
had turned into a Sunday. I was on call, and it had been a very, long
weekend. I asked the resident if it could wait until morning, maybe put
the guy in the hospital, start some anti-biotics, and do the surgery at
eight or nine. It couldn't. There was an open wound, and it needed to
be washed out. He'd make some fresh coffee.

When I arrived and entered the room to greet my new patient, I was surprised to find five men in the room, all dressed in black. Four black faces, one white.

"Hi, I'm Dr. Brady. I'm going to be your doctor. Isn't this your lucky day."

"Hey, Doc. I'm Bennie Williams. This is the band."

They nodded.

"So what happened to you? Get your hand tangled in the frets?"

He laughed. They all did.

"No. We had a little disagreement... I had a little disagreement. See, we play the blues, you know? And we were doin' a gig at Pearl's, over on Washington? And these redneck dudes in there, they must've thought I was Charley Pride or somethin', 'cause they kept hollerin' for some two-step music. Stuff like 'Bring on Clint,' 'We wanna hear some Reba!' Anyway, after the gig--they were only there for the last set--I went down and told them they needed to learn some manners. The head dude said somethin' about nigger music, and I popped him. But good."

At that point, the other four were nodding and mumbling, 'right on' and 'yes, brother,' in total agreement with the happenings of the night.

"Everyone else okay?" I asked as I looked for outward signs of injury on the rest of the band.

They all looked at Bennie. Obviously, he was the spokesman. "They all okay. Those two big bouncers stopped it before it really got started. You know those guys, Doc? Ever been to Pearl's?"

"Sure. I love Pearl's. I've never seen you guys, though. You play R & B or classic blues? You know, T-Bone Walker, Little Milton, Bobby 'Blue' Bland, Fenton Robinson?"

"Whoa, Doc." Bennie looked at his crew. They were again nodding. I was not trying to impress them, just develop a little patient rapport.

"You a blues man, Doc?"

"Well, I love the blues. I play keyboards, piano, organ. Have for years. Relaxes me. This is a stressful job, you know."

"That's cool. Really cool."

We paused for an awkward moment.

"Listen, Bennie, your hand is broken. If you let me fix it, I can have you back playing in maybe, six weeks. I assume you play lead guitar?" The head guy usually did. He nodded.

I continued, "If we cast it, it will take, oh, probably three months to heal, and the bones will be crooked. I assume you're right-handed?" He nodded again.

"So you can chord with your left, maybe strum with your right, but those riffs I'm sure you play, that's going to take months, because your fingers will be stiff from the cast. So what do you want to do?"

Although the E.R room was crowded, they gathered around Bennie and whispered to each other.

Bennie spoke. "Say, Doc. I don't know how much you know about the blues business, but the pay...it's not all that good. We get, oh, maybe $500 a night average, sometimes a little more, sometimes a little less. Depends on how bad we want to play. We all got old ladies, kids. You know, times is hard. Always has been for the blues man. So, what I'm sayin' is, Doc, I got no money, no insurance. This job don't have no benefits, shall we say," he chuckled. So did they. And nodded.

I understood the problem. I had been playing music off and on since I was five years old. But I always had kept what musicians called a day job.

"Tell you what, Bennie. I'll get the hospital to 'comp' your bill. We're set up to do some charity care. And I won't charge you. However, we'll make a deal. Every now and then, maybe once or twice a month, I can come sit in with the band, play some keys, and jam with you. Deal?"

They all nodded.

"Are you any good?" Bennie asked. "You know, we just kinda play what we want. The mood strikes, we play. We might start out in a

'G' shuffle, then cross the bridge to a Latin beat in 'D.' You know? Shit like that...Sorry, Doc."

"That's okay, Bennie. I say shit all the time. Tell you what. Try me out. When I get your hand ready to play, you call me up, and I'll come out on a Thursday, Friday, or Saturday, set up with you, and we'll see how it goes. You and the guys like it, fine. You don't, we'll see each other around."

That seemed fair to Bennie, and the guys. They nodded again.

So I fixed his hand. The last time I saw him officially was about two weeks after surgery. I had removed his stitches, x-rayed his hand to make sure the tiny screws I had inserted were in position, and given him some therapy instructions regarding moving the wrist and fingers.

A week, maybe two, later, he had called the office and invited me to sit in with the band. When I returned the call, he told me the hand was great and he could play about 90 per cent of his stuff. It had been only a month. He was grateful.

So it was that I was sitting outside Big Red's waiting for the band to show. It was a routine. I was always early, they were always late. I was excited. It was their job.

When they pulled up in a new van--they always rode together-- I inquired as to where broke musicians found the money for a new ride. Bennie explained, after I had greeted the boys, that since I had been coming out and playing with them, and had invited some friends to hear them, they had been getting some really good gigs. Private parties, paying $1,000 to $1,500 a night. Big money to guys who usually barely got by. That made me feel good, and them, even better.

I stood beside my car and smoked a luxurious Marlboro Light. The parking lot was still almost empty. I looked around the general area of the club. The Houston Heights was an older neighborhood, just west of downtown. Its main east-west thoroughfare, Washington Avenue, had been the home of many blues clubs in the late 1980's. Club

Hey-Hey, the Bon Ton Room, and the Local Charm Saloon were all closed now, leaving only Rockefeller's, the Satellite Lounge, Big Red's, and Pearl's. The 1990's were not going to be kind to blues musicians. Blues music had, for some reason, had a resurgence in the '80s, but was on the decline in the '90s. I wondered what the band would do without gigs. Play another kind of music? Not likely.

I watched the guys unload. They were doing better financially, but not well enough to afford a roadie--a set-up and take-down man. So they did all the work themselves. They hauled instruments, amplifiers, cases of connecting wire, the PA system, and a mixing sound board, which was enormous. I carried my keyboard, a Korg M-1, my Fender piano amp, and a stool. I tried to help them carry their equipment, but they would never allow me. They worried about my hands.

Setting up took a while. After the sound check, we retired to the band's dressing room, a converted closet. We had a beer and caught up on each other's lives. It had been a month since I had played with them. They had added a full-time keyboard player, but when I came to play, they put me up front and tuned me into the PA system. Bennie had always loved the way I played, from the very first time I sat in with them. I was especially good, he had said, for a white boy. So, sitting on the stage at my "rig," I surveyed the crowd. The place was packed. I briefly studied my partners in music. Bennie, comfortably seated stage front, tuned his guitar. Jake, occasional lead player and never without his dark glasses, played rhythm guitar. He saw me looking at him and nodded. Billy played drums, and was pale as starch. There was Earl on harmonica and saxophone, and Big John on bass guitar. The new keyboard player was named Jimmy. I had met him only that night. All I knew about him was that he was white, though not quite as pale as Billy.

Bennie looked around, pulled his dark glasses down to the end of his nose, smiled and winked at me. White teeth against ebony face.

"Ready, Doc?"

I nodded.

"Shuffle in 'G,' boys."

We started, and what a sound it was, especially from my vantage point on the stage. The rhythm of the blues overtook my mind. Being in the right key was all I thought about until I left for home at 2 a.m.

CHAPTER 21

AUTOPSY

I was a few minutes late for the autopsy on Harold Sanders. The anatomical pathology section of University Hospital took up a massive area of the basement. Although the hospital was comprised of five sub-hospitals, pathology was centralized in the catacombs under the ground. I hadn't been down there in years, and I got lost. Housekeeping was also in the basement, so I finally stopped in and asked directions.

Clinical pathology, involving the various laboratory testing that was required to run a major medical center hospital, was located on the second floor. Why it was separated from anatomic pathology, which was the study of live and dead tissue, I didn't know. Housekeeping personnel kindly directed me to where they kept "the stiffs." Their expression, not mine.

I entered the aluminum double doors to an office with a secretary.

"Morning. I'm Dr. Brady. I was invited to the autopsy on Mr. Sanders?"

"Yes, doctor. Straight on back. Follow your nose." She snickered when she said it.

My experience with people who worked in this field was that they were the most callous of the calloused. The patients were beyond help when they reached the basement. It bred extreme cynicism. Definitely not my thing.

After a short hallway, with many small offices off to the sides, I entered a huge room with high ceilings. Bright fluorescent lights hung from wires suspended from the open rafters, causing the room to resemble a warehouse. There must have been twenty-five or so pathologists doing autopsies. It reminded me of gross anatomy lab in medical school. The smell of formaldehyde was so pungent that I donned a surgical mask and cap, a rack of which was adjacent to the doors through which I had entered. I noticed some of the tables had more than one person standing by and assumed there were other doctors following up on patients who had died. Same reason I was there.

A technician was wandering around with a clipboard and with what seemed to be a schedule. I asked him to direct me to the Sanders autopsy.

"Station 24," he responded and walked on. Friendliness was not a prominent commodity in pathology.

I located Station 24. The autopsy was under way.

Dr. Duncan introduced himself but didn't try to shake my hand. He spoke into a microphone that was suspended over the table, adjacent to the light fixture. This freed both his hands. He dictated and described his findings as he went along.

Basically, Mr. Sanders had died of severe, and diffuse, arteriosclerosis. Hardening of the arteries. He apparently had died of a combination of a sudden narrowing of the coronary arteries, those small vessels that nourish the heart itself, and the renal arteries, the vessels that carry blood to the kidneys. I watched for an hour or so, then left the table after I felt satisfied that his death had been more or less of natural origin. It had, of course, been prompted by the unfortunate rifle wound to his leg, but how much longer he would have lived without that event was speculative.

As I meandered the tables, heading toward the exit, someone called my name.

"Jim Bob Brady. What in the hell are you doing down here?"

It was Jeff Clarke, a medical school classmate. We hadn't seen each other in years.

"Hey, Jeff. How've you been? I had a patient die yesterday, so I came down to see the post-mortem exam. Wanted to make sure I had done everything I could..."

"Shit. Same old compulsive Brady. Was that the GSW?"

"Yes, Mr. Sanders had been shot in the leg on a hunting trip. Complications set in, you know. Clogged arteries."

Jeff was short, overweight, and a transported New Yorker. His wit vacillated between hilariously funny and insultingly sarcastic. With his red, curly hair and thick glasses, I thought he would have been better suited as a stand-up comic.

"Say, you're a bone doc. Look at this."

He was doing an autopsy on a child. He had the abdomen open and was looking at a severely distorted spine. It appeared to have been affected by scoliosis, a spinal deformity that had produced an S-shaped curve in the spine that ran from the neck all the way down to the tail bone. There were long metal rods visible adjacent to the vertebrae. I then scanned the child. All the extremities were distorted, having the appearance of multiple healed fractures.

"Well, Jeff, looks like the child had surgery for scoliosis at some time. Deformed arms and legs. Some kind of genetic syndrome?"

"O.I."

"Osteogenesis imperfecta?"

"That's the admitting diagnosis. Had spine surgery this week, crashed and burned post-op. Look at these eyes." He moved to the head of the table and opened the closed lids. "Have you ever seen sclerae this blue?" he asked.

That was one of the main characteristics of O.I., in addition to soft, brittle bones that broke easily. Instead of white around the pupil, the tint was a varying shade of blue, depending on the severity of the disease. Milder cases had barely detectable shades of blue. This child must have had a bad case. The eyes were very deep blue.

As Jeff closed the eyes and went back to his work, I couldn't help but look at the child's features. A hint of recognition crept into my head. I stared, but couldn't believe it. I felt as though I were looking into the face of Stevie Huntley.

CHAPTER 22

GALVESTON

I took Mary Louise up on her offer to drive to Galveston. In the first place, I was too numb from the events of the morning to perform any physical functions more complicated than breathing and shaking my head. Secondly, she much preferred driving her Jeep Cherokee than my ten-year-old diesel.

In the '80s, when gasoline was expensive, diesel engines were the rage. The auto makers were designing smaller cars with efficient engines that required smaller quantities of unleaded gasoline, and diesel engines were available for every type vehicle from a VW Rabbit to a Chevy pick-up. My car was at this time, however, a relic. I had kept it well maintained, inside and out, and it was a source of pride to me. Round-trip mileage for me to work and home was only twelve miles, and that was perfect for a ten-year-old-diesel. Mary Louise hated to drive it, as it lacked any, as she put it, "get up and go."

As we cruised Interstate 45 south toward Galveston, I appreciated the Cherokee's comfort and speed. It was also nice and quiet. So was I.

"Are you okay?"

"I don't know. What do you think about that child? How can

you rationally explain the striking resemblance to Stevie? Was I imagining that?"

I also wondered if I was losing my mind, with the stress of the week's activity. The hit-and-run, the interview, the autopsy scene, not to mention the work schedule. I wondered if children with osteogenesis imperfecta resembled each other, like they did with Down's syndrome. I reflected that Down's was a kinder name than Mongoloid. Maybe that explained it. A physical resemblance to each other based on the genetic component of the disease. I wanted to research that. And I would. Monday. I intended to try to relax that weekend, after the phone call from Greg Mayfield, who would hopefully tell me I was not suspended from hospital privileges for a week. Surely my partners wouldn't go along with something that ridiculous, I thought.

I must have dozed off. I heard Mary Louise talking about the color of the water.

"Huh?"

"I said the water is gorgeous! Blue as the sky. Isn't it incredible?"

As I opened my eyes, we were crossing the causeway over Galveston Bay. She was right. The water was...blue as the sky. From that vantage point atop the causeway, one could see the bay, Galveston Island, and the Gulf of Mexico beyond. To my left I saw the East End clearly. The Galveston Ship Channel, the University of Texas Medical Branch, downtown, and the Strand Historical District. To the right, the island narrowed to less than a mile in width, forming West Beach. We were headed west to a beach house that we rented fairly often. Most of the rental home properties were situated in the west end, in Pirate's Beach, Indian Beach, and Kahala Beach. The farther west one went, the less crowded it became.

As we exited off I-45 onto the 61st Street exit, I rolled my window down and inhaled the fresh salt air. There had always been something magical about crossing the causeway onto Galveston Island. All the troubles that plagued you at home seemed to disappear into the mist. It was almost as if your biorhythms adjusted to the beat of the waves, and the whitecaps, gently flowing on the sparkling water had the power to lull you to sleep. Mary Louise called it "crawling back into the womb." She was probably right.

Fortunately, we had left Houston before noon, so the traffic during the 50-mile trip hadn't been too bad. Not that I would have noticed. I slept most of the way. We zipped out Seawall Boulevard, heading west. Seawall turned into Highway 3005, which led to the West End. If you drove all the way out 3005, you eventually came to San Luis Pass, where the Gulf of Mexico and Galveston Bay came together under the tall bridge.

We stopped at the Seven Seas and bought groceries for the weekend. Although we had our favorite eating spots in Galveston, we sometimes preferred to eat as many meals as possible outdoors on one of the decks facing the ocean. We traveled another mile or two, and arrived at Indian Beach.

The house we had rented was lovely. Small, but certainly large enough for two people. The ground floor consisted of a parking area for four cars, and a small storage area for bicycles, beach chairs, and fishing equipment. The first floor was large, with wall-to-wall windows extending two stories high. It provided a spectacular view of the ocean from what we called the Great Room, which consisted of a kitchen, dining area, and lounging area centered around a TV-stereo console. There were two bedrooms and two baths off to the side, each with a view of the ocean. The entire second floor was a master suite with one and one-half baths. It had its own private deck, again with a full ocean view.

We walked out onto the deck that extended out from the Great Room. It ran the full width of the house, and provided an unsurpassable view of the water, allowing a sunrise view daily, and an occasional sunset view during the winter. We had to breathe the salt spray for a while before we could unload the car.

"I think you need to take a walk on the beach, Jim Bob. You're still tense, and you're brooding."

And I thought I had relaxed.

"Walk for an hour or two, and by the time you get back, I'll have frozen margaritas made. I'll make some queso and salsa dip, too, but only if you'll walk off some of that stress. I want you relaxed, for later."

That woman had her way of convincing me to do what she thought was best for me. What could a man want other than that? I went for a walk.

I started to loosen up after the first mile. I walked east first. The Gulf of Mexico was to my right and was exceptionally beautiful that day. The March sun was bright and appeared to sprinkle glitter on the water. It followed me as I walked. The beach was not yet crowded, so I ambled fairly undisturbed until I reached Jamaica Beach. I turned around and headed back west.

My mind began to run with all the input it had received in the last week. I wished I could write down the thoughts and come back to them later. The brain was like a hard disc in a computer, without a printer. If you could get all the stuff that floats around in those little micro-processors in your head to be transcribed instantaneously, or to be transferred to a floppy disc that could be transcribed later, an astounding amount of information would be generated. However, I could only ponder the facts. Slowly.

Stevie Huntley had been killed by a hit-and-run driver, identity unknown. I had not heard if the reward offer had led to any suspects, but I could check on that through Susan Beeson, the HPD detective. If she was reticent about discussing the case, for any reason, I could go straight to her father, Police Chief Lombardo. I figured that since I had operated on him a couple of years ago, he owed me a small favor.

Next, I considered Ed Wilson's reaction, or over-reaction, to the TV interview. Maybe it was office policy, maybe not, to suspend me for not getting media permission from him or the Group. Maybe it was just bad timing. I didn't know. He had a burr up his butt.

And then, the potential twin. I wondered what that was about. I wanted to get to a medical library to research O.I. I was curious about facial features, genetics, and twins with the disease. Stevie had a mild form. The child in pathology had a severe form. Were they related possibly? If Stevie had a twin, why wouldn't he have been with Pete and Bobbie? I obviously needed to talk to Pete or Bobbie, but how could I approach that subject? What would I say? Sorry, Pete, but Stevie's twin brother, the one you and Bobbie didn't know you had, is dead. Right.

My other choice was simple. Leave it the hell alone. It really wasn't any of my business. Call Susan and have her come to the house. I could tell her about what I saw in pathology and let her investigate. She got paid to do that. She had the experience, the training, and the ability to get information I couldn't possibly get. The origin of the second boy would have to be investigated. Stevie's birth history would have to be checked out. Was it possible that he had been adopted?

See, I admonished myself, this gets way over your head. You're a busy surgeon, with very little time to yourself anyway. Why get involved with something that complicated? Hours of research, talking to people, getting hospital records that may or may not exist. An impossible task. Ridiculous to even attempt it.

The last time I gave myself a speech like that, I decided to go to medical school.

I felt better when I returned. Mary Louise said I looked better, too. She rewarded us with large, iced glasses of margaritas with a hint of Cointreau. Piles of tortilla chips, queso dip, salsa, and lots of salt. I probably wouldn't be able to get my ring off tonight or my shoes on tomorrow, I thought, but what the hell. It was Friday at the beach, and we were entitled to have a good time.

We had been sitting out on the deck, enjoying the afternoon southern breeze. I was comfortable in my swim trunks and a T-shirt. My shoes were off, and my feet were propped up on the railing that ran the length of the angled deck. Mary Louise had been inside, I assumed to get more margaritas, since we had finished a pitcher. I casually wondered who had been drinking our drinks, since certainly there was no way we could have devoured the whole pitcher.

The door opened, and she carried another pitcher with her. Also, I couldn't help but notice that she had changed clothes, if you could call what she had on clothing. A bikini that made a postage stamp look like a map.

"Mary Louise?"

"Yes, Jim Bob?"

"Do you expect me to sit here, drink margaritas, and eat chips with you dressed like that?"

"No, I do not."

"Well, you brought another pitcher with you, right?"

"Yes."

"Do you expect me to drink the pitcher now?"

"I was giving you options. I can very easily put the pitcher back in the freezer if you would like. Would you like that, sweetie?"

"Yes, ma'am, I would." I felt giddy, like a school kid.

She took my hand, pitcher in the other, and let me inside to the Great Room. Once the frozen medication was put away, and believe me, I certainly felt well-anesthetized, she took me to the sofa and made me lie down. Like she had to really force me, you know. She gently slipped off my swim trunks, and after a moment or so, although it could have been days, she looked up at me.

"You taste salty. I love salt."

Friday at the beach was tough to beat.

CHAPTER 23

UNFORGETTABLE

W e had a slight argument Saturday morning. I wanted to go into town, do a little research at the U.T. Medical Branch Library, and find out what I could about osteogenesis imperfecta. My curiosity was burning inside of me.

"Jim Bob," she started, "we had a wonderful afternoon and evening, didn't we?"

Nod.

"I brought you down here to relax, not to go running off to the library to get involved in something that's none of your business. Jim Bob, there are trained professionals to do that kind of work. Would you want an untrained person replacing your hip or fixing your broken ankle? Well, would you?"

I shook my head.

"Then why in the world are you getting involved in all this? If it's my fault because of the interview I convinced you to do, I'm very sorry. If I had known it would lead to your playing detective, I never would have agreed to it. You're not Matlock. And we are definitely not Hart to Hart. If there is something bad going on out there, I do not want you involved. I want to keep you all to myself, until you're a wizened old man. I love you, and I don't want you to take any unnecessary chances. Are you listening?"

"Yes." I felt like a school kid, but in a very different way than the night before. Maybe more like a puppy who had forgotten what it meant to be housebroken.

"But you're going anyway, aren't you? Aren't you?"

"Yes."

"Even if it makes me angry?"

"Yes. I have to check it out. It's my nature. The way I am. If I weren't this way, I never would have captured you."

She hesitated. She started a half smile. Reminding her of our courtship and romance always headed her off at the pass and got me out of trouble.

My parents and I had moved to Waco, Texas when I was a freshman in high school. Although he didn't have a college degree, my father had gathered quite a bit of experience as an engineer in the Army. He had been hired by the City of Waco as a city engineer and was reasonably well paid for his services, considering his lack of formal education. His job had good benefits and allowed my mother the luxury of staying home to take care of the household and their only child.

I had played the piano since the age of five and was considered naturally gifted, since I could play by ear. I could hear a song a time or two and then play it fairly well without seeing the sheet music. I received intense instruction in the classics, playing Beethoven, Bach, Rachmaninoff, and Schubert by day. By night, I tinkered with the new Motown sound, the blues, and music by the British invaders, who turned out to be the Beatles, the Rolling Stones, and many other groups that changed the face of American rock and roll. I worked hard at classical music. I enjoyed and relaxed with the rest. Although my dad made a fairly good living, college was beyond my parents' means. Luckily, I won a music scholarship to Baylor University and played in the Baylor Symphony, the Baylor Jazz Band, and the Baylor Golden

Wave Marching Band, when they weren't marching. On weekends, I made extra money playing in local clubs with rhythm and blues or rock and roll bands, or any other gig that provided me with some spending money.

In 1967, I faced a decision. The Viet Nam War was on, and guys that dropped out of school or finished college without plans for graduate study were being drafted. I really couldn't imagine playing the piano in a foxhole, although I'm sure the troops would have appreciated it. I developed a burning interest in medicine, the only type of graduate study that assured one of a deferment. I took some pre-med courses as electives, and although it took me an extra two summers in college, I had been accepted to Baylor's medical school in Houston.

So it was that in 1970, I found myself in Houston, deeply in debt with a Health Professions Student Loan, shopping on a Saturday for a birthday and Mother's Day present for my mother. On that day, I met a gorgeous blonde built like...something else. Fresh out of college in Dallas at SMU, she was a department manager in a ladies' clothing store. I was smitten immediately. She was, shall we say blasé. She helped me find the appropriate gifts, which I paid for with student loan money. There was precious little time for music any more, so extra money was nonexistent. She appeared to be horrified when I told her I was a medical student. She acted like I had a disease. Women who worked in the medical center always seemed impressed that I had the potential to become a RICH DOCTOR. Mary Louise, however, informed me that medical students were the worst, that doctors were the worst, and that she intended to stay as far away from that bunch as possible.

I left messages for her every day for a week. I sent flowers to the store, hoping the student loan people were not monitoring my spending. She finally returned one of my calls and consented to go out with me. After a few months, I think she fell in love with me. Not the medical student. The piano player.

Late one night, we went to the Warwick Hotel Bar. It was not crowded, and the piano player was on his break. I asked him if I could "pitch a little woo" to my date. He consented, and I went through as many Nat King Cole, Frank Sinatra, and Johnny Mathis love songs as I could remember. Somewhere between "Unforgettable" and "Chances Are," she was mine. We were married six months later.

So it was that on that Saturday morning in Galveston, I started singing "Unforgettable" to her. She smiled, then laughed, then patted my cheek and sent me on my way. Maybe I had spent all of my preceding days preparing for that night when I played the piano for Mary Louise. She had made me a happy man. What else could there be?

CHAPTER 24

UTMB

A s I traveled east on 3005, then on to Seawall and into Galveston, I discovered that I was actually in a pretty good mood. Mary Louise had definitely contributed to it.

Greg Mayfield had called Friday evening, although neither M.L. nor I knew exactly what time it had been. We were sleeping on the Great Room couch...in Margaritaville. He informed me that I had not been suspended or put on probation. The idea had struck them as so ridiculous, they hadn't even voted. He advised me that should I have any intention of lounging around the island, taking a week off, and working on my beach-bum tan, I could forget it. I must say, I was relieved, although I had seriously doubted that the Group would discipline me. I must admit, however, that during those first few minutes after my conversation with Ed Wilson, I was actually scared.

Grown men shouldn't have to be scared. Your system can't take it. Fear is for younger, healthier men, men who are in shape. I didn't fit the bill.

It had been a number of years since I had made a trip to the University of Texas Medical Branch. The UTMB was the first medical school in Texas. It remained the largest with respect to the number of students accepted. Reaching downtown, I turned left off of Seawall onto 14th Street, crossed Broadway, and started looking for "Old Red." Old Red, once the main building, was a historical monument to the thousands of doctors who had trained inside her walls. A combination of Romanesque, Victorian, and Spanish architecture, it stood four stories tall with multiple turrets, spires, and arched windows. It would have been the perfect setting for an Edgar Allen Poe tale, except for one feature. Old Red was in fact, red. Rust-colored to be exact. Why the designer had chosen that color I wasn't sure, but red sandstone was the main building component. Several other older buildings in Galveston were of the same style and color, most notably The Bishop's Palace, former home of the Galveston-Houston Diocese. I guessed the fashion of the late 1800's had been the creation dictate of these elaborate masterpieces.

As I drove around the UTMB campus, I noticed how young the medical students, interns, and residents looked. The age requirements for those professionals-to-be must have been lowered. I noted to myself that Congress had done that with respect to its senators and representatives as well. People of responsibility were definitely getting younger, or so it seemed.

I finally located Old Red and parked. I wandered around awhile before finding the library. Once inside, I looked for the card catalogue, that structure with hundreds of small reference drawers normally at the front of any library. This library didn't seem to have one. I sought help from a librarian-to-be at the central desk. She was much too young to be an actual librarian, I thought.

"Morning. I'm Dr. Brady, from Houston. I'm looking for the card catalogue. I need to do some research on a medical disease."

"Sir, we do not have a card catalogue available here. That's a fairly antiquated reference system. All our data is computer-accessible. The work stations are located along the west wall. See over there, where it says reference?" She pointed across the huge room. It must have been three stories high. The front half was completely open to a ceiling interspersed with skylights. The back half had stairs leading to additional books and periodicals. The ground floor seemed to extend a full city block, with rows of metal shelving more numerous than I would want to count.

"I'm, uh, not really familiar with computer access to reference material. When I was in school, we didn't even use calculators." I was trying to be funny so as not to appear totally stupid to this young thing. "Maybe you could let me visit with the chief librarian. She probably remembers card catalogues."

"Sir, I am the chief librarian, and I will be happy to get whatever information you need. If, that is, you have a Houston Academy of Medicine card. We have a reciprocal relationship with the Harris County Medical Society, and your access card for that library will allow you access to this library. You do have one, don't you?"

She was beginning to remind me of my son, J.J. Too damn smart for his own good. I searched my wallet, and, thank God, I found my plastic card for the Jesse Jones Library.

After I had been approved, she kindly led me to the Reference Data Access section, which was one long desk of monitors and keyboards, separated by those aluminum dividers with colored cloth. I understood entire offices were currently being designed with those things, allowing office personnel to rearrange cubicles on short notice. The "walls" and "separators" weighed almost nothing. I wondered where all the wood in the country had gone. Probably to make computer paper.

"What kind of information do you need, sir?" she asked as she sat in front of the keyboard.

"I need information on a disease called osteogenesis imperfecta. Specifically, I'd like to find out about twins with the problem and physical resemblances between children with the disease, whether in the same family or not. I'd also like to learn about the genetics of the disease and details about the various types and clinical features."

"In other words, everything."

"I guess so."

As she entered data, screenfuls of information appeared. It all went too fast for me to see what was actually there. I thought about asking her to stop, but I didn't want to appear any more backward than I already did. Finally, a small tray to the right of the monitor began to print, and many pages of reference material were produced. Included were textbook lists, numerous journal articles, and reference sources for further research.

"If you need to, you may make copies. Copy machines are scattered in strategic locations on all three levels." She turned to walk away, then looked back at me. "You do know how to use a copy machine, don't you, doctor?"

I nodded.

"I'm glad to know that. If you need assistance, let me know." She gave a little half smile.

I appreciated how prehistoric man must have felt when, freezing to death and covered with mastodon hides, he stumbled upon some strangers who had already discovered how to make a fire. I'm sure they smiled the same half smile I had just witnessed.

I spent the next three hours gathering information and reading. And I copied a few things, all by myself, thank you very much. On my way out, I stopped by the desk and showed the librarian that I had been able to use the copier without her help. She asked why I hadn't printed the data in color. Color photographs show up much better than black and white, she informed me. That half smile again. I left before I found out that there was something else I didn't know.

On the way back to the beach house, I mentally reviewed what I had learned that morning. First, young people knew a helluva lot more than I did. I knew about orthopedic surgery and music. The rest of the world was a blur. I also learned that I should get a new car. And, Mary Louise was right. My car did smell like diesel fuel, even when you drove with the windows up.

I learned some interesting facts about osteogenesis imperfecta.

It was transmitted genetically, through an autosomal gene, meaning that it was not sex linked. Transference could occur through either the mother or the father. Unfortunately, there were very few reported cases of twins with O.I. The literature seemed to imply that identical twins, who came from a splitting of the same egg in the uterus, would have the exact same disease pattern, whether mild, moderate, or severe. Fraternal twins, or non-exact twins, who came from two different simultaneously-fertilized eggs, could have a varying disease pattern from each other. The other interesting fact I learned, or maybe knew at one time but had forgotten, which I felt sure was the case, was that one particular form of O.I. was characterized by a child that appeared perfectly normal at birth, but developed fractures of a varying severity six months or a year later.

I did plan to follow up on the child I had seen in the autopsy suite. Where he had come from and who had been his pediatrician, his surgeon, his parents, etc. I needed to talk to Pete and Bobbie, too, an event I dreaded. I would definitely need Mary Louise's finesse to help me with that. Any inquiries regarding his birth history would have to be approached delicately. It might somehow be related to the hit-and-run. An unlikely scenario, but one never knew.

Vowing to enjoy the remainder of the weekend, I tried to put my thinking on hold. I called M.L. from the car.

"Hi. I'm on my way. What are you up to?"

"I'm sunning myself on the main deck, enjoying this glorious day. How about you, paleface?"

"I'm not going to be pale for long. I should be able to join you in the next thirty minutes. Are you hungry? I can stop at Cafe Michaelburger and bring you a bacon-cheese, your favorite?"

"No, thanks. I'm sipping a Chardonnay spritzer and eating fresh pâté and brie with Carr's tablewater crackers."

I hurried home.

CHAPTER 25

GAIDO'S

W e spent the rest of Saturday sunning ourselves, napping, and walking the beach, all required activities for a Galveston weekend. We had planned to meet some friends of ours for an early dinner at Gaido's, a wonderful seafood restaurant in town on Seawall Boulevard.

Our friends owned a house in Pirate's Cove, a development on the bay side of the West End. Those houses, like the one we had rented for the weekend, stood on stilts and sat on the water. The Galveston Bay water was calm and only occasionally produced the kind of cooling breeze that the ocean generated daily. I preferred the beach, or ocean side, because of the wind and the sound of the surf, which owners of bay houses sacrificed for the reduced risk of hurricane damage. I would have to take that under consideration if we ever decided to buy a home on the island.

Mary Louise spent the afternoon in her near-invisible, thonglike, so-called swimming suit. That was fine with me as long as we stayed on the deck. The West End beach houses had been designed to sit back from the beach sixty or seventy yards. Access to the sand was provided by an elevated boardwalk that passed over the vegetation, ending in a short flight of steps that led directly to the beach. With her in that outfit, I would have preferred an even greater distance between the deck and the beach. More difficult for beach-walkers to gawk at her. She thought that was silly. Who cared about seeing a 46-year old woman in a bikini, she asked, with all those young, hard bodies around. Anyone with testosterone, I had answered. She thanked me, and thoughtfully put on a cover-up before we went walking. Sometimes, I needed to be humored.

"I picked up the messages at home. Your mother called. She's staying at her sister's house, but expects to see us. I thought you'd want her to come over Sunday evening and stay for a few days. What do you think?"

"God, I forgot she was coming down. I get a little brain dead when we're here."

"Good. That's why we come here."

"Sunday night? You know what a bear I can be on Sunday. You know, the Sunday-night-I-have-to-go-to-work-on-Monday blues."

"I know, Jim Bob. But with your schedule, you won't get to visit with her on Monday or Tuesday night, and she said she was leaving Wednesday."

"I visited with her for twenty-one years. I lived at home during college, you remember."

"Yes, I know, sweetie. But she's old, and she won't be around that much longer. And when she's gone, you'll wish you had spent more time with her. That's how I feel about my parents, and I spent a lot more time with them than you have with yours."

"Your parents were great. My dad was great. Mother is just a little too much for me. She can't sit down, she can't read a book. She talks all the time and constantly tries to redecorate the house. And in between, she tells me how to live my life. I love her, but we just aren't very compatible."

"Well, she's coming over tomorrow at five o'clock. We'll take her to dinner and maybe a movie. It will be over before you know it. Besides, it might help you keep your mind off your Monday schedule.

Okay?"

"Okay."

"On a brighter note, J.J. called. He's coming home next weekend. Some kind of party one of his friends is giving. A bunch of the
kids that graduated together from high school are having a reunion."

"Good. Too bad he couldn't be coming home just to see his
dear old mom and dad."

"You sound like your mother. See? You do have something in
common. You both think your children don't see you enough."

With those words out of her mouth, she pinched me on the butt
and ran ahead. With her lithe body and long legs, I knew that catching
her was hopeless. I yelled that she was really a shit for saying that. She
cupped her left ear, saying she couldn't hear me. The surf was too
loud. She laughed and continued her jog.

We arrived at Gaido's around six. As usual, the place was
packed. The restaurant didn't accept reservations unless there was a
very large party involved. They seated those folks in dining rooms off
to the side of the main dining area. The front of Gaido's was composed
of large picture windows that faced directly to the south, toward the
Gulf of Mexico. The beach wasn't visible due to the fact that the seawall was elevated ten or twelve feet above the tide line. There had
been a devastating hurricane around 1900, and, at the time, there had
been no seawall. What the winds hadn't destroyed, the flooding had. It
had flooded across Galveston island all the way to the bay, a distance
of several miles. In an attempt to prevent a recurrence of that type of
destruction, should another hurricane of such magnitude hit the island
again, the seawall had been constructed. Gaido's view was spectacular.

We met up with our dinner companions, who were more Mary
Louise's friends than mine. The wife held the position that Mary
Louise had held at one time, that of general manager of the flag-ship
store of the retail chain. Her husband, an aerospace engineer at NASA
was a fairly quiet but pleasant sort. I liked him primarily because he

smoked an occasional cigarette, so I didn't have to go outside and sneak around like I did with other couples with whom we dined. We waited in the massive bar, drinking and watching the waves with all the other starving patrons.

Dinner was predictably wonderful. Before embarking on our respective journeys to the West End, we made a customary pit stop. It was there I ran into my neighbor, Bill Russell, fellow doctor and pediatrician.

"Hey, Brady. What's a guy like you doing in a place like this?"

I hadn't noticed him. I tried to face straight ahead when standing in a public urinal. Most men, I thought, did. Craning one's neck from side to side in a public rest room made you highly suspect. Of what, I was never sure.

"Hey, Bill. What are you doing here?"

"Taking a leak. You?"

Bill had always been a smart ass. Probably why I liked him.

"Just finished dinner. Mary Louise and I rented a house at Indian Beach for the weekend. You?"

"Med school reunion. We're at the Galvez Hotel. We're in the private dining room in the back, called the Pelican Club. Separate entrance, so we didn't have to wait around with you plebes."

As we walked out to the lobby together, I remembered that Bill had been Stevie Huntley's pediatrician. I had consulted with him on occasion when the child had sustained a fracture.

"Bill," I asked, "do you remember if Stevie Huntley was adopted?"

"Well, Jim Bob, I don't have all my patient files on me. I left the Mayflower van at home tonight," he laughed. "I think I started seeing him when he was a year or two old, but I'm not sure. The wine steward won't let your glass get below half full, so my synapses aren't too swift. I can check for you on Monday, though. Why do you want to know?"

"Just curious."

"Look, Brady, the kid is dead. I'm sure Bobbie and Pete are going through hell right now. What difference does it make if he was adopted or not, for God's sake? It's Saturday night. Chill out, guy! Call me Monday, and I'll check the file. But I can't imagine why you would give a shit!" he said as he stumbled off.

CHAPTER 26

MOM

Saturday evening we lounged on our deck, studying the constellations. It was a clear night, with an almost-full moon. I, once again, pointed out to Mary Louise the "woman in the moon." Over the years, the more I stared at the face of the moon, especially with binoculars, the more I was convinced that the face visible there was certainly not a man's. The figure I saw had large lips, a full mane of hair, and eyes that usually appeared closed. Maybe it was the light reflecting off the Galveston coast. Maybe it had something to do with the massive jack-up oil rigs in the Gulf of Mexico, visible on the horizon. Maybe it was simply my beach frame of mind. Whatever the origin, I repeatedly swore that the face in the moon was that of a woman in the midst of erotic pleasure. Mary Louise always shook her head when I said that and wondered what kind of dirty old man I might turn out to be.

Sunday brought a repeat of Saturday's weather. Sunny, a cool breeze, and a high of 75 degrees. We enjoyed the day in the same lazy and playful way we had enjoyed the previous day; in fact, in the same way we had enjoyed every day that we could remember in Galveston. Unfortunately, three o'clock brought clean-up, pack-up, and move-out time. We said good bye to the sand and the sea gulls and headed home.

We took the slightly longer route home, going west on 3005 to Free-port, then north on Highway 288 into Houston. Traffic was fairly heavy. I imagined it must have been bumper-to-bumper on Interstate 45. It usually was at that time of year, considering how fabulous the weather was.

Upon arriving at our Avalon abode, I noticed a car in the driveway. A new Oldsmobile. As we pulled in behind it, my mother stepped out.

"Where have you two been? I've been waiting here for fifteen minutes. Did you forget about me, James? Your poor old mother, wait-ing here in the driveway like this, where I could get mugged by one of the many criminals that live in this town? It's a good thing Mary Louise is responsible and cares about me. Hello, dear. I'm sorry you have to put up with my son. I certainly hope he treats you better than he treats me."

"Mom?"

"What?"

"Can I get out of the car, please?"

"I'm not stopping you, James. Why are you late?"

"Mom, I can't get out of the car and hug you hello with your face hanging in my window. Of course, maybe it would be better if I just stayed here for a day or two. What do you think?"

"I think you're impossible."

I hoped, as I always did, that I could survive the few days Mom would be there. It would be a struggle, though. Thank God she loved Mary Louise.

We unloaded the car, then went for a nice dinner at Shanghai River on Westheimer. One thing my mother and I had in common was a love of Chinese food. Afterwards, at Mary Louise's suggestion, we took her to see "The Fugitive." I didn't have to talk to her for over two hours, and the movie was great.

When we got home, it was time for me to do some office work, pay some bills, review my schedule for Monday, and be alone for a while. Mary Louise entertained our guest in the sun room with conversation and Sunday night television.

I noted that I had two cases Monday morning, with office patients starting at one in the afternoon. I planned to go back down to pathology and find out what information I could about the child with scoliosis. Unfortunately, I noticed that my first case was a revision hip replacement. The new hip prostheses were "press-fit" components, meaning that the ball and socket replacement parts were not cemented in position. This supposedly allowed a longer mechanical life due to less wear and tear. All the older prostheses, however, were cemented in position. They had to be jack-hammered out, in a sterile fashion, of course, and new parts had to be inserted. Getting out the old, loose components and pieces of broken bone cement could be a monumental undertaking. It was more physically demanding than any other operation. I wondered why Fran had scheduled it as the first case on Monday. Why not later in the week when I was warmed up?

I was tired. I said my good nights to Mary Louise and Mom and went to bed. I dreamed of salty margaritas, sunny weather, and deformed children lying on the beach on rust-colored towels. I woke up in a sweat.

CHAPTER 27

DR. JEFF CLARKE

Monday rounds were fairly easy. Since Harold Sanders had passed on, I had no sick patients in the hospital. Hattie Barnes was stirring around on a cane, having thrown her walker at the physical therapist. Hattie told me that she had instructed the young girl to give the walker to somebody who really needed it, although, I am sure, not quite that nicely. I agreed to let her go home when she said that she was experiencing less pain than before surgery. It was rewarding to have a patient do that well, even if they were a little rough around the edges and gave me a hard time. Better that any day than a bad result. Even worse was a patient who had a good result, but thought the result was bad. Woe unto any surgeon in that situation.

I finished my two cases by eleven-thirty, got a quick sandwich in the surgeon's lounge, and headed down to pathology. The ever-so-charming secretary was still there.

"Morning. I'm Dr. Brady. I was down here last Friday for an autopsy on a patient of mine, and I stopped and visited with Dr. Clarke about an unusual case he had. Would you mind telling me where he is?"

"In the lab."

"The autopsy room?"

"Negative. The lab. They do research there. Go through the autopsy area, through the set of double doors, then hang a right at the first hallway."

I followed her explicit directions and found Jeff Clarke in his lab laboring with a young Asian woman over an electron microscope.

"Hey, Jeff," I said pleasantly.

"Brady! What are you doin' down here again? Bump off another one? Heh, heh, heh. Oh, wait. I know! You're looking for fresh road kill for one of your wham-bam-thank-you-ma'am hip jobs." He laughed even harder, as did his associate, or assistant, or student, or whoever she was. "Road kill" referred to bone graft material used in certain orthopedic operations to aid healing. Bone graft could be obtained from the patient, usually from the pelvic area, or could be obtained from a "bone bank," an entity designed to harvest, purify, and distribute sterile, compatible bone graft tissue for surgical use. A bone bank harvested its material from cadavers, Jeff's area of expertise.

"No. But cute. Real cute. What I came down here for was information on that child you showed me last Friday. The one with osteogenesis imperfecta, who, I guess, expired after spine surgery. Remember?"

"What for?" he asked.

"I have a similar patient and wondered about the safety of recommending spinal fusion for scoliosis," I lied. "If the risks outweigh the rewards, then I wouldn't send my patient for the operation. See?"

"All right. Let me get my post-mortem file." He got up and left the room, leaving me alone with his colleague. She continued to study whatever was under the microscope.

"So, are you Jeff's assistant?"

She studied me with deep-set, piercing eyes before answering.

"No. I'm a pathologist. Board certified. I'm here at University doing a post-graduate fellowship in blood vessel pathology. My area of interest is arteriosclerosis, primarily the physiology of plaque. You know, that goop that clogs the arteries?"

"Oh, sure. Well, it's nice to have you here. Where are you from?" She looked about twenty years old.

"My life history or medical school?"

I smiled. So did she.

"L.A. My family is from Thailand, but I've been in the states most of my life. Undergrad and med school at UCLA. Pathology at Hopkins."

My recent exposure to young, bright, professional women who looked like they should be I.D.'d at a nightclub made me feel like the "Ancient Mariner."

"Okay, let's see," Jeff interjected. "Friday. Here it is. Jonathan Fischer. Age ten. Patient of Bill Russell's, at least he was the admitting physician."

I was taking notes, since he didn't volunteer to let me see the record. Doctors were very touchy about their records. I was no exception.

"Surgeon was Paul Gertzbein, assistant Greg Mayfield. Surgery done the day before, Thursday, March 24. Patient went to ICU in Children's Hospital post-op. Developed severe respiratory distress that evening and expired a little after midnight. I did the post, as you know. The slides haven't all been prepared yet, and the toxicology isn't completed, but I can tell you the kid basically died of respiratory insufficiency.

"Brady, that kid was a pretzel. His spine was so crooked that he probably had respiratory distress pre-op. In fact, looking at the dictated death summary from the Pedi ICU resident, that was exactly the situation. It was hero surgery. Kid dying, parents desperate, hero spine surgeons going in and trying to fix him, and...whammo! He bites the dust. Now, it'll be the surgeon's fault. Bring on the fucking lawyers! You know what we always say in this business, Brady?"

"Yes, I know. No good deed goes unpunished. But I'm sure in this case, Jeff, the parents will understand. It was a last ditch effort to save their child." Bobbie and Pete Huntley probably would have allowed anything if there had been a chance it could have saved Stevie. "Can you give me some background info? Where he was from, parents' names, that sort of thing?"

He peered at me over his bifocals.

"That sort of thing won't help you with your patient. What are you gonna do, get up a group therapy session?" He really laughed then. "I think not. If Bill Russell or one of the surgeons wants you to have that information, you'll have to get it directly from him."

"Okay. I appreciate your help. One more thing, though. Toxicology. What was the report on that?"

He looked at the file again. "The usual. Analgesics, antiemetics, anesthetic agents. They were still in his system, since he had had surgery that day. Anything else?"

"No, thanks. Do me one favor, though, if you would. If anything unusual comes up on the slides or on biochemistry, would you let me know?"

He stared at me. "What's this all about, Brady? You into forensics? You thinking of taking up a new career when the Clinton plan kicks in?" he cackled.

"No, nothing like that. Just intellectual curiosity, that's all. Thanks again." I turned to leave. "And it was nice to meet you, Miss..."

"Lee. Brenda Lee. Not the singer." They both howled.

CHAPTER 28

JONATHAN FISCHER

I had three minutes or so to spare when I arrived at the office. I called Mary Louise, and, speaking to the answering machine, told her that I had some information regarding the second child, whose name was Johnathan Fischer. I asked that she call Susan Beeson and tell her what I knew and that I would talk to Bill Russell and try to get the home address, phone number, and anything else that seemed appropriate.

I decided that if Bill gave me any trouble, I would talk to Paul Gertzbein, or better yet, Greg Mayfield. After my conversation with Paul the previous week in the Doctor's Lounge, I would rather not discuss the matter with him if I could get my answers elsewhere.

That afternoon went pretty well, except for a nice old guy from somewhere in West Texas, who needed extensive hip surgery. He had been involved in an accident on a cutting horse, herding cattle for an old-fashioned Texas round up. His name was Ed Harrison, and he had fractured his hip joint, including the pelvic bone.

The surgeon in Midland had put the joint back together best he could, but essentially the pelvic area behind the hip had collapsed. I would have to insert an artificial hip joint, and he would need a fairly massive bone graft in which to cement the prosthesis. I must have been thinking about Jeff Clarke too much, because I accidentally used the phrase "road kill" to describe the bank bone graft. I stopped talking after I said it and started to apologize, but his wife, son, and he looked at each other and fell apart with laughter.

"Just make sure you don't use one of them cow bones, Doc," he said. "With these false teeth I got, I can't chew my cud real good." He continued laughing till he cried.

When I finished up with the office patients, I made some room on my desk for the phone, shoving stacks of paper and charts around and piling them higher. I learned from his secretary that Bill Russell was still seeing patients, but she assured me that he would call back shortly.

"Is this regarding a patient, Dr. Brady?" Standard question and appropriate in this situation.

"Yes. Johnathan Fischer. Can you pull his chart for me?"

"Well, I can, but Johnathan died last week at Children's after spinal surgery. Are you aware of that?"

"Oh, sure." I lied again, "I'm treating another child with the same kind of problem, and I would like to get some information about the family, early symptoms, and development of deformity. Those sorts of things."

"I'll get the chart and have him call you, Dr. Brady," she politely said.

"Listen, uh...What's your name?"

"Emily."

"Okay, Emily. Why don't you get the chart. Most of the information will be in there, and I won't have to disturb your boss, and I can go home. He sees patients late, I hear."

"God, don't I know it. We have supper delivered up here sometimes. Can you hold a minute for me?"

"Sure."

"Thanks. Be right back."

She sounded nice. Too bad I was being dishonest, but then, that's the way it goes sometimes. From all the movies I had seen and the books I had read, private investigators were not exactly deacons in the church. As I mulled over whether to feel guilty or not, she returned to the phone.

"Let's see. Johnathan Fischer, from Port Arthur, Texas. Mother's name, Molly, nurse by training, but I don't think she worked. She pretty much took care of Johnathan full time. You know. That child had so many problems, he was in and out of here all the time. I think he had been operated on for fractures over a dozen times. And we casted him I don't know how many times."

"Emily, does Dr. Russell cast many patients himself?"

"Not really. Usually just simple stuff, but some of these O.I. kids, they have so many fractures, that they can't see the bone doctor every single time. So, we do as much as we can, and call in somebody when, well, when Dr. Russell thinks he needs to. Anyway, father's name - Nolan. He's a chemical plant operator at...let me see, Dow, it looks like. Johnathan was an only child, I think. No sibs are listed. Diagnosis - O.I. tarda. First visit was about eight years ago. He was two then. What else do you need?"

"Date of birth?"

"Let's see. January 23, 1984. That it?"

"Yes, I guess so. You have been very helpful, and I really do appreciate it. If there's something else, I'll talk to Bill. Thanks again."

"You're welcome. Bye."

I had gleaned enough information, hopefully, for Susan to leave me alone for a while. I packed up my briefcase, picking up Tuesday's charts for surgery and whatever mail would fit. I shoved the rest of the stuff around a little, messed it up on one side of the desk, stacked it higher on the other. I hoped Fran wouldn't notice the empty "out" box on my desk.

CHAPTER 29

TWINS

"How was your day, sweetie?" Mary Louise asked as I embraced her and received a welcome home kiss.

"Where's Mom? Left a day early, I hope?"

"No. She's resting in her room. Be nice."

"Time for a sneak out to the 'exercise room'?" I asked hopefully. We had an exercise area above the garage. Mary Louise used it almost daily. I, unfortunately, went out there so seldom, I never could remember where the key was.

"Interested in working out, young man?"

"Yes, in a manner of speaking. Think we can..."

"Hello, James. How are you? Tell me all about your day." My mother always had an incredible sense of timing. Bad. She loved medical stuff. I could never tell her enough, so I didn't bother to tell her much.

"Okay, Mom. First though, what did you girls do?"

"Well, we went to breakfast at that nice little place...What is it, Mary?" It was always James and Mary. None of that Texan two-name business for a sophisticated lady from Waco.

"The Buffalo Grill, Mother Brady."

"That's it. Then we went shopping at the Galleria all day. We had a salad at the cutest place. What was it?"

"A Movable Feast."

"That's it. They had sprouts, and sunflower seeds, and herbal dressing. It was wonderful, simply wonderful. I've been resting, waiting for you. How's Mildred?"

"She's doing great. She was up today on a walker, moving around pretty good. She can probably go home toward the end of the week. Are you going to stay with her for a few days?"

"Heavens, no, James. I've no time for that. I'm leaving for Dallas on Wednesday. I've got to get back home tomorrow and get ready for that trip. Busy, busy, busy. You know me. Never stop, or you'll die. That's my motto."

That was certainly true. I guessed one or more of the other sisters would stay with Aunt Mildred. Sister Lucille Brady, my mother, didn't have time to take care of anyone but herself. She was aptly named, though. A Lucille Ball look alike, she was in great shape. Five foot, two inches, one hundred and ten pounds, red headed, a ball of fire. She came from a family of long livers. Her mother died at ninety-three. We could look forward to a long relationship.

We had a nice dinner in the dining room. Candles, an aromatic Chianti Classico Ruffino, prime rib medium rare, following a Caesar salad to start. I always loved Mary Louise, but I loved her an unspeakable amount when she prepared a dinner like that. I stepped outside for a cup of espresso and my evening smoke. It was a nice spring night, the air fragrant with honeysuckle. Even the cat was nice, deftly jumping into my lap without spilling my coffee. I smoked, she purred.

The pleasantness was broken by a phone call from Bill Russell. I took it on the portable outside.

"Hey, Bill. What's going on?"

"What's going on with you, Brady? Milking information from Emily behind my back?"

"No, Bill, I just needed some background on Johnathan Fischer. You know, for my other patient..."

He interrupted me. "That's bullshit. What do you need home

address, place of employment, and date of birth for? To treat another with O.I.? No way. I want to know what the hell's this about?" He paused. "I'm serious, Jim Bob. Patient confidentiality has been breached!"

"You know as well as I do, Bill, that there's really no confidentiality in the medical business. Records are an open book, whether it's hospital or office business. All a lawyer has to do is send an official-looking release from a patient or relative, in a certified mail envelope, and we have to show them everything. So, whether I get what I asked for from you or someone else, really doesn't matter. Since we're friends, and I didn't think you'd give a damn. Do you?"

"Not really, I guess. I'm just curious. Does it have something to do with that Huntley business? Is there a plot to kill all the kids with O.I. that I treat? What's the deal? You can tell me."

"Listen, all I can say is that I'm gathering some facts for an investigation into the possible murder of Stevie Huntley. Stan Lombardo's daughter is a detective. Her name is Susan Beeson, and she asked me to..."

"Oh, I get it. They do the police work, you do the background medical work. But what, for God's sake, does Johnathan Fischer have to do with Stevie Huntley, except that they were the same age, I guess, and they both had osteogenesis imperfecta tarda, type II. Oh. Wait a minute. Shit! They looked alike. That's it, isn't it? They could be twins? Shit, why didn't I ever think about that? Too damn busy running around like a chicken with my head cut off, that's why. But Jim Bob, Stevie lived on our street. The Fischer kid lived out of town, somewhere over on the Louisiana border. Beaumont, Port Arthur, Orange."

"Port Arthur. Emily told me."

"Brady, that is just too fucking weird for me. I remember you asked me at Gaido's last weekend about Stevie being adopted. I wondered what the hell that was all about. I'll be damned. Anything else I can do for you?"

"You've certainly changed your attitude in the last few minutes. I was hoping you wouldn't make the connection between the two boys. You never had before, and you'd treated both of them for what, eight years?"

"Brady, Stevie's disease wasn't all that bad. Johnathan's was horrible. I can't even count his fractures. He was in a motorized chair most of the time. When a kid looks that bad, you really don't pay all that much attention to their face. You know what I mean?"

"I guess. Listen, you have to keep quiet about all this. If you need lessons in learning to be quiet during an investigation, I'll have Stan's daughter come over and read you the riot act. That'll get your attention."

"That's okay. I'm a pediatrician. I know how to keep quiet. I deal with anxious mothers all day. The quicker I let them say what they want to say, the quicker I get to see the next patient."

"Look, Bill. I have to talk to Bobbie and Pete Huntley at some point in time. Susan asked me if I would do it. She thought that the doctor/neighbor approach would be gentler than the police, although Susan's probably very good with that sort of thing. Anyway, do you know if Stevie was adopted?"

"No idea. I don't know about the Fischer kid either. Guess I should, huh? Being the doctor for two kids with a congenital, hereditary disease, should make me the prime candidate to know something like that, shouldn't it?"

"Well, I don't..."

"Hell, Brady. I run a hundred kids in and out of my office every day. I don't know most of their names, much less whether they're adopted or not. I will tell you this, though. The pathologist can tell you if the two boys are from the same genetic structure."

"What do you mean?"

"Stevie was autopsied, fool. Coroner's case. You know, death within 24 hours of a hospital admission gets a mandatory autopsy."

"But he was D.O.A., Bill."

"Check the autopsy. Get them to run some tissue samples. This is 1994. Those pathologists can tell you just about anything. I'm telling you he had to be a coroner's case. I signed the death certificate."

"Okay. Thanks much, Bill. I appreciate your help."

"Later."

"And Bill. Keep your mouth shut about all this. Got it?"

"My lips are sealed. Bye."

I hoped they were.

If this investigation were to remain low key, he and I both would have to keep quiet. I couldn't believe my stupidity. Stevie Huntley had had an autopsy. Since I hadn't talked to Pete yet, I hadn't heard about it, but I should have known something that elementary. Not enough experience with patients dying, I thought. Not that I wanted any more than I already had to deal with. Harold Sanders had been enough.

I sat outside with Cat and smoked another cigarette. Mom and Mary Louise were watching "Murphy Brown" on TV and laughing. Getting the autopsy results on Stevie would be no problem, since he had been my patient. I still couldn't get over the fact that I hadn't realized he was a coroner's case. I figured I needed a vacation. I asked Cat if she wanted to travel to the Caribbean. Lots of little sea critters in the sand to eat, Cat. You love fish, don't you, girl?

She didn't respond, except to purr. I puffed, and petted her. We enjoyed the rest of the evening.

CHAPTER 30

SLEUTH

Tuesday and Wednesday went fairly smoothly. Mom went home, and Aunt Mildred went home. The office patients were fairly pleasant, and surgery went well. I caught up on some paperwork, not that I would ever get it all done, but progress was being made.

J.J. was coming home on Friday, and I was looking forward to seeing him. I didn't want to make any plans while he would be here, so that I could be at his disposal if he had any time to visit with me. That is, between sleeping till noon, and partying with his friends till three or four in the morning. He was twenty, only a year from being an adult. I thought that the age of adulthood should be moved to thirty. I wondered if parents felt that way twenty or thirty years ago. I doubted it, since I was sure that collegians then were much more mature than the children of the present.

Mary Louise had made plans for us to take Bobbie and Pete Huntley to dinner on Thursday. I dreaded it. I hadn't seen either of them since the day of Stevie's funeral. They had been in hiding. I wasn't even sure if Pete had gone back to work yet. I guessed I would find out. I wondered how I could approach the adoption question tactfully. I hoped that Mary Louise would ask about it. She was much better at that sort of thing than I.

Wednesday night, Susan Beeson called the house.

"Dr. Brady? Susan Beeson. I'm sorry to bother you at home, but my husband, Gene, has a problem. He plays basketball in a league and came down on his ankle during a game. It's killing him. One of his friends had to drive him home. It's swollen and kind of looks like it has an angle to it. I'm worried it's broken. What should I do?"

It was 8:30. The thought of a long night entered my tired brain and body.

"Why don't you meet me at the Emergency Room at University? How long before you can get there?"

"Ten minutes. I'll put the red light on top of the car and turn the siren on."

I envied the luxury of taking home a police vehicle. Did that apply to all detectives or just the chief's daughter?

"Okay. I'm on my way now. I'll see you there, Susan."

"Thanks, Doc."

Gene Beeson had, in fact, fractured his ankle. Both sides of the joint were broken, and he needed surgery. He hadn't eaten since lunch, and had only had some Gatorade during the basketball game. Anesthesia agreed to go ahead and let me operate on him right away. I wanted to repair the ankle before the swelling became too bad. A fracture that bad often blistered in a few hours, making surgery next to impossible.

I took Susan upstairs to the surgery waiting area, empty at that hour. We sat and had a cup of coffee, waiting for Gene to be brought up from the ER. It took the operating room crew extra time to prepare a room for surgery at that time of night, since there was only a skeleton crew after seven. So I had time to visit with Susan. I liked her. She was smart, trained, and a professional. She was, also, a nice girl. She reminded me of a younger Mary Louise, the kind of daughter a father could be very proud of. And I knew that Stan Lombardo must be proud.

"So, how's the Huntley investigation going, Susan?"

"Not very well. In spite of the $100,000 reward, there have been no leads of any consequence. The usual worthless calls about red trucks and 'can I have the money, please, since I saw one at my apartment complex?' That sort of thing. We ran a computer print-out at DMV using compact pick-up trucks, American and foreign, using shades of red coloration, and the letters and numbers that were reported by witnesses...C, E, and 7. Do you have any idea how many vehicles were on the print-out?"

"No idea."

"Over 1,000. Do you have any idea how many man hours it would take to investigate the vehicles and the whereabouts of the owners at any given time? I'll tell you. More than we have the staff for at HPD. We can barely keep up with the murders, rapes, assaults, and burglaries with the staff we have. It's an impossible task. That's why we need a break in the case. A tip from a witness or an acquaintance of the perpetrator. Or something possibly from your end. You're trying to help us out with the medical end of the investigation, and I appreciate it.

"Your wife called me Monday and told me about the Fischer boy from Port Arthur. But I really think that's a long shot, don't you?"

"Who knows, Susan. Johnathan Fischer was the same age as Stevie Huntley, with the same disease, only much worse. He used a motorized wheelchair. Bill Russell, my neighbor, was the pediatrician for both children, so most of what I know is from his files. Since Stevie had an autopsy, I'm going to try to get my friend, Jeff Clarke, from pathology to run some tissue typing samples to see if the boys match in any way. It may all just turn out to be some inherent resemblance that kids with osteogenesis imperfecta have. I've got to check that out. We're having dinner with the Huntleys tomorrow night, so I'll broach the subject of adoption. Who knows? This may all be a ridiculous wild goose chase."

"You'd be surprised, Dr. Brady, at some of the leads that solve crimes. The smallest detail may hang somebody. You never know.

How will you find out about the Port Arthur child's family?"

"Excuse me? I thought that would be your job. Or some-body's." I paused and sighed.

"Gene's going to be out for a while, isn't he? How long would you say?"

"Well, Susan, it's a bad break. Probably no weight and on crutches for a month. Then a removable cast, followed by physical therapy. Probably six months or so. What kind of work does he do?"

"He's an accountant."

"Well, he can go to work next week. He just can't have any fun for a while."

She laughed. "About the other matter, since the information you're helping us gather isn't high priority...no offense...it would be a help if you could find out as much as you can. It would save the force a lot of man hours if there's nothing there. In your spare time, of course."

"So what do you think you want me to do in my 'spare time,' other than to give up eating and sleeping?"

"Sorry," she smiled. "First, talk to the Huntleys. Find out about the adoption. If they say no, you'll have to check birth records. They have to have a birth certificate. Try to get that from records in the city of birth. That's public record, usually, but if it isn't, for some reason, we have associates at our disposal, and they can get what you need. If Stevie was adopted, you'll need adoption records, birth records, all that. And you'll need the same on the child from Port Arthur.

"If you then get your information from the pathology depart-ment and can link the children somehow genetically, then you, or we, can ferret out who's telling the truth and who's not. Maybe it will help and maybe it will go nowhere, and you will have just pissed everyone off. That's my job in a nutshell, doc. Investigating everything down to a fine detail and pissing people off," she laughed. So did I.

About that time, the night nurse came out and said that Gene was in the operating room and asked if I would care to come to the party.

"Sure. On my way."

As I turned to leave, Susan said, "Please take good care of my man, Doc."

"Not to worry, Susan. I'm a helluva lot better at surgery than I am at detecting."

"Oh, I think that's only temporary. I'll bet you'll decide you like it if you discover you're good at it. You must have some investigative ability. You had to get through school doing a little. Right?"

"Right."

"So, you can be my silent partner, and best of all, you can enjoy the detective work. Since you don't have to do it for a living and you can walk away when this case is solved. What do you say?"

"We'll see. I'll talk to you after surgery."

The operation went well, taking about an hour. After letting Susan know that Gene was fine, I headed home. On the way, I enjoyed a cigarette in the cool, spring air with the windows down. I decided that while detective work might resemble that of a doctor, it applied more to internal medicine and diagnostics than surgery. Surgery was easy. I had fixed Gene's ankle in an hour or so, and although it would take a while to heal, I already knew that it would be all right. But, finding out who killed Stevie Huntley was a different matter. That wasn't easy. In fact, it might be impossible.

CHAPTER 31

DINNER WITH THE HUNTLEYS

Although we were next door neighbors, Mary Louise made arrangements to meet the Huntleys at The Grotto for dinner. Neither Pete nor Bobbie were sure they could make it through the entire meal, since it was their first outing after Stevie's death. I was interested in a more quiet, sedate setting for dinner. The Huntleys, however, were in favor of a crowded, boisterous Italian restaurant. This described most of the Italian eating establishments in Houston. The Grotto was no exception. Casual, yet charming, it offered splendid Northern Italian fare. Located on Westheimer Road, probably the busiest east-west running street in Houston, it was surrounded by carefully sculpted beds of azaleas, impatiens, and pansies still striving in the warm March air.

We arrived first, gave our name to the hostess, and sat at the bar. The enormous circular bar sat at the entrance to the restaurant and was completely open to the dining area on all sides. Although the kitchen was located in the back of the seating area, bins of aromatic dishes were strategically placed around the bar area to whet one's appetite. I was always tempted to reach into one of the aluminum containers, scoop out a taste of its contents, and stuff whatever it happened to be in my watering mouth. I resisted, as usual.

The bar, and the serving area, was, as always, crowded. Mary Louise ordered a glass of house chardonnay. I wanted something a little stronger and opted for an Absolut Citroen on the rocks. I preferred an unblended scotch in the fall and winter, and vodka in the spring and summer. Strange behavior, I suppose, but mine is never all that predictable or logical to anyone but me. And Mary Louise. So we sipped and discussed our respective day's activities. Her day always seemed so much more interesting than mine. Maybe it was the luxury of variety.

The Huntleys arrived at 7:20, and I excused their lateness. They ordered Jack Daniels on the rocks and gulped their drinks. As Pete ordered another round for everybody, he and Bobbie lit up a cigarette.

"I didn't know you guys smoked," I said.

"We used to. Now we've started again," Pete answered.

Neither of them looked very healthy. They were dressed fairly well, though. Pete had on black slacks, Italian loafers, and a pull-over knit shirt with an emblem on the left breast area which I could not decipher. Bobbie had on a nice, sleeveless, summer print dress and low heels.

In contrast, I had on my standard, away-from-work, casual attire. Jeans, western shirt, and black ostrich boots. My partner, and proponent of Texas chic, had on black jeans, black lizard boots, and a white western-style shirt with an embroidered horse over each pocket. And long, straight, blonde hair. The pockets of her shirt were bulging a little. In fact, more than a little. As I stared, my groin stirred. Without warning, my imagination was brought back to reality.

"Jim Bob, our table is ready," the object of my lust stated.

"What?"

"Let's eat. Dinner." She leaned toward my left ear. "You can have dessert when we get home." As we stood up, she deftly brushed the front of my jeans and smiled, "Down, boy."

We were seated on the east side of the restaurant, an ideal spot in my opinion. There were large, plate-glass windows covering the entire east wall, as well as the south wall, which faced Westheimer and through which the patrons entered. The west wall was closed, but was covered with decorative caricatures and Italian slogans. It was a friendly, lively atmosphere. We ordered calamari, Vallone salads, and dishes ranging from linguini with clam sauce to veal scallopini. And a carafe or two, maybe three, of the house chianti, a light and pleasant complement to a wonderful dinner.

We made small talk all through the dinner. Except for the dark rings under their eyes, they seemed to be doing fairly well. They chain smoked between courses, which bothered even me, the old closet smoker, a little. They got a little giddy on the wine and seemed to be enjoying themselves. I felt like shit for what I was about to do.

As Mary Louise and I sipped our cappuccino, and they their respective sambuccos, I brought up the subject of Stevie.

"I hate to bring this up, but have the police made any progress in the investigation?"

It was as though I had slapped them both. Bobbie sort of bowed her head.

Pete responded with an informative, "No, nothing yet."

"Well, I hate to bring this up, but..."

"Then don't," Pete said loudly. "Leave it be, Jim Bob. We live with this every day. We thought we'd have one night to get drunk and maybe not think about it." He was slurring his words a little. I didn't blame him one bit for getting angry.

"Pete, Bobbie, I wouldn't do anything, or say anything to hurt you or upset you. But I have been exposed to something that may affect you and Stevie, and I have to talk to you about it."

They stared at me, then at each other.

"What is it?" Bobbie asked.

I told them an abbreviated story of my discovery of Johnathan Fischer and Susan Beeson's request that I gather information in a discreet sort of way. I explained that what I was doing might have no bearing whatsoever on the death of their son, but that I had to ask them a very important question.

"WHAT, for God's sake?" Pete was looking a little steamed.

"Was Stevie adopted?"

Their reaction resembled the pattern of a balloon when its air has been suddenly let out. They deflated over a second or two and were then left wilted and still. Bobbie and Pete leaned back in their respective chairs. Bobbie started to cry. Pete lit a cigarette off the butt of the one that was still burning.

"Jesus H. Christ, Brady. You do know how to fuck up a good evening." He comforted Bobbie as best he could, but she left the table anyway. Mary Louise followed her.

"Pete, your answer to the question will make the difference in whether there may be a window of possibility of finding someone that maybe had something to do with Stevie being run over or not. It's that simple. If you say no, then the resemblance between the two boys may be simply a coincidence. If you say yes, then there are all kinds of possibilities to consider, all of which may simply be coincidental as well. It may turn out that Stevie was the victim of a random, hit-and-run driver.

"I will tell you, though, that the pathologists at University can run tissue samples on both children and can tell us if they are genetically compatible. So, if your answer is no, that Stevie wasn't adopted, and the pathologist says the boys are twins, you'll have some explaining to do to the police. They are going to be investigating every aspect of this case," I lied a little, again. Susan Beeson had told me HPD didn't have the time to check every detail. That's why I was playing Matlock.

He glared at me for a few seconds, then crushed out his cigarette as violently as he could. He probably wished that he had my head in the ashtray. Pete wasn't a large man, probably five nine or five ten, and maybe 170 pounds, but extreme violence could be carried out by anyone of any size in a volatile situation.

"Yes, you asshole. Are you satisfied?"

"Pete, I'm really sorry. I just happened to stumble..."

"Shut the fuck up, Brady. No one has ever known that Stevie was adopted, except Bobbie, of course, and our parents. It was a very discreet, private adoption, arranged by an attorney friend of mind. We never intended for anyone to know. Not even Stevie, not that it matters now. But I can't imagine how that could have any bearing on Stevie being run down in the street.

"The son of a bitch who killed him will, I'm sure, never be found. Some kid in a hurry to pick up some dope, or to get his girl-friend laid, or some goddamn thing like whoever was driving that car had done a hundred times before. It's just that Stevie happened to wander into the street. He was in the wrong place at the wrong time. That's all it was! We'll never know what really happened.

"And all this bullshit from you about twins, and osteogenesis imperfecta, and all that crap, is RIDICULOUS! You've ruined dinner, and I'm sure Bobbie will be up all night crying again. Thanks to you, pal. What a good neighbor you turned out to be."

He turned to walk away, then stopped. He leaned down into my face.

"You know, Brady, if you had really wanted to help us out of this situation, you could have done something to save Stevie when he was lying there in the street dying. Helping us out now, well, it's not helping. Now leave us the hell alone!" He pulled out a few bills and flung them at the table. People were staring at both of us.

"There! I don't want you buying my fucking dinner."

I sat there for a minute, watching him storm out of the restaurant. I wanted a cigarette, but didn't want to light up in public. Mary Louise came walking back to the table shortly. I added a few bills, too upset to really figure the tip accurately. I erred, hopefully in the waiter's favor.

We left through the side door and walked between tables set up on the patio.

"How's Bobbie?" I asked quietly.

"Upset, obviously. How's Pete?"

"In another time, another place, another culture, I would be dead. At least that's the way he acted. I'm not sure it was worth it. I feel like...shit."

"I know, so do I. That interview I arranged started your involvement in this investigation business, so it's my fault as much as yours. I'm sure they'll get over it in time. Bobbie was as upset about Stevie being adopted as she was talking about his death. It doesn't seem all that important to most people, I don't think. Maybe I'm out of touch, Jim Bob. It's nothing to be embarrassed about. There's no stigma to infertility. It's a prevalent diagnosis, but physicians treat it like it's a disease now. People adopt babies all the time, don't they?"

"Maybe it's more popular to be infertile and to be artificially inseminated than it is to adopt. Who knows? Anyway, I really don't feel like being involved with all this anymore. Pete and Susan are right. The pathology analysis will amount to nothing. The police will never find the truck or the driver. The Huntley-Fischer twin O.I. thing is probably a colossal waste of my time, and all I've done is piss off two good friends."

"You never know, sweetie. You just never know." She patted my thigh. Then she moved her hand over a little. My groin stirred again. I wondered why I always thought of sex when a terrible situation arose. Maybe that was normal, and then, maybe it wasn't. I decided I really didn't care.

CHAPTER 32

J.J.

I made thorough rounds on Friday morning, not that I didn't on other mornings during the week. Patients who were required to stay in the hospital over the weekend always acted a little clingy and resentful on Friday, saying things like they hoped I had a nice weekend. Fortunately, I could afford the luxury of hiring a resident or a fellow to see patients on Saturday and Sunday, a benefit of being associated with the hospital teaching program.

Of course, when I had been in training, it had been the custom for the house staff to perform such services for free. Maybe the difference was that during the '70s, our alternative was to be in Southeast Asia. Personally, I preferred making rounds for the staff orthopedic surgeons and taking their calls on the weekend to playing honky-tonk piano in a "Mash" unit. The thought of playing Elmore James' "Stormy Monday" under a tent surrounded by machine-gun fire had never appealed to me.

I did three small cases, all outpatients, and went to the office. I dictated the "have to do today" stack of charts, opened my mail, and bid adieu to Fran and Rae.

Mary Louise had left me a note, saying she had a luncheon and two meetings to follow, and that I should relax and enjoy my afternoon off. I constructed a pastrami sandwich on toasted white bread with all the trimmings. I selected an ice cold beer, sat in the kitchen, watched HBO, and enjoyed myself.

I meandered into the backyard after lunch, inspected our gardening handiwork, and plopped into my rocking chair like a man twice my age. I concentrated on Lawrence Sanders' newest novel about the continuing adventures of Archie McNally. I flipped to the back cover periodically, noting to myself that his cat must like him a lot better than mine liked me. Cat would never pose for a photograph like that. His cat seemed to be serenely pleased to be held next to his face for the picture that adorned all of Mr. Sanders' recent novels.

I pondered the arrival of J.J., and thought about him as a little boy transitioning to an adult. He was too smart for his own good. J.J. was now twenty, and had grown up in the era of complicated video games, Nintendo, and computer wizardry. We bought his first computer, an early Apple model, when he was in the second grade. Although J.J. did fairly well in school, he was no straight-A student. He preferred to spend his time playing intricate games on his computer, or on his television conversion that served as a monitor for his video games. I tried to play his games with him, but, by age ten, he was unbeatable.

I will never forget that Sunday afternoon, when he was twelve. I was working in my study, paying some bills and leafing through correspondence. I had an unfortunate habit of forgetting to record checks in the check register after paying the bills. I was absently muttering about having no earthly idea as to the balance in my checking account. J.J. had come by and stood by the desk with his usual question of, "Whatcha doin', Dad?"

I mentioned that I wished the banks were open on Sunday for purposes like retrieving a checking account balance. ATMs allowed that sort of after hours thing at some point in history, but in 1986, either it was not available, or I didn't know how to access the service. Probably the latter. At any rate, he borrowed a pen, wrote down something on a note pad, and ran up the stairs.

Later that afternoon, around dinner time, he proudly strolled into the sun room with a computer print-out of my checking account, including check numbers, their amount, and a current balance as of the closing of the bank the previous Friday afternoon. I was amazed.

We had recently invested in an updated computer system with a modem, because J.J. claimed he needed one to communicate with his friends. Thinking, oh, that's nice, Mary Louise and I had proudly purchased a state-of-the-art system for him, complete with printer. Not bad for a kid in the seventh grade. I was very proud of him and wondered how in the world he had obtained the information that I had wanted. J.J. was proud that he could help out his old man.

By Monday afternoon, however, there were federal agents in our home. Mary Louise had called me at work, said there was an emergency, and told me to get home right away. One of my partners took over my office for me, and I streaked home like a madman. It seemed that J.J., and perhaps my generous wife and I, were guilty of a federal offense. Specifically, one that involved illegal entry into the data banks of a federal institution. It was called computer hacking, done with a modem, through some sort of system that was far too complex for a mere doctor and his wife to understand. We spent the next several days explaining what had happened to banking officials, local police, and numerous federal agency personnel. Even though it had been an innocent gesture on the part of J.J., we had to hire a lawyer. We ended up paying a ridiculous fine, and went through a very embarrassing scenario to get J.J. and ourselves off the hook, so to speak.

I have always suspected that J.J. probably knew exactly what he was doing, but he persistently maintained his innocence, as only a cute, twelve-year old can. His modem privileges were suspended for two years. Eventually, he got back in the "business," as he called it, of sharing computer information with other modem users, but it seemed that the scare of his two-year penalty had cured him of anything that could be construed as illegal. Or so I hoped.

As I mentally reviewed the incident of the past, I wondered if J.J. could still get information that was, oh...relatively inaccessible. I wondered if I could take him into my confidence and find out any background data on the adoption of Stevie Huntley, since I was quite sure that neither Bobbie nor Pete would be speaking to me for quite some time, if ever. I thought that he could help me gather some data about the Fischer boy in Port Arthur, also. I wouldn't expect him to do anything illegal, of course...just save me some leg work, help out the police, that sort of thing.

There was a problem, though. I didn't know the birth mother, the birth father, the actual registered name, or even the place of birth. I wondered how I could get that information. I considered calling Stan Lombardo and letting him know what I was up to. To cover my butt, in case I got myself, or J.J., more importantly, into any activity that was outside the realm of legality.

With those complicated thoughts of skullduggery swimming in my head, I fell asleep. Or so I assumed, since the next thing I remember was the sight of Cat's face staring at me no more than an inch away. Get the cameraman, I thought, she's finally ready for a photo.

CHAPTER 33

COINCIDENCE

Mary Louise and I decided to make our favorite meal, home-made tacos. We didn't know exactly what time J.J. would arrive. I had no idea what his class schedule was, but I assumed that since he was not an early riser, he would leave Austin around four o'clock or so. College kids didn't seem to know how to use the telephone to call home. They simply arrived with dirty laundry. We figured he would be home around seven, starving. So, we made something that would keep for a while if we guessed wrong.

Although J.J. had been accepted to several schools, he had decided to attend the University of Texas. He loved the Austin campus, not to mention the town itself. Seated in the incomparable Hill Country, U.T., which sported over 50,000 students, was a sprawling campus in the middle of town. Austin had almost too much to offer a student, making studying a low priority to many young minds. There was the State Capital and the Legislature, Lake Travis, the numerous night clubs on Sixth Street, and the beautiful Hill Country towns such as Kerrville, Fredericksburg, Johnson City, and Luckenbach, the latter made famous by Willie Nelson and Waylon Jennings.

J.J. had done a marginal job in school the first year, but revived himself the second year to qualify for the UT Business School. Currently in his third year, he was doing very well, taking the courses he enjoyed toward his degree in, naturally, Computer Science. I could picture him after graduation, holed up in a dark room with wall-to-wall monitors and electronic surveillance equipment, breaking computer data bank entry codes and spying on the bank accounts of the entire planet. Mary Louise had told me that was my mind's eye view of the best and worst of the movies "Sliver" and "Sneakers." And I always reminded her of J.J.'s sixth-grade incident.

And so, we occupied ourselves with the slow, yet enjoyable process of making tacos. She expertly took corn tortillas, fried them, and made tortilla chips and tacos. I acted as her assistant, first chopping red onions to fry with the ground chuck, then branching off into my own version of pico de gallo. I chopped fresh cilantro, scallions, tomatoes, and jalapenos, taking care to avoid adding fresh filet of fingertip to the concoction. I often thought, as I did that night, that chefs would make the best surgeons, though I didn't know any who had made the transition.

We sipped our iced Corona with lime and nibbled on chips with salsa and queso. We started the ritual by playing a Joe Sample compact disc, listening to his unusual brand of jazz piano combined with an occasional country motif that revealed his Beaumont, Texas roots. Midway through our second beer, we moved into an Etta James mood and danced around the kitchen to her stirring blues rendition of "Nighttime is the Right Time." We must not have heard the front door open, because we were startled to see J.J. and a companion staring at us.

"Sorry, Brad. My parents are a little weird," J.J. exclaimed over Etta's thundering alto voice.

I hugged the boy and shook hands with Brad, his roommate, whom I had met only once. I turned down the music to a near-conversational level, not wanting to completely tune out Etta James. She was not Muzak, after all. Her music was a joy to be savored. Mary

Louise meanwhile hugged both J.J. and Brad. She was that kind of girl.

"You guys hungry? We're making tacos," Mary Louise said lovingly as she patted J.J.'s cheek.

"Mom! Please! I'm not a kid."

"Yes, you are." And then she patted Brad's cheek, too. He liked it, I think. Most grown men would love to have my bride pat their cheek. They would, of course, have to die after the experience, which is why she didn't do that.

"Things are about ready. Why don't you two get cleaned up," she said. "Are you staying the whole weekend, Brad?"

"No, ma'am. Just tonight."

"Fine. Use the guest room across from J.J.'s room."

They went upstairs to get ready for dinner. I looked for laundry but didn't see any. J.J. was probably hiding it somewhere.

"Did you know Brad was coming, too?" I asked.

"No. Did you?"

"Of course not. I'm never sure J.J. is coming until he actually shows up."

"It's fine. We have plenty of food and plenty of room. I like Brad."

"You don't even know Brad. You only met him that one time."

"He's J.J.'s friend, right?"

"Right."

"And he's J.J.'s roommate, right?"

"Right." I knew where this was headed.

"So, I like and love J.J. Right?"

"Right."

"So, I must like his friends, right?"

The rationality of all women, even my darling Mary Louise, ended when it came to children.

"He could be a convicted felon, or a drug addict, or..."

"He's a nice boy. He said ma'am to me. And he's J.J.'s friend.

That's enough for me. Now set the table, young man, and quit being Mr. Suspicious. I'm a good judge of character, don't you think?"

I set the table. Yes, she was a great judge of character. She had married me, hadn't she?

Dinner was great fun. The tacos were superb, and the boys, it turned out, enjoyed the blues music I played. They had been to Antone's, a blues nightclub for which Austin was famous, "a time or two."

As we digested the meal, we sat drinking coffee. Playing Mr. Inquisitive, I asked Brad where he was from.

"Lafayette...Louisiana."

"Where is that in relation to Lake Charles?"

"Just south of Interstate 10, between Lake Charles and Baton Rouge. Bayou country. Actually, Cajun country, Dr. Brady. Boudin, red beans and dirty rice, fried alligator, you know," he answered.

"Sure, Brad," I said. "I have a lot of patients who come from over there. I'm surprised that you didn't go to LSU. How did you end up at UT? Don't you have to pay out-of-state tuition?"

"Dad? Is Brad on trial or something?" J.J. asked.

"No, J.J. Just curious. Sorry, Brad. I didn't mean to pry."

"It's okay, Dr. Brady. My folks sent me to Texas to get away from, oh, the friends I had in high school. I got in with a pretty rough crowd, and my grades weren't exactly what my dad expected. They did pay out-of-state tuition the first year, but then I established residency in Texas. I lived with my aunt here in Houston and worked for three months. So now I, or they, pay resident tuition."

"Well, that's good for you, and them. I thought the residency requirement was six months."

"Well, we fudged a little. I liked UT, and especially Austin. So, my aunt helped me out. She's picking me up tomorrow. You can meet her if you like."

"Fine, Brad. What does she do?"

"Dad!" J.J. exclaimed.

"It's okay, J.J. He's just curious. No prob, man. She's a nurse, or was. Or still is. She's some kind of big-wig at one of the hospitals over here."

"Really?" I asked. "Which one?"

"Oh, I don't know. Somewhere in that big medical center you have here."

"Huh. I work at University Hospital. I was just wondering if I might know her."

"Yeah. That's where she works. Her name is Beverly Richard."

"What?" I think the color left my face at that point.

"Beverly Richard. Do you know her?"

I was at a loss for words, a rare occurrence for me.

"Sure," I answered. "She used to work in orthopedics before she became a nursing administrator."

"Cool. She's a neat lady. She's taking me over to Port Arthur tomorrow to see my Aunt Molly. Her kid just died. I couldn't make it to the funeral, with school and all."

"Really? What happened?" Mary Louise interjected.

"Oh, he had some kind of back operation or something. Poor kid was crippled all to he...well, he was really crippled. I don't know what exactly was wrong with him, but his bones broke real easy. He rode around in this electric wheelchair. You know, the kind with the hand controls. Everybody thinks it's for the best and all. Life was pretty hard for Aunt Molly and Uncle Nolan, with Johnny being so bad off and all."

Mary Louise and I looked at each other, stunned.

"Wait a minute. What was the child's name?" I asked.

"Johnny Fischer."

I stared at Brad. The odds on that had to be a million to one.

"So, Molly Fischer, Beverly Richard, and your mother are..."

"Sisters! Great, Dr. Brady. You want to know about the rest of the family?" Brad asked laughingly.

J.J. laughed and shook his head at his old man's inquisitiveness. "Sorry, Brad. I didn't mean to get so personal."

"No prob, bro...I mean, Dr. Brady."

Things were quiet for a minute. I asked if anyone wanted an after-dinner drink. They all declined. The boys got up from the table and started helping Mary Louise remove the dishes, an old habit of J.J.'s that Brad picked up on. J.J. and his mother enjoyed some of their most intimate conversations cleaning up the dinner dishes. It had been that way as long as I could remember.

I excused myself and scurried to the bar, where I poured myself an eighteen-year-old MacCallan unblended scotch, taking care to omit the ice and water. I wandered outside to ponder these recent revelations and to concur with my confidant, Cat. She was nowhere to be found, so I positioned myself in the rocker and confided in myself. About what, I wasn't really sure, except that I had, by serendipity, found a link to the Fischer family. The fact that Brad was Beverly Richard's nephew and Johnathan Fischer's first cousin was an incredible coincidence, the first I had experienced that rivaled my cosmically-directed chance encounter with Mary Louise, the woman of my dreams.

CHAPTER 34

AUNT BEVERLY

By the time dinner, conversation, and clean-up had ended, Mary Louise and I were ready for quiet time. After she bathed and I showered, we cozied up in our bedroom chairs to read and allegedly watch one of the late-night talk shows, although we couldn't read or watch TV, because we couldn't quit talking about the connection between Johnathan Fischer, Beverly Richard, and Brad. We also wondered about Brad's last name. Mary Louise couldn't believe I hadn't asked. After a while, we must have dozed off, so I was startled by J.J. shaking my shoulder.

"Huh?"

"Dad. I thought you and Mom were going to watch Letterman tonight. Bonnie Raitt is his musical guest."

"Oh, sure we are. We just dozed off for a minute."

"Dad, it's eleven. I came to tell you that Brad and I are going out for a while. You haven't changed the alarm code again, have you?"

"No." I remembered the time I had changed it, though, when, in spite of my warnings after J.J. had been accepted to college, he persistently came home at all hours of the night during his senior year of high school. I, of course, needed my beauty sleep and could not function in the morning after I had been awakened at two or three o'clock as he entered the house, shut off the alarm, and then restarted it. The night I changed it, of course, the sirens blared, the police came, and my darling son was quite shocked. That had been the last night he stayed out late during a school week. He obviously hadn't forgotten.

"Where are you guys going?"

"Out!" he exclaimed. "It's only eleven. The night's young, dude!"

"Right. Be careful. Houston's full of crazy people this time of night, including probably, you and Brad."

"No prob, it's cool."

About that time Brad wandered into our bedroom. I was glad we had our robes on. Mary Louise was still fast asleep. The boys could have been brothers. They both stood at five feet eleven and were thin. I hated both of them for what had to be a size 28 waist. Faded jeans, hiking boots, and plaid shirts with Tommy something on a sideways label was their style.

Each wore a baseball cap turned around backwards, which I failed to understand. J.J. had a beautiful head of blonde hair that he had inherited from his mother. He wore rimless glasses, a preferred fashion statement among his computer-literate friends, and like his father, had hazel eyes, large lips, thick eyebrows. Good looking boy. So why did he ruin the look with that baseball cap?

Shortly after they left, I woke up my sleeping wife and helped her get into bed, since she remained half asleep. I tried to watch the last half of ol' Dave Letterman, but I couldn't make it. I felt old. I was glad I didn't have to take my teeth out.

Saturday morning was beautiful, a little cool and one of those rare cloudless days in the former swamp now called the Texas Gulf Coast. Mary Louise and I puttered around, read the paper, and even made a second pot of blended breakfast coffee. We wondered about the boys, since we hadn't heard them come in. I saw J.J.'s bright, metallic blue Mustang in front of the house, so I wasn't worried. Brad had said that Beverly Richard was taking him to Port Arthur on Saturday, meaning that she would probably be coming to our house.

The telephone rang about ten o'clock.

"Dr. Brady? This is Beverly Richard. How are you?"

"Doing fine, Beverly. And you?"

"Great morning. I guess you know by now that your son and my nephew are roommates at UT."

"Well, yes, I do. I'm embarrassed to say that J.J. isn't very communicative about that sort of thing. Mary Louise and I met Brad last year, but we had no idea that he was related to you until last night at dinner. I was sorry to hear about your nephew."

There was silence on the phone for a moment.

"How do you know about that?" she asked. She seemed very nice, for a change.

I told her about our conversation the night before regarding Johnathan Fischer, then made up a story about how Greg Mayfield, my partner, had showed me his x-rays before surgery and how I had learned he died post-op. I didn't tell her that I had seen him in the autopsy suite or that I had made a connection to Stevie Huntley. I also left out the fact that I was looking into the possibility that the boys were twins.

"Well, it's a shame Johnny died, but we all think it was for the best. He was so crippled and miserable most of his life. So was my sister. A blessing, I think."

"Well, you're probably right."

"Listen, the reason I called was about Brad. He gave me this number. I need to pick him up at noon. We're going to Port Arthur to see my sister and brother-in-law. But you probably know that."

"Yes. I'll let the boys know, or at least, I'll let Brad know. I would expect they were out late. But he'll be ready, Beverly."

"Thanks, Dr. Brady. See you at noon."

She seemed much nicer than I remembered. Maybe the years

had mellowed her, or me, or both of us. Or maybe the fact that Brad linked our families together made the situation better. Whatever the reason, it was a relief to think that she and I could finally get along.

I woke up the boys at eleven. They were both pretty groggy.

"Late night, huh?"

"Yeah. What time is it?" J.J. asked.

"Eleven. Brad's aunt is picking him up at noon. I rousted him first. You okay?"

"Sure. Guess I have to get up, too, huh?"

"Well, if you want to see Brad off, you do. It's the polite thing, don't you think?"

"Yeah. Anything to eat down there?"

As I viewed him laying there in his rumpled bed with his tousled hair, he seemed to still be a child.

"I'm sure your mother has something for the two of you to eat. You know how she is."

"Yep. The greatest." He got up and went into the john and shut the door. That was my signal to leave.

Mary Louise had managed to rustle up breakfast tacos. Scrambled eggs with red and green peppers, cheese, and bacon bits rolled in fresh flour tortillas with salsa. Sometimes I thought I married that woman for her wonderful Tex-Mex cooking. The boys ate like they had been starved for weeks. So did I, for that matter.

The doorbell rang promptly at noon. I greeted Beverly Richard at the door and invited her in. She was more attractive than I remembered. I had spent the last eight years or so avoiding her. She was dressed very well, in fact, better than a nursing administrator would be expected to dress. I guessed they made a lot more money than I realized. She had on a beige Chanel suit, higher heels than I would expect for a drive to Port Arthur, a lady's gold Rolex, and diamond stud earrings. Her well-manicured nails were painted a day-glo red. I remembered her hair as being red, but on that day, it appeared to be a muted, strawberry blonde. Overall, she was a good-looking woman, with a decent figure to boot.

"Hello, Dr. Brady. Beautiful day, isn't it?" she said as she offered me her hand.

"Yes, it is, Beverly." I returned her handshake. Her grip was firm, but not overly so.

"Beautiful home. Have you lived here long?"

"Oh, about eight years now, I think. You are certainly looking well." I think she saw me scanning her wrist and ears.

"Yes, thank you, I am. I've done well for myself. I've been fortunate to have been successful with my career. Going back to school to get my Master's in Nursing and then an MBA was a smart thing to do. Of course, while I do make a nice living at the hospital, I supplement my income."

I guessed she was volunteering that for my benefit, sensing my reaction to her display of Houston glitz.

"Really? Doing what?" She could be a call girl, I thought.

"Blackjack. You know I'm from Louisiana. We've had legalized gambling there for as long as I can remember. First, it was horse racing. Delta Downs, you know, and those places. In the last few years, gambling ships run out of New Orleans and Lake Charles, and I've been fortunate to have the time to perfect my skills. I'm a helluva card player."

"You mean, you actually win?" I asked incredulously.

"Oh, yeah! I started going on some Las Vegas and Atlantic City junkets a while back. Now they comp my food and my room just to get me out there, or up there, to gamble. I love it. I've thought about giving up my position at the hospital to do it full time, but I like the security of my day job. Know what I mean?"

I did, and I was impressed. It seemed a bizarre story, but no less likely than the one my twisted mind envisioned.

About that time Mary Louise came out of the kitchen and into the foyer.

"Hello. I'm Mary Louise. I apologize for my husband's failure to ask you to come in, sit down, and have something to drink. Can I get you some breakfast? Brad's still eating."

Mary Louise, the ever gracious hostess.

"Sorry," I said.

"7-UP and ice, please," Beverly said. "I'm addicted to that stuff. Buy it by the case. It doesn't have any caffeine, but it has something."

We walked her into the kitchen. She and Brad hugged, and she shook hands with J.J. We all chatted quite respectably, and I continued to be surprised.

After a bit, Beverly told Brad to get his things, since they had to get started. She asked to speak to me in private for a moment. We went into my study, but I left the door open. I thought that if she stabbed me or something, at least Mary Louise would hear the groaning and rescue me.

"We haven't spoken in so long," she started. "That incident many years ago was at an unfortunate time of my life personally. I have regretted it for a long time, but I never had the courage or the opportunity to tell you how I felt. You were right to bring that young boy to surgery. I was a bitch about it, and I'm sorry."

I was stunned. I mumbled something like sure, okay, no problem. I was speechless again, a rarity that had become more common in recent days.

"If you ever need anything at the hospital that I can help you with, let me know. And don't be a stranger." She once again extended her hand. I once again shook it back.

We all walked outside to see them off. J.J. said it first, although I could have thought it first.

"Wow! Cool car! Turbo Carrera?"

"Yes. Isn't it wonderful?" Beverly said.

"Do I get to drive today, Aunt Beverly?" Brad asked as excitedly as a twenty year old could without foaming at the mouth in public.

"Sure, Brad. I'm looking forward to catching up on some reading. It's not often I have a chauffeur."

It was a fabulous, red, Porsche 911 Carrera with the typical extra-wide rear axle, racing tires, and a spoiler. And a sunroof, no less. I thought it resembled the Porsche I had seen at Stevie Huntley's funeral, but I couldn't be sure.

"Great car, Beverly. You weren't by any chance at Stevie Huntley's funeral, were you?" I asked, immediately wishing I could take the question back. Too much of my mother in me.

"No, I don't think so. Who's he?" she asked innocently.

"My next-door neighbors' son. He was a hit-and-run victim a couple of weeks ago. Right here in the street. A woman sat next to us at the funeral who drove a car almost like this one. Just curious."

"There must be two dozen of these cars in Houston, Dr. Brady. I'm depressed every time I take it into the shop for a tune-up, thinking I have the only one. And, to my dismay, there are always others just like mine waiting to be serviced. Well, thanks for your hospitality. We'll be back tomorrow afternoon, so Brad and J.J. can get back to Austin before nighttime."

"Sorry about your loss. Your nephew and all. Give my regards to the family, please."

"Thank you, I will. I do think it is a relief for all concerned. He had been ill for so long. Well, bye now."

She waved, Brad saluted, and they mounted their turbo-charged steed and blasted off. There was no sound to compare with the start-up and take-off of the Carrera. I envied for a moment as they sped away.

"Jim Bob? Did you notice the license plate?" Mary Louise inquired. "That's so bizarre. It said "ACES HI." What in the world did that mean?"

I told her. She thought the story was as strange as I did.

"What did she want to talk to you about?"

"She wanted to apologize for that mess back in '86 or '87."

"That's surprising. Maybe she's not such a bad person, Jim Bob. I cannot get over the coincidence that she's the Fischer boy's aunt. And a gambler? With a Porsche? Did you see that jewelry? I wonder about all that. She has the appearance of a kept woman to me."

"Huh," I intelligently said. A kept woman. By whom, I wondered. She claimed she was a good blackjack player, and the license plate was certainly indicative of that. I decided I needed a nap to recharge and wondered if Mary Louise needed to recharge with me. I hoped J.J. had errands to run.

CHAPTER 35

ANNOUNCEMENT

W e didn't make it to nap time until three o'clock or so. J.J.'s reunion party was to start in the afternoon, so he hung around the house
for a while. He filled us in on all aspects of college life, academic and
social. It sounded to me like he was having a lot better time than I was.

The party was to be held at a friend's parents' horse farm in
Hockley, Texas. About thirty miles or so northwest of Houston, off
Highway 290, Hockley was dotted with small horse farms and cattle
ranches. In fact, some of the best thoroughbred and quarter horse
breeding farms in the state of Texas were located in a triangular area
bounded by Hockley, Brenham, and Magnolia. Maybe it was the grass.
Or maybe it was the proximity to Houston, where people of means
could live in the metropolis during the week and travel only a short
distance on the weekend to enjoy the country life. Some folks went to
the beach, some went to the farm. Houston wasn't exactly deserted on
the weekend, but many people left to get away from the maddening
crowd.

So it was, finally, that Mary Louise and I snuggled in our
roomy bed and listened to Charles Brown sing the blues. He had been
well known in the '50s and '60s, until music turned into rock-and-roll

and he sought another occupation, but he had been rediscovered in the '80s. He toured with Bonnie Raitt, one of his biggest supporters, and had quite a following. They packed the local clubs when he played in Houston. After all, he had grown up in Texas City, a community on Galveston Bay about ten miles northeast of the island.

"You know, Charles Brown is the only man I would ever leave you for," Mary Louise softly said as we listened to "Driftin'."

"I'm glad he's in his seventies. Would you come back to me after Charles died?"

"Of course. I might stay gone only for a week or two, just so I could hear him sing and play every day."

We kissed gently, then passionately. She was wearing nothing at all. Neither was I, but she looked so much better in the buff than I did. We worked ourselves into a minor frenzy, then a major frenzy. The woman always made me feel, and act, like a teenager.

Panting, I asked, "Good God a'mighty, woman! Am I alive still?"

"Very much so, young man. As alive as I've seen you in a while. You sort of, wore me out."

"Sorry."

"Apology not accepted. I said you sort of wore me out. I want you to really wear me out."

"I don't know, sweetie, I'm a little..."

She massaged me gently and ran her tongue along my neck.

"You're not little at all. In fact, you're a growing boy."

I was.

Afterwards, we took a real nap.

"Jim Bob. Time to get up. It's six o'clock. Jim Bob!"

I awakened slowly and groggily.

"We have to get ready for Ed's party. Wake up, boy!"

"Ed, who?"

"Ed Wilson. His party is tonight."

"You're kidding. Why didn't you tell me?"

"I just did."

"I mean, before now?"

"Because you would have thought of an excuse not to go."

"I don't want to go after our blow up last week. Actually, his blow up. He tried to get me suspended!"

"Jim Bob, he's been a friend of ours for twenty years. I'm sure there's a good explanation for what he said and did. All the partners will be there. It's an annual event, and we're going. Go shower."

I hung my head and did as she told me. I resented it, though. I just wanted to lay in bed and sleep.

Of course, once we were there, I was glad we had gone. As Mary Louise had anticipated, most of the partners and their spouses or companions were there. Sixty or seventy people in Ed's house seemed like a small crowd.

He lived in a prime section of River Oaks, west of River Oaks Boulevard and north of San Felipe Road, on Chevy Chase. The house could aptly be described as a mansion. It was set back off the street with a long circular drive. An English Tudor, it was three stories of massive rooms with twelve-foot ceilings and impeccable furnishings. Huge Oriental rugs adorned polished, hardwood floors in every room. Well, at least every room I had ever been in. There may have been a bathroom somewhere with an old marble floor, but I hadn't seen it. The grounds were landscaped with ligustroms cut into shapes of birds and forest animals. Beautiful blooming flower beds covered the areas adjacent to the brick patio and around the oak trees. The pool must have been sixty feet long. It was well lighted and decorated with floating magnolias.

I was doing my usual wandering around, talking to people when Ed stopped me and asked if he could speak to me in private. That was the second time that day someone wanted to speak to me in private.

"I wanted to apologize for my behavior towards you last Thursday. It was inexcusable. We have been friends too long for that kind of...confrontation."

It was his confrontation, not mine, but I was, for a change, silent.

"I had received some especially bad news that day," he continued, "and my frame of mind was poor. I'm going to make an announcement after dinner, but I wanted to tell you specifically how sorry I was for my outburst. Your partners found my tirade quite ridiculous and refused to even vote on your possible suspension. No hard feelings?"

"No, sir. Not at all."

"Will you ever quit calling me sir? I'm only seventy-two."

"No, sir. I'm sorry, Ed. Just a habit from my youth. Not one most of the young people have today, is it?"

"No, James, it isn't. Well, let's eat, shall we?"

Everyone gathered outside, and helped themselves to a buffet-style dinner catered by Ninfa's. I had heard that Ninfa Laurenzo was a friend of Ed's. She was one of the most famous and successful women in Houston, and her chain of Mexican restaurants spread throughout the state. The caterers served fabulous chicken and beef fajitas, spicy tamales, shrimp guadalupe, traditional rice and beans, pico de gallo, chili con queso, and fresh flour tortillas. Followed by flan and Mexican coffee, dark-roasted and strong.

"While you are all finishing your dessert and coffee, I'd like to share something with you." Ed stood as he talked. "I have gathered my orthopedic colleagues, partners, and friends together tonight as I have every year for the last fifteen years. When Mrs. Wilson was alive, God rest her soul, this was one of her favorite crowds. And, as most of you remember, we entertained quite a bit when she was alive.

"I want to thank you all for coming, and also to thank you for helping make University Orthopedic Group the largest and, if I do say so myself, the best subspecialty group in the country."

There was a round of applause for ourselves.

He continued, "Unfortunately, I have developed a health problem. A rather serious one, I must say. Prostate cancer."

The crowd was hushed as he spoke.

"I have not been as good a diagnostician of my own problems as I have of my patients'. I assumed I had a little prostate trouble, as most men my age do, and I ignored it. I had a cystoscopy ten days ago, along with a bone scan and an MRI. I have prostate cancer that has invaded the bladder and probably the lower spine and pelvis area as well. I know that prostate cancer usually has a good prognosis, but when it's diagnosed late, well, the outcome isn't so good."

Most of us had stopped eating dessert by that time.

"Anyway, I am having surgery Monday. Dr. George White, Chief of Urology, will perform the operation to try to remove as much of the tumor as he can without destroying vital tissue. I have told him that I do not want to live as an invalid wearing diapers due to lack of bladder control. I will have to have radiotherapy, and probably chemotherapy, following the healing of the surgery. And who knows, I may be here next year laughing about this speech. But, if things do not go well, I wanted to tell all of you how much I appreciate all your hard work and your friendship over these last fifteen years. Thank you all, so much."

We applauded in unison, but the party for all intents and purposes was over. We all mingled and whispered about Ed's speech, but I think most people were deflated and wanted to go home. I was, and so was Mary Louise. She had cried during his little talk, and so had I. Ed had been like a surrogate father to me. It was a sad time. His speech had certainly justified his behavior the previous week.

CHAPTER 36

OSTEOGENESIS IMPERFECTA

Sunday morning found me groggy. I had stayed up late watching one of my favorite movies of all time, "Chinatown." It was an excuse not to worry about old Ed Wilson and his cancer. The reason I had been awake in the first place at that hour was that I couldn't get him off my mind. I was concerned about the practice, not that Ed really practiced much any more. He was, however, a powerful political figure and a master of negotiating managed-care contracts for our group and the hospital. He had arranged the first capitated orthopedic contract in Houston, capitation being the wave of the future for most medical care.

In a capitated arrangement, an insurance company with a large population of patients negotiated their care. In our case, it was orthopedic care that was negotiated for a specified dollar amount. If the surgeons spent more than the allotted amount on patient care, the group lost money. If not, then the remaining money was profit. Unfortunately, in my opinion, this promoted less care or even no care, in order to save money. Although the concept was a turnabout in our traditional American system, it had already become regrettably predominant in several states before being implemented in Texas.

I felt sorry for Ed. No children, his wife gone, and probably few friends. Most rich and powerful people didn't have time for many casual friendships, I reasoned. Otherwise, they wouldn't have had the time to become rich and powerful. They would have spent too much time goofing off, socializing, playing golf, or doing whatever people who weren't rich and powerful did.

As I pondered these weighty subjects from my vantage point in the rocking chair, Mary Louise ventured out with the portable phone.

"It's for you. Jeff Clarke."

"On a Sunday?"

"Well, it's Jeff, and it's Sunday. Want some more coffee?"

"Love some. Thanks, you cute thing you."

She wiggled her rear end in my face and went inside.

"Hello, Jeff. What's up?"

"Well, Brady, some of us are working today. Obviously, not you."

"Are you on call or something?"

"Yep. Every five months, unless the guy on call gets a barrage of bodies, then one of us on second or third call has to come in and help. So I'm up here catching up and thought I'd do you that little favor you asked. About the O.I. kids."

"Great, Jeff. I really appreciate it. What do you think?"

"Well, in the first place, you're a lousy detective."

"I know that. I'm not in this willingly, you know. In fact, Jeff, it's your fault. If you hadn't stopped me that day and shown me Johnathan Fischer's spine, I wouldn't be in this mess. And neither would you, compadre."

"Touché. Anyway, the Fischer kid's date of birth was January 23, 1984, right? Well, the Huntley kid's DOB was April 23, 1984. So, if you had checked the simplest thing first, you would have realized that they couldn't possibly be twins. Twins are born at the same time, or at least a few minutes apart. Now, admittedly, there are a few case reports of twins being born several hours apart, and even one that was born a day later, but it would be impossible to have twins born three months apart. So, they couldn't be twins, right?"

I had to admit, I hadn't even thought of that. Well, at least I could tell him thank you, be on my way, and go back to being one of the "goof offs."

"Well, that was pretty dumb, Jeff. I appreciate you..."

"Wait a minute. I have more. I pulled out all the tissue samples that we had. Since both boys had bone pathology, we had even frozen some bone. I went over their tissue with a fine-toothed comb, made some more slides, looked at their bone specimens, then did electron microscopy on some of the tissues. I even checked their haptoprotein levels. I did it all, man."

"What is a haptoprotein, Jeff?"

"Brady, did you go to med school? No, that's right, you didn't. You guys go to auto mechanic's school and work as an apprentice carpenter, then go into orthopedics. My mistake." He laughed so loudly at his own joke that I had to take the phone away from my ear.

"Sorry," he said, "I have a sick and twisted mind. That's why I can't work with live patients," he continued laughing.

He calmed down and resumed his lecture. "Look, there are three basic criteria for twins, at least identical twins. Identical twins are monozygotic, meaning they are fertilized from one egg. Stop me if I get too complicated, okay?"

I was silent.

"Fraternal twins are dizygotic, meaning they are fertilized from two separate eggs. Fraternal twins can have some of the same characteristics, but identical twins have most of the same traits, since they form from the egg actually splitting into two parts after it's been fertilized.

"Three criteria must be met to say with certainty that twins are identical. They have to be the same sex, they have to have the same blood type, and they have to have identical haptoglobin, which is a protein of the blood. The point is, Brady, that while they were the same sex and had the same blood type, their haptoglobins were different."

"Meaning they weren't twins?"

"Meaning they weren't identical twins. I kept looking at tissue samples, bone content samples, and even ran some DNA protein analyses on the analog computer. I did all that, because I thought they had physical features far too similar to be coincidence. I did a little research on O.I., and there is no typical "phenotype" that one sees in Down's syndrome, Cri-du-chat, chondrodystrophy--that's dwarfism, Brady, in case you don't remember--and some of the other chromosomal abnormalities. O.I. involves collagen abnormalities, and although it's inherited, there is no chromosomal abnormality involved, which would preclude phenotype similarity. Understand?"

"I think so. It's inherited, but O.I. involves abnormal collagen, which makes up bone. And it is carried on a DNA protein somehow, but doesn't involve a bad gene, like in Down's syndrome."

"Excellent."

"So, Jeff, what's the point of all this?"

"I might be wrong, but I doubt it. I believe they're twins, but fraternal, not identical."

"But they look so much alike. How can that be?"

"It happens, Brady. When those DNA molecules get together, it's like a party in there. Hair color? How about a little red, a little blonde, a little auburn? And whammo, those little molecules start rearranging themselves to make whatever color they want. And so it goes with all of our characteristics. Sometimes, in fraternal twinning, the molecules line up very similarly, thus the testing for true identicity. If some doctor before us hadn't been curious about the problem of identical versus fraternal, there wouldn't be a hapto test. Got it?"

"So that would explain the difference in the severity of the osteogenesis?"

"You bet. Different little DNA micro-globules in unmeasurable quantities make the difference in good bone, mediocre bone, and incredibly shitty bone."

"Well, Jeff, that's an enlightening piece of work. I thank you."

"There's one more thing."

"What?"

"One of the birth dates is wrong. I wondered why."

"Well, that's a good question. I know the Huntley boy was adopted. I don't know about the Fischer boy. Maybe he was adopted, but maybe he wasn't. I have no idea why they were separated. That's for someone else to figure out. You've hopefully finished my job for me. I owe you one, big time."

"Well, my pleasure. It was fun. Let me know how it all turns out."

Mary Louise came back outside. "That was a long conversation. What was that all about?"

"You're not going to believe this."

J.J. returned from his overnight stay in the country about two o'clock. Brad arrived about three and was apparently dropped off, but none of us saw Beverly.

"You boys hungry?" Mary Louise had asked. Silly question, I thought.

"Sure. You bet." An answer in unison.

She pulled out fresh pastrami and ham with all the condiments and sliced a fresh loaf of sourdough bread. We enjoyed our late lunch at a small table out on the patio.

"How was the party, J.J.?" I asked.

"Great," he said between bites. I waited for an elaboration, but, as usual, there was none.

"How about you, Brad? How were things in Port Arthur?"

"Dad! Give him a break!" J.J. exclaimed.

"It's okay, J.J. Fine, Dr. Brady. Aunt Molly and Uncle Nolan are handling things pretty well. Johnny had been sick for a while, so they expected it, I guess. My mom and dad came over, too. It was good to see them. Too bad about the circumstances, though."

"Listen, Brad, I hate to pry, but was your nephew adopted?"

"Dad! Brad's never coming back here! Why do you keep asking him so many questions?"

"Sorry, Brad, I'm just..."

"It's cool, guys. I don't mind." He and J.J. eyed each other. "I don't know. I guess Johnny was born when I was ten. I really didn't pay much attention to that sort of thing, since I was into Little League until I was twelve. Did I tell you that we went to the semi-finals in the Little League World Series when I was eleven?"

"No, you didn't. That must have been a fun experience," I said.

"Man, it was great. I guess I didn't care much about family stuff for three years. I stayed with my friends when my parents visited my relatives, so I could play ball. But I don't think Johnny was adopted. I think I would remember something like that."

As we finished lunch, J.J. glared my way a time or two. Even I knew when to keep my mouth shut. Sometimes.

As the boys gathered their things to make the trip back to Austin, I asked Mary Louise to have J.J. come down to my study before he left. She was lovingly folding freshly-washed jeans, khakis, and shirts and packing them into suitcases. She even did Brad's laundry.

"J.J., I have to take you into my confidence on something. It's important that it remain between you and me. Don't interrupt me until I'm finished, okay?"

He nodded, and I proceeded to give him an abbreviated version of what I had learned in the last two weeks.

"So let me get this straight, Dad," he said. "You want me to gather some information for you about Brad's family. Right?"

I hated the way he put it. "Yes, but..."

"You know, Brad's my best friend, and I don't want to do anything that would hurt him. I mean, I love you and all, but everybody has limits. You know what I mean?"

I did, and I felt bad. "Well, you're probably right, J.J. Why don't you just forget it, okay? We'll just let the police investigate the situation, and if they want more information, they can figure out a way to get it. Just leave it be. It's fine. Really."

J.J. was such a good kid. I loved him more than I needed to help Susan Beeson or, for that matter, the Huntleys, who hadn't spoken to us since our Thursday dinner fiasco.

"On the other hand, though, if I could help you out and not hurt Brad, what do I get out of it?"

Bribery! The world's oldest game. How could I have forgotten to play that game, especially with a twenty year old?

"Well, what would it take, J.J.?" I asked smilingly.

"Well, let's see, Dad. I have to legally, sort of, break into the Records Division of City Hall in Port Arthur, Texas and Lafayette, Louisiana and find out about the births of twins between January and April of 1984, looking for the names Fischer, Broussard, and Richard. That it?"

"Well, I'm not sure about Broussard. Why that name?"

"Brad's last name, Dad."

"Oh. Okay, but Richard for sure, since that's Molly Fischer's maiden name, and Fischer, since that was Johnathan's name. But, J.J., it's possible I guess that Johnny, as Brad calls him, could have been adopted, and that none of these might even be his birth name. You see, it gets complicated."

"Well, Dad, Brad and I usually do this kind of thing together. We provide a little, service, I guess you'd call it, in Austin."

Fear gripped my heart. "What ever do you mean, child?"

"Well, over the years, he and I separately, and for the last year or two, together, have compiled a massive fax-modem-computer-data-access list of organizations and institutions down to entry data information, code numbers, and..."

"Wait. I don't want to hear this. Remember the sixth grade?"

"Yes, and very well. It's just that I've gotten a lot smarter since then. I've learned how to get in and out of a data bank and erase any evidence that I was there. Look, Dad, there's nothing illegal about what Brad and I do. We know that major corporations do it all the time. We are hired on occasion by certain companies to check out their security systems and to retrieve data of a...sort of sensitive nature. We get paid well for it. That's why I don't have to ask you for money."

"Does your mother know about this?"

"Sure. She helped us get started. She bought some equipment we needed, cosigned the note, and got us our first job."

I couldn't believe what I was hearing. "Which was?"

"Well, an unnamed charity organization she was working with at the time was being de-funded, and we..."

"De-funded? What kind of word is that?"

"A nice word for stealing. Brad and I figured out the system that caught the thief, and even deciphered a code that led us to the destination transfer point, so the money that hadn't been spent was re-transferred back into the charity coffers with a new entry code that the woman didn't have. She was dead in the water. See? No fuss, no muss, no cops. Unless there had been an enormous amount of money spent, and the company we worked for decided to prosecute. That's their business. Mostly, we do recovery and investigative work and let whoever we're working for do the rest. It's a fairly clean business."

I was speechless. To think that my wife was in collusion with my only son, and I didn't know a thing about it.

"How long have you been doing this, J.J.?"

"On a small scale, since the eleventh grade. But, on this scale, since my freshman year at Texas. With Brad, only about a year and a half. Anyway, there's a piece of equipment I could use to access certain computer systems faster. I'll see what I can do for you. If you like my information, you can buy it for me. Deal?"

I didn't know what to say. "Okay, I guess." I shook his hand on the deal. He hugged me.

"I love you, Dad." He started to walk out the study door, since we had both seen Brad come down the stairs with Mary Louise.

He turned around. "One more thing. I'll have to tell Brad what I'm about to do." We work in the same office, so he'll have to know. I'll tell him all about it, so it'll be like a job to him. Besides, he wants that enhancer as bad as I do."

"You guys have an office?" I asked incredulously.

"Sure. We can't do all that work in the dorm, now can we? See you. I'll call you when I know something. Bye."

I watched the boys leave. Mary Louise gave them both a tearful hug.

"Mary Louise? We have to talk," I said as the boys drove away. "J.J. just told me this incredible story about a business..."

"Setec Astronomy?"

"What?"

"The name of his and Brad's business. Setec Astronomy. From the movie 'Sneakers.' It's an anagram for TOO MANY SECRETS. Cute, huh?"

"I can't believe you and J.J. kept this from me. How could you do that?"

"You don't have the heart for that sort of thing, cutie. Besides, some things are just between a mother and her son."

"But, Mary Louise, I..."

"Jim Bob? Hush." She kissed my cheek and went inside.

CHAPTER 37

AFFIRMATION

Sunday evening failed to produce the usual, comfortable mild depression to which I was so accustomed. Perhaps it was because I preferred to relish my mood as a prig, an aptly descriptive term that I had picked up in the latest Jack Higgins novel, On Dangerous Ground. Having finished Lawrence Sanders' rendition of Archie McNally's latest escapades, I had moved on into the world of British espionage and international terrorism featuring Sean Dillon.

As priggish as I felt, I remained relatively silent, brooding over the insult brought down on me by the secrecy shared by my wife and our son. Mary Louise went about her business as usual, but at one point in the evening, she remarked that I reminded her of the famous Freida Kahlo painting "The Wounded Deer." I pictured myself full of arrows, yet undying. I had to laugh and put an end to the "peacock period" of the day.

I enjoyed the passing of my bad mood. We ate delivered Chinese food and watched "Sleepless in Seattle" on cable, and I realized I much preferred to be happy and to have fun with my Mary Louise.

Monday brought no surprises. Rounds were routine. The surgery schedule was lighter than normal, probably because there were only two weeks left before the IRS tax deadline. I figured no one could afford surgery.

On my way to see office patients, I checked on Ed Wilson. He was still asleep from his operation that morning but was extubated and breathing on his own. George White, his surgeon, happened to be in the recovery room.

"Well, how'd it go, George?"

"Technically fine. However, the MRI did not show the extent of the cancer. He had metastases around the bladder, into the pelvic nodes, and even up into the sacral area. It looks bad, Jim Bob. Even with chemotherapy and radiotherapy, I would be surprised if he lasted a year. I'm still upset that he waited so long to get help. Damn doctors! They continue to treat themselves, not that they know anything about medicine outside their own field. You remember that, Brady. You remember that!" He emphasized his point by turning directly into my face and pointing his finger at me.

He walked away, shaking his head and staring at the tiled floor.

I had some spare time before the day's first office patient was due to arrive, so I made a feeble attempt at catching up on my still-growing mound of paperwork. Distraction from the drudgery of doctorhood, came easily, and my thoughts wandered to J.J. and Brad's business, whatever it was. Worry took over, and I called Police Chief Stan Lombardo's office.

"Chief Lombardo's office," a pleasant-sounding woman answered.

"Hi. This is Dr. Jim Bob Brady. I wonder if I could speak to the Chief for a moment, please?"

"Is he expecting your call, sir?"

"No ma'am, but he does know me. I'm his orthopedic surgeon, at least I was when he broke his hip last year. Did you work for him then?" I was being so polite.

"No, I did not. But he still limps!"

Great. She probably had a sideline business as a part-time diagnostician, like Lucille Brady, with her certificate from the Good Housekeeping School of Medicine.

"Well, he had a bad fracture. He fell out of an elevated deer blind."

"Serves him right for shooting God's innocent creatures."

I concluded that there was no way to get to first base with that woman.

"Listen, can you just give him a message that I called? Do you have my name down?"

"Of course. I can't promise he'll call back, though. He's very busy. Goodbye."

After witnessing her bureaucratic attitude, I suspected she'd never give him the message. So, I was surprised when Fran buzzed me on the intercom to say that Chief Lombardo was on the line.

"Hey, Chief. How are you?"

"Busy. You?"

"Doing drudge in my office and I thought of you."

"Funny. I should sue you for this limp I have, Brady. It hurts me all the damn time!"

"Well, if you hadn't been drinking Bloody Marys at seven in the morning, you probably wouldn't have fallen out of that deer blind."

"You know, I should never have told you that. You'll hang that over my head till the day I die."

I laughed. "Yeah, it's nice to have a guy like you owe a guy like me for a change." I paused. "Listen, I won't keep you long, but I do need to ask you something about J.J., my son."

I briefly gave him an abbreviated sketch of J.J. and Brad's part-time Austin business, or at least as much as I could, since I had been left out of the picture at its time of creation.

"I see. Well, I've been meaning to call you to say thanks for helping Susan out with her investigation. And also for fixing Gene's broken ankle. Do you think he'll limp, too?" He began to laugh, loudly.

"No, he won't limp, I don't think. He's a lot younger than you. He'll heal better." I began to laugh. Then we both laughed.

"Look, Brady, I know about J.J.'s sideline occupation. Mary Louise talked to me about it, oh, several years ago. I have kept a close eye on him to keep him out of trouble. We've talked a few times, and I've given him advice. So, it looks like you're a little behind the times, shall we say!"

Once again, I was stunned and speechless. It had become my modus operandi.

"Besides, J.J. and his buddy, Brad, have done some investigative work for the department, and each time, they did an excellent job. They have talent, those two. I hired them on an anonymous basis, of course, since they're both under age and still in school. And, by the way, I think it's about time you involved them in that little project you're helping Susan with, if you know what I mean. If there is anything about the Huntley boy's death that relates to any of this business that Susan has told me about, then those boys will discover it. And a helluva lot quicker than you, old boy. In fact, Mary Louise wanted to involve them earlier, but since you didn't know about their business, we had to wait until you came up with the idea. And boy, are you the slow one." He started laughing again.

"So I guess this means there's no problem with J.J. and Brad helping me access some data..."

"Hell, no, Brady. The quicker we find out what there is to find out, the quicker we can move on to something else if there's nothing there. Got it?"

"Sure, Stan. I got it."

"One more thing, Brady."

"What's that, Stan?"

"Send me some of that arthritic medicine. What's it called?"

"Relafen."

"Yeah, that's it. I want those free samples you get. I can't afford that stuff on a cop's salary." He hung up.

I stared out my office window at other buildings in the Medical Center and past them at the Astrodome. It was another beautiful day. I wished for an afternoon baseball game, a hot dog, and an ice cold beer. I wished my dad was around to go with me. I wanted to be a kid again, even for just a little while.

CHAPTER 38

DEATH

M onday afternoon's patient load wasn't that heavy. Fran attributed it to a combination of Spring Break and the upcoming Easter weekend.

I arrived home before six and had time to enjoy the last thirty minutes of evening sunlight before dinner.

"Can I get you anything, sweetie?" she asked.

"Just a Coke, thanks. How was your day?"

"Well, I played tennis like a teenager. I'm in a new league, and those younger girls gave me a run for my money. I'm so sore I can hardly move."

She came back outside with a glass full of ice and a 7-UP.

"Sorry, Jim Bob. No Coke, no Diet Coke. I didn't make it to the grocery store today. I bought a case of 7-UP for J.J., and it's all we have left. I'll go to Randall's first thing in the morning."

"That's okay. This is fine."

"I thought it was interesting that Beverly Richard likes 7-UP so much. She said she was addicted to it? Sounds like J.J."

"Yeah. She was telling me about her gambling career, if you want to call it that. 7-UP is clear, so it looks like vodka when she drinks it at the blackjack tables. Said it throws the dealers off, as well as the pit bosses. I guess a woman who drinks vodka continuously while playing cards wouldn't appear to have the ability to count what's been played."

"I guess not, Jim Bob, but I think that whole thing is a little bizarre. Don't you?"

"I totally agree. Yet, she was much nicer than I remember. So, maybe she's not so bad. Who knows?"

"We're having leftover pastrami and ham sandwiches with sourdough. Hope you don't mind."

"Ambrosia of the gods, Mary Louise. Ambrosia."

She smiled and patted my head, then went inside to prepare dinner. 7-UP and ice. Not bad, I thought. I admired J.J. and Beverly for their good taste.

My sore, tired wife declined my after-dinner offer to join her in her hot bath in the whirlpool tub. She really wanted to soak, but suggested I give her a rub down afterwards with some new, deep-penetrating oil she bought at the tennis club. Apparently, it was being pushed by more than one of the instructors.

"I'm interested in deep penetration, but I'm not sure I need the oil," I had said. She playfully gave me a wet, open-mouth kiss before she slithered into the bathroom and shut the door.

I watched a new show called "Dave's World." Starring Harry Anderson of "Night Court" fame, it was based on the comedy writings of Dave Barry. The show was hilarious, and, as usual, Dave Barry's sense of humor was admirable. I had read his weekly Sunday column in our newspaper. It seemed he could make light of anything, a talent I truly respected.

My thoughts turned to other things as Mary Louise exited the bathroom wearing only a towel.

"Hmmm. Lose your clothes?"

"Yes...I thought I would save you the trouble of taking them off. I brought my oil. Interested?"

"Well, I just happen to be available," I said as I raised my eyebrows and gave her my best deep John Belushi imitation.

As we were beginning to get the oil massage down to a fine art, the telephone rang.

"Shit," I said.

"Let the machine get it. You can pick it up if it's more important than what you are doing. Although, I can't think of many things that would be. Can you?"

"No, my dear, I cannot."

Unfortunately, the call was not a pleasant one. It was the answering service informing me that Dr. T. Edward Wilson, my friend and partner, had died.

Mary Louise and I quickly dressed and left for University General. We went first to the Recovery Room, but the head nurse on duty told me that Ed had been moved to a room about three that afternoon. He had been doing well, talking, breathing on his own, and Dr. White had authorized his transfer. Standard procedure after surgery. She gave me his room number, and I got Mary Louise out of the waiting room and went upstairs to the urology wing.

The answering service must have called all the associates in the group, since ten to fifteen of my partners, some with wives, were already standing around the nurses' station.

"What the hell happened?" I asked of the group.

"Not sure," Greg Mayfield answered me. "He was doing fine, then about six o'clock, he quit breathing. The nurses called the Code Blue team, but they couldn't get him started. They called it off about six forty-five. George White was up here by then and gave the okay to stop the resuscitation effort. He called our office number, got the answering service, and asked them to call all of us. So here we are."

"Where's Ed?"

"The body's still in the room. The transport people have to take him to the morgue, then for the post. Hospital rules, you know. It was a less than twenty-four hour death, so an autopsy will be required. Of course, Ed probably would have wanted to have one anyway," Greg noted.

I went into Ed's room alone. There were the remains of a resuscitation attempt everywhere. Small vials of drugs, syringes, IV bottles and tubing, and a "crash cart" with the paddles thrown over the top. All the signs of life, and death. Ed's chest was bare, with the conductive grease spread all over it. Blood from his surgical bandage covered his lower abdomen. It was not a pretty sight. I went to the head of the bed and noticed that Ed's eyes were still open. I closed them gently and patted his already-cooling arm.

Mary Louise wanted to see him, but I thought it better if she didn't remember Ed that way. She cried, and I held her. Greg walked over, and put his hand on my shoulder.

"We lost another good man, Jim Bob. Not many like him anymore."

"No, Greg, there aren't." I paused. "I wonder who's making the funeral arrangements. Ed's wife is dead, and there aren't any children. Any idea?"

"Nope. I don't even know who his friends are, except us. Hey, there's George White. Let's ask him if there's anything we can do."

The three of us wandered back over to the nurses' station. More of our partners and their wives had arrived. I wondered how many people my death would attract.

Dr. White spoke. "The Code Blue team did everything they could to save Ed, but nothing worked. He was doing so well this afternoon, that I let him go to a room. I would have preferred that he stay in ICU overnight, but he absolutely would not hear of it. I saw him about five o'clock in his room. He was doing great, so I went to my office. I received an emergency call at six or so and ran back over here. The team was working on him, but without any response.

"Since he wasn't in ICU, he wasn't being monitored. The nurses have no idea how long he was in arrest, or whether it was cardiac or pulmonary. It could have been as long as thirty minutes, or as little as three minutes. The nurses took his vital signs at 5:30, and all was well. When catering went in to deliver his clear liquids, they came out to the nurses' station and reported that the man was blue. That was at about five minutes to six." He paused. We were all silent for a moment.

"What about now?" I quietly asked. "Did he make any arrangements?"

"Yes. Before surgery, he gave me a sealed envelope that I was to open in case something happened to him and he didn't make it through the operation. I have it here."

He handed it to me, why I don't know. I opened it while Mary Louise and as many of my partners who could manage looked over my shoulder. It was a single page, typed on legal stationery. It basically stated that in case of Ed's death, arrangements had been made through the law firm of Baker, Elkins, Butler, and Henderson. And whoever was reading this note was to contact the firm for explicit instructions regarding funeral and burial arrangements. The letter was actually a power of attorney, allowing the law firm to make whatever arrangements Ed had wanted.

There was more legal terminology that I skipped, but my eyes drew themselves to the signature at the bottom of the page. The name was typed and signed above. The attorney of record who had prepared the document was...Peter B. Huntley.

CHAPTER 39

SEXUAL HARRASSMENT

I slept erratically and awoke feeling like I had not been to bed. I let Mary Louise sleep, fixed my coffee, and headed to work. I had a light breakfast after rounds.

The word was out about Ed's death, and several physicians gave me their condolences, as I'm sure they would to any of Ed's partners.

I had only one case that morning, a revision of a total knee replacement in a 300-pound, former football player. Moving his leg was like trying to lift a log. Although the surgery went well, it took me three hours, about an hour longer than usual. I felt somewhat distracted throughout the entire case. When it was over, I went outside the operating room to the scrub sink and washed my face and glasses, an act that was absolutely forbidden in the OR. I, therefore, did it every chance I got.

"Sorry about Dr. Ed," Loretta said. "He hadn't done much surgery in the last few years, but he was a real pistol in his day."

"How long had you known him?"

"Oh, let's see. I came here in '78, when I was 22 years old and just out of nursing school. You started right after that, didn't you?"

"Yeah, I think it was '78 or '79."

"Well, I was a hot little number back then. I mean, I'm good looking still, but back then? I was damn good looking! Dr. Ed would have been, how old?"

"Well, he was seventy-two, so he would have been about fifty-six years old then."

"Well, I started working down here in the trenches right off, and he was after me every day. I mean, every day!"

"What do you mean, 'after you,' Loretta? You mean he was on your ass about doing a good job, or what?"

She laughed. "He was after my black ass, all right, but not like you might think. He couldn't keep his hands off me. He tried to touch me every time he had a chance, especially when I scrubbed with him. He had that damn elbow of his in my tits all the time! If I was circulating the case and he wasn't scrubbed, and he had the resident workin', he would grab me from behind and rub his 'thang' against my butt. And, oh, my God, you could never bend over in the OR or pick somethin' up. He's have his hands on your hips and start bouncin' up against your crack."

I must have looked at her like she was crazy. I had never heard any such thing about Ed. He was the picture of propriety. At least, I always thought he was.

"Where you been, Doc? Everybody knows how he was. Everybody. It just wasn't me he was after. It was any young skirt. Black, brown, white. It didn't matter to him. That's just the way he was. Now, he didn't get all vindictive or anything. If you just shoved him off, and made a joke or somethin', he'd back right off. You never had to worry about your job, see. But some of the young ones, they didn't know that, so a lot of them took the bait."

"You mean, slept with him?"

"Oh, yes. A lot of them. A lot of young nurses and OR techs quit over that man."

"I can't believe no one ever complained or filed an incident report. What about sexual harassment?"

She laughed. "Sexual harassment is a new thing, Doc. You ought to know that. A thing of the nineties. Man, talk about your big companies and law firms all you want, but the worst offenders at hittin' on the women are the surgeons! Where you been all these years, boy? Your head been in the sand?"

I just stood there and shook my head. I could not believe what I had heard. Loretta was very reliable, though, and one of the best nurses I had ever worked with. I didn't think she would make all that up.

She patted me on the shoulder. "We all love you, Doc Brady, 'cause you treat everybody with respect. The fact that you had no idea Doc Ed was hittin' on people speaks well of you. You ain't no gossip, never was, never will be. You're a good man. There just ain't many like you. Now git on out of here, and quit washing your damn face in my scrub sink!" She winked and waved me off.

I meandered to the office after Loretta's little speech. I plopped down in my chair and stared out the window at nothing.

"You okay, Pop?"

I turned and saw Fran and Rae looking a little concerned.

"Yeah, I guess. Just tired."

"We were sorry to hear about Dr. Wilson. Were you at the hospital last night?" Fran asked.

"Till about ten. I didn't sleep well."

"Well, with those dark blue bags under your eyes, I would agree," Rae remarked.

"Why don't you take a few days off? It's been a rough few weeks for you. Your neighbors' kid gets run over, Harold Sanders dies in the hospital, and now Dr. Wilson." Fran was always sympathetic.

"Well, I guess I could. I wonder when the funeral for Ed will be?"

"Tomorrow. We've all been notified. They're going to close the clinic in his memory. We're all invited to the funeral."

"They're going to close the clinic tomorrow?"

"Yes. The beloved administrator sent out a memo. I've already cancelled your surgeries for the morning, and we've almost got the clinic rescheduled. It would be easy to cancel Thursday, too. Friday's a holiday, and the clinic is closed anyway."

"It is? What is it?"

Fran and Rae looked at each other and shook their respective heads.

"Good Friday. Don't you ever go to church, Pop?"

"Oh, sorry." I was embarrassed. "There's just been so much going on lately. I can't think straight."

"Don't be sorry to us," Fran said. "Take a few days off. You owe it to yourself."

"Right. Okay, go ahead and cancel Thursday, too."

They turned to go, already making their plans for the next five days. Fran and Rae liked my days off as much as I did. Maybe more.

"Oh. One more thing. I've known Ed Wilson for over twenty years. I trained under him as a resident, he recruited me to work with him in this group, and I practiced with him for fifteen or sixteen years. To me, he's always symbolized the ideal example of a physician and surgeon. Kind, compassionate, and proper. A good surgeon, and a wonderful physician. A pillar of the community, active in church work and civic affairs, and very charitable. Am I missing something?"

Fran and Rae looked at me for a second, then at each other. Then, they inexplicably burst out laughing.

Rae approached my desk and put her hand on my shoulder. That amounted to two shoulder pats in the last hour.

"You know, Pop, it's a good thing you have Mary Louise to watch out for you. You're an adorable man, but uninformed. Very un-informed."

She and Fran continued laughing as they left and closed my office door behind them.

I finished patients somewhat in a daze, almost to the point of distraction. It had been difficult to concentrate. I just wanted to go home. I looked forward to having the next five days off. I needed the time. I was concerned that the rescheduled surgery and office patients would be upset, but I, also, knew that a distracted doctor could not do his best job.

"Go on home. That stack will be there next week," Fran said as I surveyed the mass of charts on my desk.

"I just can't do any more, Fran. I'm sorry."

"Get out of here. I called the resident, and he'll make rounds for you while you're out. Don't worry. I told the patients that you had a death in the family, and you would be out for a few days. Only a couple of people were mad, and you really don't need that kind for patients. So, go home, and get your head together. The world can't afford to lose a good doctor like you. Get some rest, and I'll see you Monday."

"Okay." I felt like I had the mind of a child and that I sounded like one. I gave her and Rae a hug, wished them a Happy Easter, and started home...to Mama.

CHAPTER 40

TONY'S

O nce again, I had forgotten to call Mary Louise and let her know that I was on my way home. Nevertheless, she greeted me at the door in an incredibly form-fitting, black, cocktail dress. Pearl necklace, matching pearl earrings, and high, black heels with an unusual scalloped border.

"Whoa, mama! Where are you off to?"

"To dinner at Tony's. With you, big boy. Get showered and dress up. We're having fun tonight."

"Wait a minute. How did you know..."

"Fran, Rae, and I conspired to give you a few days off. You don't mind, do you? I mean, after all, when a person has spent as many years as you have working your tail off, don't you think you deserve a little break? And don't you think Tony's is the place to start a little mini-vacation. Want a drink?"

I declined. "I'll wait until we get there, thanks. A conspiracy, huh? Sounds like something you and the girls would do. I'll get ready." I kissed her perfumed cheek and headed upstairs to shower and dress. My mood was improving.

At the restaurant, we headed straight for the bar. Tony's was always a treat. While we didn't go there often, maybe once or twice a month, the staff always made us feel as though we were their best friends. At the hostess station, Ann assured us that our table would be ready shortly. As we sat on two of the available bar stools, Jerry greeted us from behind the bar and prepared our libations of choice. An eighteen-year-old unblended MacCallan scotch for me, and an Absolut Citroen vodka over ice, in a martini glass, with a lemon twist for Mary Louise. We sipped, made small talk with Jerry, and gazed.

Tony's attracted the cream of Houston society, not to mention well-known personalities from all over the country, who happened to be visiting Houston for whatever reason. They offered incomparable Continental cuisine and impeccable service fit for a king, or a queen for that matter.

As we finished our cocktails, Ann retrieved us from the bar, and Rueben, consistently our "best man," showed us to our table. Tony Vallone, the proprietor, was present that evening, making his rounds and greeting his guests. While he had four other restaurants in Houston, only this one bore his name. He shook our respective hands, then went on to thank his other guests for coming. Among the diners, were Chuck Norris, Kenny Rogers, and Beverly Sills. He also greeted Maxine Messenger's party, which included Liza Minelli, in town for a benefit concert. Maxine was ubiquitous, jetting between Houston, L.A., and New York to keep Houston readers informed in her "Our Town" column.

Although we dined alone that night, people occasionally wandered over to say hello. We did the same. It was one of the routines at Tony's, and perfectly acceptable. In fact, one did not ignore one's acquaintances when at Tony's. If anything, it was considered bad taste not to mingle among the tables of this most unusual, yet most exhilarating, restaurant.

We enjoyed beef carpacchio, Caesar salad, and rack of lamb, along with our favorite bottle of red wine, a 1986 Chianti Classico Ruffino Reserva. In my mind, and in Mary Louise's, the French did not have the corner on the market of excellent red wines. The Italians had done their homework as far as we were concerned.

We indulged ourselves with Tony's wonderful dessert cart, accompanied by an espresso for me and a capucchino for my bride. With a little Irish Mist on the side, straight up, of course. A wonderful experience and a guaranteed mood-elevator for me on that particular night. Who needed Elavil, I thought. Just go to Tony's.

Mary Louise picked up our messages as soon as we arrived home. J.J. had phoned and requested that I return his call as soon as I could. Not wanting to interfere with my good mood induced by Tony's, I chose to head immediately to my spot on the patio for my first Marlboro Light of the day. I had a sudden desire to visit Cat. After all, communing with the ever-roving feline took extra time, so I was justified in enjoying a second cigarette. Cat purred while she wove herself back and forth between my legs and then finally decided it was worth the effort to leap onto my lap. She circled my lap for a minute or two, looking for the perfect spot on which to make herself comfortable. As we sat together, I refused to worry about anything.

After a while, having given me the required amount of attention, Cat deftly dropped onto the flagstone in search of a more interesting agenda. I went back inside and heard the sounds of Charles Brown coming from upstairs. I flipped off the foyer lights and eagerly went up the stairs, where I found my darling wife lying on the bed with her eyes closed. She was dressed in something flimsy, an obvious cast-off from the Victoria's Secret collection due to its X-rating.

I rotely performed the usual bathroom necessities and perfumed myself as best a man could. When I opened the bathroom door, I noted candles glowing in the evening moonlight. It made a spectacular picture. My woman, good music, candles, and the moon visible through shadeless windows. Our lovemaking was gentle and sweet. I feel asleep amidst the smell of Dona Karan perfume and the sound of Charles Brown singing, "You Changed My Life, And I Thank You."

CHAPTER 41

PSEUDOCHOLINESTERASE

F or the second time in less than two weeks, I entered the George
Lewis Funeral Home on Kirby Drive. Mary Louise and I spent the first
fifteen minutes of our early arrival visiting with various friends and
colleagues. We all assured each other that Ed's sudden demise was far
better than a slow, agonizing death from metastatic cancer, and, as
surgeons, we wished aloud for such a death. We had seen too much
misery to discount his sudden passing as anything but a blessing.

There was no casket. Ed had wanted to be cremated. The service was simple, consisting of only a homily from the minister at
Christ Church. No eulogies were given. Either that was his wish, or Ed
had no friends close enough to eulogize him properly. That was something we would never know. I also wondered about the destination of
the ashes, since, with cremation, there would be no graveside service.

We visited for a short while after the service, then snuck away
for a Wednesday lunch at Carrabba's. My associates obviously envied
the fact that I was off duty and grumbled about having to hurry back to
work.

Mary Louise and I ate wonderful pasta and drank more Chianti.

On my second glass, I wondered if I should periodically get some liver function tests. I, unfortunately, wondered that aloud, and she whipped out her portable phone and called my internist for an appointment. The next day. I decided to keep my mouth shut from then on, at least when I wondered about my health.

When we returned home, there was another message from J.J., one from Jeff Clarke, and a call from Pete Huntley. After Pete's reaction to the questions I had asked him and Bobbie at dinner the previous Thursday, I was very surprised that he called. Of course, he had drafted Ed's power of attorney, so there was a possibility that he might want to discuss Ed's will. I gathered up my courage and decided to return his call before the others.

"Baker, Elkins, Butler, Henderson. May I help you?" the switchboard operator answered.

"Hi. Dr. Brady here. Could you ring Pete Huntley's office, please?"

"Thank you. One moment, please."

I held for the required moment.

"Mr. Huntley's office. May I help you?"

"Yes, this is Dr. Jim Bob Brady. I'm returning Pete Huntley's call?"

"Yes sir. One moment, please."

Another moment.

"Pete Huntley."

"Hey, Pete. Jim Bob. You called me?"

There was a pause. "Yes, Jim Bob. How are you?"

"Well, okay, I guess. How about you?"

"Tolerable. Under the circumstances. Listen, about the other night. Sorry about all that. Bobbie and I have been under quite a bit of stress lately, as you might imagine. I haven't really understood your profound interest in our adoption of Stevie up until now, but I may have discovered something that will answer any questions you might have. In fact, I have some information in my hands that may raise a few more questions. Anyway, I don't want to get ahead of myself. Can you come to my office this afternoon after you finish work? I want to show you something."

"Well, Pete, as it happens, I've got the day off. What time do you want me there?"

"Oh, five o'clock or so is good for me. I'll buy you a drink."

"Okay, sounds good. See you about five."

I put my curiosity as to what that was all about on hold, and I decided to call Jeff Clarke next. I'd save J.J. till last.

"Pathology Department."

"Hi. This is Dr. Jim Bob Brady. I'm returning Dr. Jeff Clarke's call?"

"Hold." Politeness still had not blossomed in that department.

"Jeff Clarke," he answered, after what seemed like an interminable hold on my part.

"Hey, Jeff. Brady here. You called me?"

"Well, Mr. Detective. How's it going?"

"Okay. Except for all this death and dying around me."

"That's life, Brady." He broke into his irritating laughter. I waited until he stopped.

"Well, I've visited with you more in the last two weeks than I have since I've been in practice. I hope you don't have any more of my patients down there."

"Nope, just Ed Wilson's cold, stiff carcass. I thought I'd give you a call, since you seem to be so interested in all the orthopedic stiffs we have down here lately."

"Well, Ed Wilson's not really an orthopedic death, is he?"

"Not really, but since he is, or was, one of you bone docs, I thought you might be interested in something his autopsy showed. Bone docs, bone patients, they're all the same to us."

"Well, Jeff, Ed was a good friend of mine for a long time. I'd like to think of him in better terms than just another one of your 'stiffs.'"

"I guess. We barely had time to look him over before the funeral people grabbed him up and burned him to a crisp. We did most of the work yesterday and picked a few more specimens to review today. Takes a while to deep fry the body for cremation, so we had to hurry."

"Jeff, is there a point to all this? I'm off today, and I'd really rather spend it doing more pleasant things than having this morbid conversation with you. No offense, but..."

"You can't offend me, Brady. I'm a pathologist. Anyhoo, the reason I called. By the by, I didn't call any of your so-called partners, because I can't stand most of them. A lot of self-serving pricks, I think. But then, most of you surgeons are. I wanted to let you know that Wilson had a pelvis full of cancer. The prostate lesion, which, by the way, could have been treated early and saved his pompous ass, had spread all over the lymphatics and into the sacrum. It was even up into the lower lumbar spine. The bladder wall was invaded, and even along the suture line, where the great George White cut the so-called 'visible' tumor out. All in all, he was a goner from the get-go. Another case of a dumb-ass doctor trying to treat himself. Message there is, Brady, that if you can't pee, see a real doctor."

I paused for a moment, so that I could manage to be as polite as possible. He had helped me out with the Stevie-Johnny twin thing, so I felt I owed him a little courtesy.

"Is that all, Jeff?"

"Hell, no, amigo. I wouldn't call you about a little cancer growing in ol' Ed Wilson's prostate. That's not very interesting. What's interesting is that Wilson had a pseudocholinesterase deficiency. Does that ring a bell, Mr. Carpenter?"

"Huh? Something about an enzyme deficiency, right? Has to do with anesthesia?"

"Oh, you're getting warm. Let me save you some mental stress, since I know you bone docs can't afford to stress out what little white matter you have in those miniature skulls of yours," he laughed, while I steamed, silently.

He continued. "You know, Brady, you're a helluva lot of fun to shoot the shit with. You can take a joke. I like that. That's why I talk to you. Anyway, pseudocholinesterase deficiency means that if you have an operation, and the anesthesiologist gives you succinylcholine, or a chemically related drug, to paralyze you, so he can get a tube down your throat and breathe for you during an operation, you can't metabolize it. It means that you can't breathe on your own for an undetermined period of time. Without the enzyme, you will eventually break down the cholines, but it will take hours. That's why taking a history of previous problems with anesthesia is so important. Well, Wilson had had previous surgery, right here at this hospital, and this enzyme deficiency was well-documented in the chart."

"So? Aren't there other drugs the anesthesiologist can give in those cases, like Propaphal or fentanyl?"

"Good, Brady. They can also give sodium pentothal, Pavulon, nitrous oxide, stuff like that. Point is, the gas-passers can give a patient a lot of stuff to keep him or her asleep and relaxed without using choline compound, especially in those cases where either there is no history of surgery, and the enzyme content is unknown, or in those cases where the enzyme is known to be absent. Right?"

"Sure, Jeff. I just don't see the problem."

"Well, on toxicology, we ran the usual chromatographic studies for drugs, medication, etc. Wilson had all the usual analgesics in his system, and some anesthetic agents that hadn't been metabolized yet. All that rubbish. But guess what? Guess what, Brady!"

"What, Jeff?"

"He had a whopping succinylcholine titer in his blood, and some in his tissue. What do you think about that?"

"Jeff, that's not possible. I saw him Monday afternoon in Recovery Room. He wasn't awake, but he was breathing on his own, off the ventilator, and even extubated. That's just not possible!"

"True, in that it's not possible that he got any during surgery, because he would have been breathing on a respirator until the cows came home. He had to get it later."

"What?"

"Somebody dosed Wilson with succinylcholine after he was off the ventilator--in his room more than likely--since, if he wasn't breathing, they wouldn't have released him from recovery, now would they?"

"Jeff. Do you know what you're saying?"

"Yeah, buddy. He was torched. Either some dumb-ass nurse gave him some by mistake, although not likely, since that's not a common floor drug, or maybe an injectable bottle of morphine or demerol was mislabeled, or...somebody iced him."

"Jeff, I can't believe all this. Are you absolutely sure?"

"No doubt in my mind, Brady. No doubt whatsoever."

"Well, can you hold on to this information for a while?"

"I dunno. What'll you do for me?"

"What do you want, Jeff?"

"Aren't you guys the team docs for the Astros?"

"Not me specifically, but two of my partners are the designated team physicians."

"I want two seats behind the Astros dugout for Friday night's game with the Mets. You deliver, I'll sit on this for, let's say, 48 hours. That's Friday at...Friday's a holiday, isn't it?"

"Yes. Good Friday."

"Any Friday that's a holiday is good, Brady. Tell you what, I'll hold it until Monday, so it buys you an extra day or two. Deal?"

"Are you breaking the law by withholding that information?"

"Brady, you dumb shit, there is no law in pathology. We're eccentric. We take our time. Nobody ever tries to rush a pathologist. We can fuck them over, give them the wrong frozen section diagnosis, all kinds of mayhem. We run the show down here. I can do what I want, and say what I want. That's why I'm such an asshole. Do we have a deal?"

"Deal. I'll get you the tickets by Friday."

"No dice. I want them on my desk by eight in the morning, or you're dead meat. Got it?"

"Okay."

As he hung up the phone, I rued the day I saw Stevie Huntley run over, the day I saw Johnny Fischer in Pathology, and the day I asked Jeff Clarke to check on a possible connection between the two boys.

Mary Louise had left to run errands, or so read the note she had handed me during the phone conversation. I wanted desperately to discuss the new information with her. Jeff had laid something extraordinary in my lap, and I neither wanted it nor had any idea what to do with it.

I went upstairs, removed my blue suit, white shirt, and tie, and opted for something more casual and comfortable for my downtown meeting with Pete Huntley. I chose faded blue jeans and a wild-print, short-sleeved shirt. I didn't want anyone to think I was an attorney.

CHAPTER 42

THE WILL

T o me, downtown Houston had always been a maze. Surely, somewhere down there was a large piece of cheese, like in the old experimental psychology labs I had to suffer through in college. I had left home early in case I needed extra time to find Pete's office. There were an incredible number of high-rise office buildings, and I routinely got lost. If possible, I avoided downtown like the plague.

One of its unusual features was the underground tunnel system. Mary Louise and I had become familiar with part of it through our attendance at various concerts, operas, and plays. Jones Hall, the Wortham Theatre, and the Alley Theatre had spectacular events throughout the year, including an opera series, Broadway musicals, and first-rate live stage performances. These theatres and concert halls were linked with an underground parking facility that spanned several blocks. Security was always present, so play-goers and theatre goers could park safely, close to an event, and never walk outside. This was certainly advantageous in a town where heat and humidity were predominant nine months out of the year.

However, there were massive office buildings linked by a section of the underground tunnel system that was probably as confusing to me as the University Hospital complex was to a patient. While I accepted that as only fair, I struggled with various entrances off of Louisiana, Milam, Texas, and Lamar Streets before I found something that looked like an exit to the Texas Commerce Tower. Between Allen Center Towers, Houston Center Towers, Pennzoil Plaza, and God-only-knew-what-else Towers, I longed to be in a town in Texas where you could park in front of a building and walk right through the front door.

The tunnel system provided indoor access, or so I was told, between the various buildings for clients, attorneys, bankers, and delivery men. There were restaurants, bars, Federal Express stations, and every imaginable kind of retail outlet one could want. As I walked and looked for a way to the elevators that would take me to the 44th floor, I realized that I was vastly underdressed. Most of these skyscrapers had a major tenant, for whom the building was named, with the remainder of the lessees being attorneys. I felt certain that I was the only non-lawyer in the tunnel.

More than once, I tried to stop someone to ask directions, but the people seemed to shy away from me. I was puzzled at first, since I was dressed like a true Texan in my jeans, garish shirt, and ostrich boots. But then I realized the problem. I had no briefcase. To people in the tunnel, that probably meant I was homeless. Or at least destitute, and certainly not very important.

I finally stopped at a Whataburger and asked directions. The kitchen smelled so good that I ordered a Coke and an order of french fries. I had about ten minutes to kill. I tried to sit as obscurely as possible, since in this hamburger joint, the patrons wore three-piece suits.

I located the elevators to the offices of Baker, Elkins, Butler, and Henderson and stepped off onto the 44th floor. They apparently had the whole floor, since the elevator emptied onto an enormous two-story foyer surrounded by glass windows. There was a 360° view of the city, and rather than waste it, I stopped and gawked. It made my view from University tower seem like one seen through a telescope. I wandered around for a few minutes, then found the receptionist's desk. Even she wore what appeared to be a designer suit. I wondered how they achieved that level of affluence.

"May I help you, sir?"

"Yes. I'm Dr. Brady, for an..."

"Oh, for the deposition? You're late. It started at 4:30 doctor. Right this way, please." She seemed worried.

"I don't think I'm here for a deposition. I have an appointment with Pete Huntley at five o'clock."

"Oh. You're not one of the defendants in the medical malpractice case?"

"God, I hope not."

"I'm very sorry. We've had doctors in and out of here all afternoon. When you said 'doctor,' I assumed...Well, never mind. I'll call Mr. Huntley's office. Please be seated."

I sat, thankful I wasn't a part of the medical malpractice case. I wondered who was there, what the case concerned, whether I knew the doctors, all those things that pop into a surgeon's brain.

"He's running a little behind. Can I get you something while you wait?"

"No, thanks. I just had a Coke downstairs. I'll just sit and enjoy the view," which I did for another fifteen minutes or so, reading magazines that were current. Unlike a doctor's office, where magazines could be three months old or three years old, they had the latest editions of Time, Newsweek, People, and U.S. News and World Report. I also noted that month's Texas Monthly, Houston Metropolitan, and National Geographic. I again wondered how the law firm handled the expense of the view and the up-to-date magazines.

I walked back over to the secretary. "Excuse me?"

"Yes, sir? Change your mind about some refreshment?"

"No. I was just wondering how many lawyers are in this firm."

"Two hundred and eleven."

"Do they do some kind of specialized legal work or what?"

"Our firm does everything. We do have specialists in every aspect of the law. We do not do medical malpractice on the plaintiff's side, only the defense. Other than that, we do the gamut--wills, trusts, probate, corporate litigation, banking, oil and gas. You name it, we do it. Two of Texas' Supreme Court Justices have come from this firm."

"You seem very loyal."

"Yes, sir. My father's a Butler. Not the original Mr. Butler. That was my grandfather. But Butler, Jr., he's my father."

"Interesting. I'm glad to hear you do only medical malpractice defense."

"Why's that, doctor?"

"Well, because I'm a doctor, and..."

"Oh, I forget sometimes how sensitive you physicians are about lawsuits. It's never anything personal, just something lawyers do. The responsible party is actually an insurance company, anyway. Many times, it's no reflection on a physician's reputation or quality of work. It's just business. You people always take it so personal," she smiled.

"Yes, we do take it personally. It would be like one of your men getting sued for legal malpractice."

"Oh, that rarely happens. Can't find an expert witness to testify against another lawyer," she laughed. I shook my head.

As I walked back to my seat, she called to me and said that Pete Huntley was ready to see me. To the right, down the hall to the end, then right again. He would meet me in the hallway. I thanked her and made my way to see Pete.

"Sorry to keep you waiting," he said. "Clients. This wouldn't be a bad business if it weren't for clients."

I laughed. "I sometimes say that about my patients."

"I understand. What can I get you, Jim Bob?"

"Have any scotch?"

"Sure. Glenlivet or Chivas?"

"The Glen, of course. Rocks and a splash, please."

He went to a liquor cabinet in the corner of his plush office and mixed. Massive oak desk, thick pile carpet, framed diplomas, a few family pictures. An attorney's office. It seemed much more important than mine.

He brought me my drink, poured one for himself, and sat behind his desk. I hated that. I felt like the lesser one. He could have sat in the other chair opposite his desk, next to me. I wondered if I would do the same in my office.

"Well, I guess you're wondering why I asked you to come down here."

"Yes, I am."

"Well, it has to do with Ed Wilson's will. Actually, it goes back a lot further than that, so I'll start from the beginning.

"Bobbie and I moved here after college, so that I could attend the University of Houston Law School. I finished there in 1977 and came to work in this law firm. They had recruited me during my last year of law school, as most law firms do. I interviewed with several of the large firms and selected this one. At the time Baker, Elkins had 120 or 130 lawyers, and I thought that if I worked hard and did a good job, then becoming a partner would be fairly easy. Some firms have the reputation of hiring more lawyers than they could possibly take in as partners, so a lot of young lawyers work for a firm for a few years for the experience and then go out on their own or join a smaller firm. Not Baker, Elkins. They usually hired, at least at that time, about the number of people that they wanted as partners, minus the normal attrition rate of attorneys deciding they really wanted to do something else. There's a lot of that in this business, Jim Bob. Lawyers often move around and do other things, because they end up hating their jobs.

"Anyway, I joined the firm, and worked my ass off for six long years, which was one, maybe two, more than I thought I would need to become a partner. During that time, Bobbie and I tried to have a child, but we were miserably unsuccessful. I had a low sperm count, and she had 'egg trouble.' For two or three years, she saw fertility experts and did all that temperature measuring. We had sex at all the 'right times,' which, I guess, ruined our spontaneous sex life. Fertility work wasn't then what it is today. It's much more refined now, I understand. We tried IVF--that's in vitro fertilization--twice, which cost me about $25,000, but we had no luck. She was miserable, and she made me miserable, wanting to have a kid. I was spending so much time at work, that I wasn't real supportive and never seemed to be home at just the right time when she needed me to be her 'sperm donor.' I guess I didn't care as much as she did, but then I don't think most men do. Do you?"

"I don't know, Pete. I think it varies a lot among men."

"Figures. Anyway, she's trying to get pregnant, I'm working like a son of a bitch, and there is no peace. It seems that the firm doesn't want to take all six of us that were up for partnership that year. They want to take four. Well, I wanted to be one of the four, Jim Bob. You can understand that. Right?"

"Sure." I wondered where this was going.

"Okay, so old man Henderson comes to me. I'm like one of his favorite 'boys.' He knows from our conversations in the office, and sometimes at parties, how bad Bobbie wants a baby, and he knows that the fertility thing just hasn't worked. He says he can arrange a private adoption. No hassles. Seems he provides that service on occasion to 'selected clients,' and he suggests that he could help me out.

"So, I ask him where the baby was coming from, and all those questions that someone would ask. Is it healthy? Is it deformed? Is the mother a drug addict? I mean, there are a million questions you start to think about.

"Bobbie and I talked about it for weeks. Back and forth, back and forth. Should we, or shouldn't we? Finally, I talked Henderson into letting us see the baby. He said that was highly irregular, but as a favor to Bobbie and me, he would try to arrange it.

"About that time, he brings up the fact that the partnership is down to choosing between me and another guy. And that my accepting this child, and talking Bobbie into it, would be looked upon as a sign that I could be depended on and would probably guarantee me a partnership position.

"Well, Jim Bob, I was determined to like that kid. Fortunately, the day we saw the little boy, Bobbie fell in love with him, immediately. Didn't want to let him go. Henderson said we could arrange the transfer...he said it was like a legal document, or a package...in a week, once 'arrangements' had been made.

"Well, it turns out that...You want another drink?"

Desperately did I want another drink.

"Sure. Want me to pour?"

"If you want."

"What are you having, Pete?"

"Black Jack, straight up 'cept for one ice cube."

I made the drinks, strengthening mine a bit.

He continued. "Anyway, Henderson tells me that a private adoption of a healthy child is not cheap. There is the legal work and care of the child's previous medical expenses--birthing costs, all that shit. The price? $50,000!"

"$50,000? You've got to be kidding!"

"I kid you not. This is after Bobbie has held this child and fallen in love with him. So what do I do? I told Henderson yes, we want the boy, but I don't have that kind of money laying around. I'm on a salary, not making much more than the adoption fee per year. He says no problem, he'll pay the money, and I can pay him back out of partnership proceeds over the next year or two, or three. He draws up a private contract between him and me. We sign it, and Stevie Huntley is 'born,' at least to us. At the time, he was just barely three months old.

"That's kind of late for an adoption, isn't it, Pete?"

"I guess, man. By then I didn't care. I wanted Bobbie to have that baby, and I wanted the partnership, so I took the deal."

He stood up, said he had to take a leak, and left the office. I got up and walked over to the window, taking in all the city at twilight.

When Pete returned, I asked directions to the john and proceeded to try to empty my distended bladder. I hesitated a moment, standing at the urinal, and wondered if I had prostate trouble like Ed Wilson. I lit my first, or my second Marlboro Light of the day. The water flowed as I relaxed, and I presumed myself to be okay.

I returned to Pete's office. He immediately continued with his catharsis.

"So anyway, Jim Bob, Stevie was the love of our life. Such a sweet kid. He had the osteogenesis imperfecta problem, but it was never all that bad. He was normal until he was a year or so old, and then he broke a bone occasionally. But, never bad enough that I wanted to break old Henderson's neck. I got the partnership three months after we adopted Stevie. I was able to pay Henderson back in eighteen months, and everything has basically been great, until two weeks ago last Saturday. Bobbie is still a basket case. Me? I'm back at work doing my thing. I miss the hell out of the kid, but maybe men are different than women. What do you think?"

"I think it varies among men, Pete."

"I figured you'd say that. Wanna another drink?"

"No, I'm okay right now." He was slurring a little, but I didn't blame him. I probably would be, too, in his situation. He mixed himself another Jack and ice, and sat down.

"So, Henderson died last year. His files and cases were divided among several partners, but I got the lion's share. Including Ed Wilson's business. I met him for the first time last summer when I drafted a power of attorney for him in case of his sudden, unexpected death. Man, that guy had some portfolio. You know he married well, don't you? Very well."

"Yeah. Old oil money, wasn't it?"

"Big time. I know from Henderson's old files that she left an estate of about sixty million. She left forty million to various charities and twenty million to Wilson. Wilson had a good practice, I'm sure, so he only spent a small part of the interest. He didn't touch the principal, which was invested through our trust department. The weird thing is that with all these papers Henderson had in the file, there was made mention of Wilson's will, which was in a safe deposit box that was to be opened only after his death. Well, I've been curious about that for the last year, but I couldn't get to it, because the key wouldn't be available to open the box until after he died. The Trust Department had it. Anyway, I have the will, and I've read it, and that's why you're sitting here now."

"What does Ed's will have to do with me?"

"Well, Bobbie was a little embarrassed about the adoption thing, so very few of our friends knew anything about it. At dinner last week, you asked me if Stevie was adopted. How would you know to ask that question? We've only lived next door to you for three years or so. Why did you ask me that?"

I thought about it for a minute or two. I got up and walked around his office. I told him what I knew about Stevie and Johnny, how I found out that they could be twins, and why Susan Beeson had asked me to do the background work. I explained that I was trying to help find out if there was any reason for Stevie's death except an accident, since there had been no clues forthcoming from any sector about the red truck. I told him all that I had done for the past few weeks, and then I waited.

"I really can't tell you what the will says, since it won't become public until the probating. I'll paraphrase it, though, since I think it has bearing on other peculiarities you've uncovered. Wilson left ten million to University Hospital, five million to various charities, including Christ Church. You know where the other five million is to go?"

"No, Pete."

"$2.5 million goes to my son, Stevie Huntley, and $2.5 million goes to a Johnathan Fischer of Port Arthur, Texas. They are the beneficiaries of a five-million dollar health, education, and welfare trust, the trustee of which is a Beverly Richard of Houston, Texas. The name Johnathan Fischer rang a bell from dinner last week. Now, I don't know about you, but how the hell would Wilson know these kids even existed, much less leave them money...unless he was their natural father. And who the hell's this Beverly Richard woman? I ask that, Jim Bob, because she is now a very rich lady!"

"How's that," I asked. "She was the trustee..."

"The will states that, if neither child is surviving when the trust is activated, the trustee, who is Richard, gets all the money."

CHAPTER 43

TOO MANY SECRETS

Mary Louise had not fixed dinner. Since I was on vacation, she was on vacation. She wanted sushi, which was fine with me. I picked her up at home and slowly traveled down Kirby to Miyako. Pete Huntley's revelations weighed heavily on my mind.

She ordered, as usual. Over a large Asahi beer, which we shared, I filled her in. Mary Louise was a good confidant, and could be relied upon to keep any secret that I divulged. Since I couldn't keep anything from her, it was a good thing that she was reticent to share confidential information with anyone.

"So what do you think?" she asked over our usual array of raw fish and seaweed.

"I don't know, sweetie. What I know for sure is that Stevie Huntley was a hit-and-run victim. I also know that he and Johnny Fischer were fraternal twins, at least according to Jeff Clarke. I have been told by Pete Huntley that Ed Wilson left $2.5 million to each child, and therefore assume, along with Pete, that he knew who those kids were, and agree with him that the most likely explanation for that generosity is that Ed knew he was the father of the two boys.

"Do we assume that Molly Fischer was the birth mother of both boys? If so, why did she keep Johnny and put Stevie up for adoption? And how did Ed know Molly? And why did Ed name Beverly trustee? What kind of relationship did she have with Ed? Was Stevie's death an accident, totally unrelated to those other facts?

"I mean, Mary Louise, Johnny Fischer died after surgery, but he was a respiratory cripple. Would he have died anyway? Probably so. And Ed Wilson? He had metastatic cancer. He died after surgery, too. But would he have died anyway? Yes, although he probably would have hung on for six months, maybe a year.

"And how did Ed know about the two boys? Did he have some kind of guilt late in his life and seek out their whereabouts? Or did he know all along who they were and where they were? There are just too many questions. Or, according to J.J. and Brad, too many secrets.

"By the way, did you hear from J.J. today? I never called him back."

"Well, he sent a huge amount of fax material through my computer this afternoon. I printed it and read over most of it, but I think you need to see it yourself. It's fairly complicated, but I'll help you sort through it."

"Well, that's fine, but I think that my only need and desire at this point in time is to go home, have a smoke on the patio, and get some sleep. I've had way too much input for one day. Especially a day off. I'm supposed to be relaxing, you know."

She laughed. "Yes, dear, I know. Poor baby. Everybody always wants something from you, don't they?"

"Yes, they do." I did my best pout, ordered some sake, and tried to finish dinner without further regard to recent events and problems. As we drove home, Mary Louise held my hand but slipped into a quiet mood.

I had my visit with Cat and smoked two cigarettes. Upstairs, Lou Rawls was singing on the compact disc player. It was one of our favorite songs, "At Last," our replacement for "The Wedding March" at our nuptials.

When I entered our bedroom, Mary Louise was wearing my favorite outfit...nothing.

Thursday morning presented me with a mild hangover. It could have been from alcohol, or from hearing that Nurse Richard was a multi-millionaire. After reminding me to read through the info sent by J.J., and to keep my doctor's appointment, Mary Louise left to play tennis.

Great, I thought. A rainy day reading faxes from my son, highlighted by an appointment with my doctor, who with the way my luck had been going, would decide I needed a rectal exam.

I finished an entire pot of coffee, Seville Orange flavor, while waking up. I read the paper, watched the "Today Show," and fed Cat. I wanted more coffee, since I had to sort through J.J.'s faxes and made myself another pot using a blend called Twin Peaks. We used a wonderful little coffee shop on West Gray Avenue, which had coffee beans of every imaginable flavor from countries I didn't know existed. Every morning, I removed a different package from the freezer, ground the beans, and enjoyed a fresh pot of coffee. It had become a science, almost. We all need our little pleasures.

I poured my Twin Peaks blend into the insulated pot, went up to Mary Louise's office, and gathered up the faxes from my always-amazing son. They didn't look like the faxes I received at work. The pages all appeared to be freshly typed.

Although I was computer illiterate, I knew that both Mary Louise and J.J. had a fax-modem. Somehow, he transmitted information through this system onto her computer, and she printed the data. I learned this the previous year, when I inquired of her how J.J. had the time to type such precise letters. She informed me that he just typed a letter into his computer, sent it by fax-modem, and she printed my copy. She always read the letter off the monitor. I seemed such a backward fool to myself sometimes.

Mary Louise's office was in one of the two guest bedrooms on

208

the second floor. When he had lived at home, J.J. had used it as his computer center, preferring to use his bedroom for sleeping, watching television, and listening to his always-too-loud stereo. He had left some outdated equipment behind for his mother to use, and she had added enough hardware, or software, or whatever it all was, to become current. At least, she was current enough to communicate with our son, which was a lot more than I could do. He respected her intelligence and adaptability. I think he just tolerated me, since I was married to his mother, a woman he loved dearly.

I felt uncomfortable in her office, so I picked up the computer-typed paper she had left for me and headed down to my office on the first floor. I felt at home there, since the only two mechanical devices in it were a telephone and an old-fashioned Smith-Corona typewriter, both of which I was familiar with. I began to read.

Date: March 30, 1994
From: Setec Astronomy, Inc.

To: Dad

I wanted to talk to you, Dad, before you got this fax, but Mom said you were stressed out, and could I just send you this info through Mom's f-m. That's cool with me, but I wanted to let you know in person on the phone, dude, that Brad helped me out with this stuff. He's cool and all, and hey, we work together on everything. What is really COOL is that he did some work for his Aunt Beverly last year that relates to your inquiry. What is even COOLER is that we also did some work for Dr. Wilson last year, that all relates to what Brad did for his aunt and the stuff in Lafayette that you wanted me to look into. So, it all ties together. And Brad and I? Man, we are the A-number-1 dig-it-out-and-find-it duo, dude! Some of the reports aren't the original, since our investigations are supposed to be confidential. So we've retyped it, leaving out a few particulars to be legal and all!

So, what you're reading through there, Pops, is a summary of Brad's report to Aunt Beverly Richard, donated with his full permission, and he by the way, apologizes to you for not telling you the truth at lunch last Saturday. He was protecting his client, something you have to do in this business to get more business. Anyway, there also is a summary of the work we did for Chief Lombardo's friend, Dr. Wilson, whom we know you know, or at least knew, Dad. Also are birth records you wanted, repro-duced on regular phone fax, not modem, which explains their poor quality. But you can read it, dude. Following that is a print out of extensive personal and financial data that Brad and I gathered, that we think you might have wanted but were afraid to ask for.

Brad and I don't know exactly what you're up to, but from the information we have reviewed, we have summarized a series of events that holds up to Logic Testing, with a variable accuracy percentage of greater than 98.4%. You may plug some more pieces of the puzzle in, and if you want to share that data with us, we'll give you the over-all 'accuracy of logic' percentage with its coordinated variable. If you've done well, old man, we might offer you a job, once you complete computer training classes. You're a good guy, but a fossil when it comes to '90s communication skills.

Any questions, call. And Dad, keep your copy of the documents. We moved the data onto floppy disc and erased the hard disc. Wouldn't want any 'Prodigy Pirates' snooping around Setec's files, would we?

Later. Your ever-more-brilliant son, J.J.

Well, as usual, I was surprised, yet almost expectantly, at the latest piece of electronic information-gathering work that my son had done. He was too far ahead of me to ever catch. But could he 'nail' a broken hip? Could he play "Statesboro Blues" in A-minor on the Hammond B-3? No. But I could do both. I somehow felt better about myself as I reflected on the things I could do, rather than on the things I couldn't, and read on with interest the pile of data J.J. and Brad had sent me. I read over the copy of the birth record of the twin boys born to Molly Richard several times. No listing of a father was noted. The informant was listed as Beverly Richard, so I assumed that Molly couldn't give out any information at the time of her delivery, which didn't seem all that unusual.

Both Beverly and Molly gave their home address as being the same, on Calder in Lafayette. I had forgotten exactly when Beverly had left University Hospital, but I calculated that it must have been around that time. Perhaps she had gone home to take care of her sister. Interestingly, the record showed Molly's occupation as a nurse, but it didn't specify a hospital.

If Pete Huntley's and my theory was correct, Ed Wilson had

been the father, but there was yet to be a clue as to his connection with Molly. There were still too many unresolved questions.

Finding it impossible to figure out what that would be, I read on. Of particular interest were two memos, one from Setec to Dr. T. Edward Wilson, and the other to Beverly Richard.

Date: January 6, 1993
From: Setec Astronomy, Inc.
To: Dr. T. Edward Wilson

Dr. Wilson,

Thank you for your confidence in hiring our firm for your discreet inquiry. We are pleased that Police Chief Stan Lombardo had the confidence in our abilities to recommend us to you.

Enclosed is a copy of the birth record of the said twins in question. As you can see, we obtained this information on November 22, 1992. We have delayed sending it to you due to a personal conflict one of staff had during this investigation. That conflict has been resolved, and this inquiry will, of course, remain discreet. You have our assurance on that.

It would seem from our data that Johnathan Lenoir Richard is in fact Johnathan Lenoir Fischer, since the marriage records in Port Arthur, Texas show that Nolan Fischer married Molly Richard October 15, 1984. There is record of a name change for the child approximately one month later, November 17, 1984. There is no record, however, of any name change of Gregory Rougeau Richard. In fact, there are no records of that name after the birth record, at least in Port Arthur or Lafayette. We therefore are unable to obtain data on the whereabouts of that child. Perhaps if you could give us more information, we could find out his whereabouts for you.

Thank you again for your employment of this firm.

Our bill for services rendered is enclosed.

Sincerely,

J.J. Brady

Unfortunately, the bill was whited out, so I couldn't tell how much my enterprising son and his partner made off this venture. It seemed that they hadn't done all that much. Johnny Fischer was with his mother, Molly, who married Nolan Fischer, whoever he was, and lived in Port Arthur, Texas. I thought Nolan Fischer must have been a helluva guy to marry a woman who had a nine-month-old child with osteogenesis imperfecta. I wondered what symptoms Johnny had exhibited at that age. Surely, he must have broken a bone or two by then.

I also wondered about the other child, Gregory. If he was Stevie Huntley, which most certainly he had to be, how did it come about that he was adopted during this time? Did Ed Wilson know that he was the twin and help arrange the adoption? Why would he do that? And why did Molly Fischer give up a relatively healthy baby and keep a crippled one? I read on.

Date: April 22, 1993
From: Setec Astronomy, Inc.
To: Beverly Richard

Aunt Beverly,

When you asked to employ my company, which I own with J.J. Brady, I had no idea that it would be so difficult to perform this job. From the professional and technical standpoint, it was difficult. From the personal side, it was especially hard, since I have been essentially investigating my own relatives. I have been exposed to some things I would have preferred not to know. However, there should be no emotional ties if I am going to continue to work in this field, which I think I want to do. So, this is a summary of what I have discovered at your request.

Using the birth certificate of Johnny and his twin brother that I didn't know about, I traced every normal route I would use in both Texas and Louisiana to try to find out about adoption information on a Gregory Rogeau Richard. I found nothing. I was trying to keep J.J. out of this, at your request, but he's better at some of this data-gathering than I am, so I asked him to help me. You didn't provide us with much in the file that you had, but after coming up negative looking for legal adoption information, we decided it must have been a very private matter. You had a copy of a check made out to you from a James P. Henderson, attorney at law, from a Houston bank. We looked up his name in our telephone directories, including the criss-cross, and deciphered that, at that time, it was the senior Henderson, and not the junior. Senior is dead now, by the way.

We made a trip to downtown Houston to the Texas Commerce Tower, and found the marquis listing of Baker, Elkins, Butler, and Henderson. J.J. thought that maybe a private adoption had taken place to keep the identity of the adopting parents secret, not the child's. So, we put all 212 lawyers' names in alphabetical order, and ran them against birth records in Houston during the first six months of 1984, just in case there had been a falsified birth certificate, which J.J. said wasn't all that unusual, especially with lawyers handling the deal.

Well, we found eight births during that period. We then searched each birth record carefully for any discrepancy. And bingo! J.J. found it. There was a Stephen Ray Huntley, born, according to the record, April 23, 1984. That's three months to the day after Aunt Molly's twins were born. However, the thing that caught our eye was that the birth wasn't registered until July 21, 1984, almost three months after the supposed birth. Normal registration is ten to fourteen days.

Bottom line, we think Stephen Huntley is Gregory Rougeau Richard. Enclosed is his address. The father, listed as Peter B. Huntley, is a partner in the law firm of Baker, Elkins, etc., so J.J. and I think that Henderson arranged the adoption in secret for him. For what reason, we don't have a clue.

I don't know what you want this info for, but I hope it's satisfactory. The bill is enclosed.

Sincerely, Brad.

After mentally forgiving Brad for not telling me that he knew his nephew was adopted, I again studied the birth certificate of the twins and re-read the letters from Setec to Ed Wilson and Beverly Richard. I tried to piece it all together as best I could.

Ed must have known Molly through Beverly and known that they were from Lafayette, Louisiana, since he knew where to tell J.J. to start looking for the birth record. I assumed also that he knew Stevie Huntley to be the other twin, since it didn't appear he had asked J.J. for information on him. Ed must have already known that part of the story.

Beverly, for whatever reason, had hired Brad to find out what had happened to the other twin, Stevie. J.J. and Brad had discovered the answer via a check issued to Beverly from old man Henderson.

Why he had issued a check to her, I didn't know. She, of course, knew Johnny's whereabouts, since her sister had kept the child who was subsequently adopted by Nolan Fischer. Nothing, however, explained the role of Beverly as the boys' trustee.

I figured that Ed sought the second twin, so that he could leave money to both of the boys when he died. Why Beverly sought the other twin, I didn't know, but I did know Stevie, Johnny, and Ed were all dead. Stevie's death was suspicious, and Ed's death was very suspicious. Only Johnny's death could be interpreted as somewhat expected, but was it? I could not ignore the fact that Beverly Richard was now rich due to the deaths of three people in less than the same number of weeks.

There was a lot more in the file that J.J. and Brad had provided, but by then it was almost noon, and I had a one o'clock doctor's appointment. I stored the information in my desk and went to change clothes for my upcoming torture, wondering how extensive and personal the remainder of Setec's data would prove to be.

CHAPTER 44

DR. MORGENSTERN

D r. Jim Morgenstern's office was in the University Towers complex, so I parked in my usual spot, wound my way through the many walkways, and took the elevator to his suite on the 26th floor. After my latest experience with the downtown tunnel system, I mentally vowed to get my office staff to give new patients explicit directions through the maze.

Jim's nurse was waiting with the usual array of medical implements, including a blood pressure cuff, a tube for collecting urine, and too many needles, syringes, and red-topped, purple-topped, and blue-topped tubes for my precious blood. After draining me dry, she instructed me to collect a sample of my urine.

"You want me to use this little tube?"

"Yes, sir, I do."

"What happened to those little jars?"

"Gone with the wind, Dr. Brady. These are easier to process."

"Huh. It just seems...so small."

"Well, you don't have to put yourself in the tube, Doc. You just have to aim."

"I know that, it just seems like I'll get it all over myself, and the tube."

"Dr. Brady, just do the best you can, clean off the tube, and bring it back to me. How you do it is up to you. I would think a man who got through medical school could figure out a simple thing like that." She smiled, patted my arm, and left.

I did the best I could with the microscopic tube, but it was not a pleasant experience. I returned to my examination cubicle, and almost immediately, my friend Jimmy walked in.

"Jim Bob! How you doin', boy?"

"I'm great, how about you?"

"Busy as shit, and hearing nothing but complaints. I'm thinking about quitting, moving to Galveston, and opening a taco and bait stand. I'll have a few beers, sell some shrimp and mullet, fry a few tacos, and relax. And, if I drink too much and mix up the bait and the taco meat, my customers can pretend they're in Mexico." We both laughed.

"So, are you sick?"

"No. Mary Louise made the appointment. She worries I'll die and leave her a grieving widow. I've told her I'm a lot more valuable dead than alive, what with all that insurance I have to carry."

"Yeah, but she wouldn't have your smiling face to see around the old homestead then, would she?"

"I guess. That's exactly what she says."

Jimmy proceeded to give me the once-over, doing all the usual peering, probing, measuring, and clocking.

"Okay, Jim Bob, now for the fun part," he said as he slipped on the dreaded glove. "Turn around, and bend over."

"What? No kiss first, Jimmy?"

"Nope. I only kiss Mary Louise. Spread 'em boy."

I think internists delighted in this humiliation. It humbled me to think I was just another asshole.

"You're okay. Get dressed. Then go to my office."

I did that gladly and left the exam room for his private domain.

"Well, B.P., heart rate, and the exam is fine," he said as he walked in. As he looked over my chart, I realized what a fondness I had for my old friend. We had trained together, and had been both friends, and on occasion, patients of each other. He was about five foot nine, thin, with a close-cropped graying beard. His glasses were so thick that they distorted his eyes. He had had some serious health problems about ten years earlier, but he seemed to have been cured by a surgeon who removed three-fourths of his ulcerated stomach.

"You need a treadmill and an Echo. I'll schedule it for next week. Friday's your half day off, isn't it?"

"Yes, but next week..."

"No buts. I'm scheduling it, so be there or Mary Louise will kill us both. Got it?"

"Aye-aye, captain."

"Good. Oh, by the way, sorry to hear about Ed Wilson. Tough break. That cancer just ate him up. I wished he had let us treat it. Never could figure out why he let it go like that. Must have had a death wish or something."

"What are you talking about? I thought he'd only been diagnosed in the last week or two?"

"Are you kidding me? I found it last year. He got cystogramed, had a bone scan, an MRI, the works. It was all repeated a couple of weeks ago, but that prostate CA had gone everywhere. Why in the hell he decided to have surgery then, I don't know. Anyway, I won't let you make a stupid move like that, even if I have to drag your hairy butt to the OR myself. Now move along. I have paying patients to see." He shook my hand, and we both left to our respective duties.

On the way home, I was puzzled by the Ed Wilson story. He had cancer for a year, and went without treatment? He probably could have lived at least five or ten more years if he had been treated when first diagnosed. I couldn't imagine why he would make a decision like that. I wondered about the sealed will in the safe deposit box, and I called Pete Huntley's office on the car phone.

"Baker, Elkins, Butler, and Henderson. May I help you?"

"Yes ma'am. Pete Huntley's office, please."

"Thank you." I waited a few seconds before Pete's secretary answered.

"Mr. Huntley's office."

"Hi. Dr. Jim Bob Brady. Can I speak to Pete, please?"

"Is Mr. Huntley expecting your call, sir?"

"No, I don't think so."

"Please hold." I waited for a while, which was okay, since traffic on Fannin at that time of day on Friday was miserable.

"Jim Bob. What's up?"

"Hey, Pete. I need to ask you something, and I hope it won't be too confidential for you to tell me. I'd like to know when your senior partner Mr. Henderson died, and when Ed Wilson made out that sealed will you read from last night."

"Why do you want to know that?"

"Just curious, Pete. Can you tell me?"

"Hang on," he said with some exasperation in his voice. I waited for a few minutes.

"The will is dated May 17, 1993. Henderson made it out. I think it was one of his last wills, though, because if I remember, he died in...Hey, Jeannie! When did old man Henderson die?" I heard them talking, but I couldn't understand her side of the conversation.

"First part of June, Jim Bob. Why is that important?"

"I don't know. Just curious, as I said. Thanks."

"You have anything else to tell me? About that matter we discussed last night?"

"Not yet, Pete. I'm still working on it. I'll call you when I know something. Thanks again."

On the way home, I reviewed what I could remember from the files J.J. had sent. Wilson hired Setec in January and found the whereabouts of Johnny Fischer. Beverly Richard hired Setec in April and found the identity of Stevie Huntley. Wilson executed his will in May, leaving money to the boys in a trust and making Beverly Richard the trustee. Henderson died in June, and the Wilson family files went to Pete Huntley, except for Ed's will, which was locked in a safe deposit box, not to be opened until his death. Some time later, Wilson was diagnosed with prostate cancer, neglected treatment, and had Pete execute a power of attorney in case he died a sudden, unexpected death.

I called home, hoping Mary Louise had returned from tennis.

"Hello?"

"Hey! I'm glad to hear your voice! How was tennis?"

"Great, but I'm beat. Where are you?"

"Leaving Jimmy's office."

"So, are you healthy?"

"So far. It'll take a couple of days to get the blood results back, and I have to have a treadmill test and an echocardiogram next Friday. Purely precautionary. He didn't find anything wrong with me, but he insisted on running the tests, mostly to make you happy, I think."

"Good. Are you hungry?"

"Yes, starving. Want me to pick up something on the way home?"

"Took the words right out of my mouth. Tacos?"

"Taco Bell, baby. I'll get one of those cartons with 10 or 15 in it. I think they're dietetic, aren't they?"

"Right. But it's okay, 'cause I'm in the mood for a cholesterol binge."

"Good. I'll be along." I paused. "Listen, one more thing. Jimmy told me that Ed Wilson had cancer for a year, not just two or three weeks like he told us all at that party. What do you make of that?"

"Interesting. Did you read J.J.'s file?"

"Most of it. You know, I think I need to meet with Susan and bring her up to date on what all we've found out. Don't you?"

"She'll be here at five."

"What?"

"I called Susan. It's time to let her run the show. I think you've done enough. Bring me tacos!" As she hung up the phone, I realized once again that she knew what I was thinking before I did.

CHAPTER 45

PAYOFFS

"I think you should read the rest of J.J.'s file before Susan gets here," Mary Louise had said.

We were sitting on the patio at the small, white, ornate table she had bought at an antique show several years before. We had pigged out on tacos and used so much hot sauce that after four or five tacos apiece, we were required to concoct our second iced Coronas with lime. We had been mulling for a while as she petted Cat.

"There's important 'stuff' in that file that may affect the police investigation," my bride continued. "I read through it yesterday."

"Well, it's after three o'clock, Mary Louise. I want to type up a chronology of events for her to sort of review what I've discovered these last three weeks. Why don't you just go through J.J.'s file, highlight the things you think are important, and show it to Susan when she gets here. You're going to give her the file anyway, right?"

"Sure, although there is some rather sensitive information in there about the people involved in all this mess that J.J. says was obtained in a surreptitious fashion."

"Meaning illegal."

"Probably. But then, Stan Lombardo has been very supportive in the past. I'm sure it will be fine, Jim Bob."

"I hope you're right."

I went inside and typed the chronologue of recent and past events, which forced me to organize my thoughts. Although I planned to give Susan a copy, since she knew very little about the recent discoveries, I wasn't sure how much I really knew.

CHRONOLOGY

*Beverly Richard comes to work at University Hospital in 1981--check on date.

*Molly Richard comes to work at University also and if so, when?

*Ed Wilson knows both women, has an affair with Molly, she gets pregnant?

*Richard twins born in Lafayette, La. Jan. 23, 1984

*Molly gives up second twin (Stevie Huntley) in July, 1984. Why? Adoption private, arranged by Henderson through Wilson?

*Beverly comes back to work at University--1986.

*Wilson hires Setec Jan., 1993--finds Johnny Fischer.

*Bev. Richard hires Setec April, 1993--finds Stevie Huntley.

*Wilson revises his will--May, 1993.

*Wilson power of attorney--Summer, 1993.

*Stevie killed March 12, 1994.

*Johnny dies post-op March 17, 1994.

*Ed dies post-op March 24, 1994. Succinylcholine injection?

There were gaps, but I felt that I had done what Susan had asked me to do. And Mary Louise was right. I had done plenty. More than enough, and none of it had been fun. I figured we would have the meeting in thirty minutes, I would give Susan the info I had, and Mary Louise would show her the highlights of whatever else J.J. had sent. Then, armed with that new knowledge, the detective might be able to go out and solve whatever mystery she thought she could solve, that began with Stevie Huntley's hit-and-run. The part of the story that I knew seemed a little sinister, and I felt it was time for it to become a police matter. I was ready to relax and get brain-dead in my spare time again.

In order to celebrate, I poured myself a thirty-year-old Usquebach unblended scotch, with one ice cube as recommended, and returned to my wicker rocker for my second smoke of the day.

Mary Louise retrieved me from my solace after an enjoyable half hour. Susan had arrived, and her husband, Gene, had come along. I greeted them both as Mary Louise seated them in our formal dining room.

"So how's the ankle, Gene?" I asked.

"It's doing great, Doc. It's only been a week, and I'm back in the office doing paperwork. I guess you'll change this cast next week, huh?"

"Maybe, if you behave yourself. Otherwise, you have to wear that smelly thing for six weeks."

He stared at me for a moment, then realized I was joking.

"Right, Doc, I get it. It's already starting to smell. Any chance you can change it sooner than next Thursday?"

"Nope."

Susan interrupted. "Listen, guys, let's get going on this. What do you have for me, Dr. Brady?"

I went through my chronology of events and gave Susan a copy of the one I had typed. I had run the original through Mary Louise's fax machine, which I recently learned was a sort of copy machine. It wasn't perfect, but it would save her from peering over my shoulder.

Once I had finished, she made some notes and questioned me on details. I told her what I knew and what I didn't know, such as Molly's work history, her relationship with Wilson, the fact that Wilson knew of the twins, where Beverly had been for the two years she was absent from University Hospital, and how she had risen to the level of Nursing Vice-President of the hospital from a surgical nurse's position.

"I don't know any more than what I've told you. Mary Louise has some more data that J.J. discovered, and she'll go over that with you now. After that, we feel like we've done all we can, and should do, to help you out. We'd like to turn over all this info to you, and if it helps, fine. But, my wife and I are retiring from this case after today. Right?"

Mary Louise nodded and began talking. The folder in her lap was bulging, and I couldn't imagine what all was in there. I didn't know when she had had the time to look at all that. She had to be smarter, and quicker, than I. She was also much better looking.

"What I have here is compliments of Setec Astronomy, which as you know, is a company that our son J.J. owns with his friend and roommate, Brad Broussard, who happens to be the nephew of Beverly Richard and her sister, Molly Fisher. Since he was so closely involved with the personalities, I have to commend Brad on his cooperation and lack of bias in helping J.J. obtain all the data.

"In the process of both Ed Wilson and Beverly Richard hiring Setec, they each filled out an application form which included their social security number. J.J. tells me that once you know that bit of information, you can find out anything about anybody. He and Brad require that before taking on a case, since, so often, he tells me, the person paying for an investigation often needs to be investigated as well. How he got the Huntleys' social security numbers, I don't know. I assume Brad somehow got Nolan and Molly Fisher's numbers.

"This stack of paperwork is a compilation of credit reports, through TRW, of all the parties involved here. Also, Setec has listed properties owned by these folks, with tax records to show their valuation as of 1993. In addition to the charge account listings, and every other financed item on every individual concerned for the last ten years, my son and his enterprising partner have obtained bank records for the last ten years or so on those he could. He could only get Beverly Richard's bank data since 1986, which is apparently when she returned to Houston. The Fischer's bank records begin in late 1984, which I think coincides with their marriage in Port Arthur."

She handed me my copy, which was quite professional. I stared at her. I was stunned, both at J.J.'s abilities and her competence. And at her nonchalance with all the very personal and private data, that we all so casually reviewed. I wondered how many people had reviewed my bank records, property valuations, and credit card charges. It had to be a new world out there if two twenty-year-old kids could find out that much about a person with a computer. I shuttered to think of what the IRS, the CIA, and the FBI could do.

My wife continued, "I've highlighted what I think are the most interesting aspects of the file. Susan, I think you should review this in meticulous detail on your own, since you may know to look for things that I don't."

"I seriously doubt it, Mary Louise. This is absolutely incredible. You've done a wonderful job. You too, Dr. Brady. I'm impressed."

"Let me point out a few things," Mary Louise continued. "Since 1986, there has been a monthly transfer of $10,000 electronically from Ed Wilson's personal account at Nations Bank to Beverly Richard's account at Med Center Bank. The following day, in every instance, there has been a transfer of $2,000 from Beverly's account to an account in Port Arthur in the name of Molly Richard. I would assume this is Mrs. Fischer, her sister, using her maiden name. Why this would be, the file doesn't speculate.

"Also of interest is that Beverly owns a townhome, or patio home, on Potomac, between San Felipe and Woodway. That area has been remodeled in the last few years and consists as you know of luxury, updated homes. She owns hers free and clear, with a tax valuation of $375,000. She also owns her Porsche free and clear. She also owns a Honda Gold Wing motorcycle, again, free and clear. I don't know if

Jim Bob mentioned it, but her Porsche license plate is ACES HI.

"There doesn't seem to be anything out of order in Ed Wilson's data base other than the electronic transfers. Nor is there anything glaring in the Huntley segment, although their house is valued much lower than ours, and I intend to complain to the City of Houston about that."

We all laughed. She continued, "Other than the $2,000 from Beverly's account to her sister's account on a monthly basis since 1986, the only item I found peculiar was...actually, there were two things. The Fischer's home in Port Arthur is valued at $63,500. They've lived there for 10 years and owe $41,000 on it. What Molly does with her monthly stipend, I've not a clue. Maybe she used it for medical expenses on Johnathan, although according to that segment of the file, Nolan Fischer has excellent insurance through his job at Dow Chemical. I know it's hard to believe, especially for you, my darling husband, that this much information is obtainable on we United States citizens. It makes you wonder about whatever happened to the privacy of the American people that we are supposed to enjoy. Well, I'm here to tell you, it doesn't seem to exist any more.

"Anyway, my last point. Nolan Fisher drives a red, 1987 Chevrolet SR-7 pick-up truck. It's a small bed pick-up, which could be compatible with the truck seen by eyewitnesses, including my husband, at the time Stevie Huntley was run over. However, the license plate is GUF 883, which isn't even close to what was initially described as a C, an E, and a 7."

Susan remarked, "Looks like our friend Beverly is living high on the hog to me. Looks like she had something on Ed Wilson, but what, there's no way to know. It appears that she was sending her sister money, but kept the lion's share for herself. And I don't know what to make of the Fischer pick-up.

"Dr. Brady, is there anything else you can tell us that might help?"

I honestly couldn't remember whether I had told her about the succinylcholine business that Jeff Clarke related to me. I asked. I hadn't, so I gave her the scenario that Jeff postulated.

"So," Susan continued after my narration. "Stevie Huntley is run over, and Johnny Fischer and Ed Wilson die after surgery. And maybe Wilson was suspicious, maybe not?"

"Well, I would prefer you get with Jeff Clarke about all that, Susan."

"Fine. Now, somebody needs to talk to Beverly Richard, and somebody needs to make a trip to Port Arthur to talk to the Fischers. I'll round up a colleague to talk to Ms. Richard. I want to go to Port Arthur myself tomorrow and see what I can find out.

"What about you, Dr. Brady? Want to go to scenic Port 'Artur' with me?" She used the Cajun French pronunciation.

I looked at Mary Louise. She nodded. I must admit that I was very curious about the Fischers.

"Sure, if you'll buy me some boudin," I replied.

CHAPTER 46

PT. ARTHUR

$\mathbf{I}$t was a little after ten in the morning when Susan picked me up at home and we started out.

I had asked Mary Louise to accompany me on the trip to Port Arthur. I was a little worried about making conversation with Susan Beeson for that length of time, since it was a one-and-a-half hour drive each way. That included neither the waiting time, should the Fischers not be at home, nor the time it would take for Susan to ask whatever questions she had planned for them.

I hadn't quite begged Mary Louise to go, but I had come close. She had insisted that the trip was something I had to do on my own, since I was the catalyst behind this entire investigation. I whined, but she continued to decline, informing me that she had meetings, a luncheon, and other charitable duties to attend to. She added that Susan was very nice and assured me it would go fine.

"Gene and I stayed up half the night reading through those TRW statements and personal records looking for something to tie all this together," Susan began. "I know there's a key to all this, but neither of us could find it. We were both fairly tired last night, so Gene said he would spend the morning going over everything a second time.

It's got to be there somewhere, don't you think, Dr. Brady?"

"I don't know, Susan. My mind is burned out, both from all this, and from work."

"You have a fairly intensive job, don't you, Doc?"

"I guess. There never seems to be any time to really relax and forget about your patients. They're with you in your mind, even when you're off. We have to dot the i's and cross the t's, just to keep the vultures off our backs. And it's not just the lawyers any more. It's all the government agencies and insurance company peer review boards that really bother us these days. I think that in the beginning of all this 'policing' of medicine, the idea was a good one. Ferret out those few doctors who practiced bad medicine, for whatever reason--incompetence, alcoholism, drug abuse--and get them out of the business. Now, all these groups watch every move even the good guys make. If you add all that to all the HMO's, PPO's, CPO's, and IPA's, and the capitated plans, it makes life for the average doctor fairly miserable. And in the final analysis, guess who suffers? The patient."

We headed east on Interstate 10, passing Highlands, Baytown, Winnic, Hankamer, and other small Texas towns on the 90-mile trip to Port Arthur. We were silent for a time.

"So, what did you two do last night after we left?"

"Oh, I played the piano for a while. Relaxation therapy, you know. We ordered Chinese food and watched two of my favorite shows, 'Seinfeld' and 'Frazier'."

"Oh, I love 'Seinfeld.' I forgot all about it, with all the paperwork we were reviewing."

"I can understand about paperwork," I had said.

"That Kramer cracks me up, especially the way he can fall down and pop right back up. I can understand why the women are so attracted to him. He's totally honest. He's who he is. No pretenses. Women love that, you know. It's endearing."

"Really?"

"You bet. You know, Jerry is a very nice-looking man, but he has all this stuff going on in his head all the time. He's confused about what he wants, so his dates respond accordingly. What happened last night?"

I related the episode of the previous night, which happened to be a re-run. It was about Jerry's friend George parking in a handicap zone at a shopping mall in his father's new car. The patrons coming out to the parking garage somehow found out that the owner wasn't handicapped and basically destroyed the car with tire irons and base-ball bats. I couldn't help but laugh when I described the events, and soon we were both laughing. After that conversation came easily, and we talked about everything from my growing up in Waco, to her being a policeman's daughter. It turned out to be fun. Mary Louise had been right.

Like all the cities along the Texas-Louisiana Gulf Coast, Port Arthur was centered around refineries and chemical plants. Although the size of the cities varied greatly, Houston, Beaumont, Port Arthur, Lake Charles, Baton Rouge, and New Orleans had much in common. Including the weather, which on this day was overcast and in the eight-ies, with the humidity at "drip" level.

We stopped at Homer's Barbecue in Port Arthur. I had a sliced beef poor-boy, with pickles, onions, jalapenos, and a side order of Ca-jun boudin. Boudin was a concoction of pork or beef, chopped finely and mixed with dirty rice and hot spices, then packed tightly into a thick, skin-like membrane tied at each end like a sausage.

Homer's was an old, clapboard, dilapidated restaurant, a sure sign in Texas that the food was excellent. Susan had something that looked a little healthier, although I wasn't sure what you could find in a place like Homer's one would consider "healthy."

I had a Lone Star beer, she had iced tea. She asked me what the cook used to wrap the boudin. I told her she didn't want to know.

We both made a pit stop before leaving. I sneaked a cigarette, not wanting to smoke in front of such a nutrition-minded person as Su-san. When we returned to the car, she pulled out a city map and located the street, and we proceeded to the home of Molly and Nolan Fischer. I became nervous, or excited, or both. I think that I was a little afraid. Kramer would admit to that, so I felt comfortable doing the same.

We eventually turned onto a street in a middle-class neighborhood, with numerous tract houses, differing only slightly in their coloration and configuration. We found the house, pulled up to the curb, and got out. The red Chevy truck was in the driveway, and as best I could determine, the license plate matched J.J.'s report. Amazing kid, I thought.

The door was answered by a rather tall, thin man with a pleasant face.

"Yes?" he asked.

"Hello. Mr. Fischer?" Susan asked.

"Yes?"

"I'm Detective Susan Beeson, Houston Police Department. This is Dr. Jim Brady, an associate. May we speak with you and your wife a moment?"

"What's this all about?" he asked as he opened the door and came out on the porch. "My wife is under sedation. We lost our son last week, at University Hospital. In Houston."

Nolan Fischer appeared gaunt, probably still suffering from the pain that only losing a child can bring. He was dressed in faded jeans, a work shirt, tennis shoes, and had a "gimme" cap that had a Dow Chemical emblem on it. He was one of those people with a pleasant demeanor, who you could like the moment you met them.

"Well, sir, that's part of the reason we're here," Susan continued. "We have discovered, quite by accident, that your son Johnathan had a twin brother. About three weeks ago, his twin was the victim of a hit-and-run accident. We are investigating that accident, and we are hoping you or Mrs. Fischer might be able to shed some light on the situation."

If he could become visibly paler than he already was, I thought he did. He looked down, then up, then into the distance. Susan was being a little cagey with her information, but maybe that's how detectives operated. Feed the fish a little line, see if he would take the bait. Mr. Fischer continued to stare, seemingly at nothing.

We all stood there for an uncomfortable moment or two, but then turned toward the door at a sound that sounded like metal being dragged across a floor. The door started to open, and Nolan Fischer pulled the handle to complete the process. There stood before us a slight woman, frail, with crutches. I viewed her slim body, down to the brown, high-top, lace-up orthopedic shoes, then up to the stainless steel and leather long-leg braces that ended almost at the hips. She wore them outside shorts.

"What do you want?" she asked hoarsely.

"They're police, Molly. From Houston. They said some kid was run over in Houston, and they think it's a twin brother of Johnny's. I told 'em you were sedated and all, but they..."

"It's all right, Nolan." She viewed him tenderly, like I would have expected a damsel in distress to eye her knight in shining armor. He helped her out onto the porch, where we all stood in silence for a moment.

"I don't know who you people are, and I don't really care. I lost my only son last week after an operation to try to straighten his back, since he couldn't breathe any more. He had the same curse as I do, this lousy bone disease. He got it from me, and it killed him. That's all I know, and that's all I can tell you." She resembled Beverly, though not all that much. Her short stature was probably due to her growth having been stunted by the disease, but I couldn't tell about the braces. Maybe some bad fractures, or bad surgery. She was a pitiful sight, and my heart grew heavy for these poor people. This was such a contrast to the wealthy, attractive Beverly, that my emotions switched to anger.

"Mrs. Fischer, we wanted to ask you about an adoption ten years ago. Apparently, your son had a twin, and died under..."

"Listen, young lady, and listen good. My life has been shitty, except for two things. Nolan here, and Johnny. The past is dead and gone, and I got nothing to say about any of it. Now I figure that you got no authority here in Port Arthur. So, unless I see the Sheriff on my front doorstep with a piece of paper that says I have to talk with him, I got nothin' to say. Now get off my property." She looked at her husband. "Nolan? Please make them leave." She then turned around, with difficulty, and made her way back into the house, with Nolan holding the door.

"I'm sorry about all that. She's under a lot of stress. I guess I'll have to ask you to leave."

We turned to walk to our car. Susan knew she had no jurisdiction there, so I figured there wasn't much she could do. Nolan Fischer followed us to the car, however, which surprised me.

"That adoption was a long time ago. I married Molly after that, when she just had Johnny. We never really talk about it. Her sister, Beverly, handled it for her. Beverly's been real good to Molly. Gives her money and all. They're best friends, you know. I don't really know why she gave the other boy up. She won't talk about it. I always figured it didn't really matter. Johnny was all we could handle, with him being sick or hurt most of the time."

I had to ask, "How long has your wife been in leg braces?"

"Ever since the accident, I guess."

"What accident?" Susan asked.

"She was in some kind of accident when she worked in Houston with Beverly. When she left Lafayette, in '82, I guess, she didn't need braces. She limped a little, but wasn't nearly as bad off as she was after the wreck."

"So you knew her before, in Lafayette?" It was my turn for a question.

"Oh, yeah. We grew up together. I've loved that girl all my life. Just about did me in when she moved to Houston."

"So, you married her after the accident, and after she had the twins?"

"Oh, yeah. Johnny was about nine months old then. He was in a body cast for something; and she, bless her heart, walked down that aisle in long-leg casts. We got out of Lafayette, her being an unmarried mother and all. Came here in '84, since Dow was hiring, and Molly and I got married."

"So you were never bothered by the fact that Johnny wasn't your child?" Susan retorted.

"I said, I've always loved that girl. No matter about Johnny. I raised him like he was my own. I loved him more than anything, except his mother. He was a fine boy."

Nolan Fischer was turning out to be even more of a saint than I had imagined.

"One last thing, Mr. Fischer. That's your truck?" Susan asked.

"Yep."

"Where were you three weeks ago? Were you in Houston by any chance?"

"Let's see. That would be about the time Johnny had his surgery, which was on the 17th. Yeah. We came over to Houston the Friday before. We wanted to take Johnny to an Astros game. That was on Saturday. We stayed at Beverly's a few days after that, since he was having surgery on the next Thursday."

"So when you went to the game, did you drive your truck?" I suddenly started to get where she was coming from. The Astros game was the day Stevie Huntley was run over.

"Nah. I hate to drive in that Houston traffic. Beverly hired us a big Lincoln with a driver. Johnny loved it. She was supposed to go to the game, but she got called into the hospital on an emergency. We had a great time at that game. Season opener, you know. We had box seats. Johnny thought..."

He broke down at that point, putting his head into his hands and weeping. I became very emotional myself and had to turn away.

"Thank you so much, Mr. Fischer. I'm very sorry about Johnny," Susan said in leaving. All I could do was pat the man on the shoulder and get into the car.

Susan and I were both silent for a while on the trip back to Houston. I felt as though she had been as affected emotionally as I, but didn't say anything. After all, she was a cop, and cops supposedly saw horrible things every day.

I continued to picture Nolan Fischer ten years earlier, marrying a crippled girl, his childhood love, who had to walk down the aisle wearing long-leg casts. And somewhere in that church, or chapel, or wherever, was a nine-month-old child in a body cast. Basically, Nolan would never be "anybody" in the social sense of the word, but I would never forget him as long as I lived. He was a man to be respected and admired, although probably no one but his wife would ever really appreciate him. It was sad.

I had somehow thought that maybe the red truck was the key, and that in some form or fashion one of its owners, either Nolan or Molly, had run over Stevie Huntley. It was apparent to me after meeting them that that wasn't possible. Nolan Fischer was as gentle as a lamb. I doubted Molly could even drive with those braces. I did think that Molly probably knew a whole lot more than she was willing to talk about, but as for her running down a child, I doubted it. It wasn't physically possible for her to do so, and for some reason, I didn't think she had the heart for it.

I still didn't know why she had given up one child, the healthier of the two, for adoption. Maybe she had tried to give up both babies, but because Johnny's disease was bad at birth, she had to keep him. Although sister Beverly, according to Nolan, had been generous with them, I doubted he knew that she was pocketing $8,000 a month from Wilson, by sending her sister only $2,000. I wondered again why Wilson had been giving Beverly money all those years.

The clincher, though, was the last little thing Nolan told us, about going to the Astros opening game in a limo of some sort. Probably a big thrill for all three of them. And wasn't it coincidental that the loyal and faithful Beverly Richard, nurse extraordinaire, had been called in to the hospital for a supposed emergency. She could have used the truck herself, since the Fischers were staying at her house. But then, the license plate wasn't even close.

Although I didn't pay much attention to Susan, preferring to remain isolated in my thoughts, I noticed on occasion that she was making calls, both to home and office. She had trouble trying to hold the steering wheel, dial the car phone, and refer to her file-o-fax. I almost suggested my tried and true method of driving and negotiating other duties. I simply put on the cruise control and steer with my left lower thigh, just above the knee. This allowed both of my hands to be free to eat fast food and drink Coke. I thought about explaining it to her, but remembered she was, in fact, an officer of the law. I could imagine the police radios blaring: Be on the lookout for a man driving with his leg and using his hands to eat and drink. Armed with tacos, and very dangerous.

Fortunately, Susan interrupted my dreamy state. "Got it!"

"What?" I said sleepily. I had dozed off.

"I've been trying to get hold of Gene for an hour. He finally called me back. Dad put out a warrant for Beverly Richard's arrest, and they've put an APB on for her. He went to her house, and to her office at University, but she's nowhere to be found. Dad said the Porsche was in the garage, but the motorcycle was gone."

"What in the hell did Gene find in those papers that allowed the chief to get a warrant for Beverly's arrest?"

"Gene didn't find it, Doc. Your boy did. Actually, Brad discovered it, which is especially ironic, since it's his own aunt whose goose he cooked."

"What?!"

"Brad told J.J. that his dear Aunt Beverly had new personalized plates this year. He wondered why she had changed them and asked J.J. if he thought it was important. So, J.J. called Mary Louise, and she called Gene, and Gene called Dad. The license plate change from last year was buried in those files Gene poured through, but he never connected it, until J.J. called your wife. Guess what the old plate read!"

"Please, Susan, I'm going to have an arrhythmia if you don't hurry up and tell me."

You'll love it, Doc. '7UP ICE'!"

CHAPTER 47

THE SHARD

F riday afternoon was a time to stay off the freeway--any freeway--going into or out of Houston. Traffic was bumper to bumper. It was after six o'clock in the evening before Susan dropped me off at home. Mary Louise greeted me at the door.

"Hi, sweetie. How are you holding up?" she asked.

"Pretty good. Some day, though."

"Can I get you something?"

"Twist my arm." She playfully did just that, after which I held her tightly for a moment. "I'm very glad to see you, my dear."

"Likewise, mon ami."

I stepped into the bar, prepared her an Absolut Citroen, and myself, an eighteen-year-old MacCallan unblended, with two ice cubes as recommended. We sat in our respective wicker rockers and watched the family of doves eat the fresh bird seed Mary Louise had placed lovingly in the bird feeder. She spread a little extra for the baby doves along the parking area in front of the garage, since they were apparently still afraid of the metal feeder.

"What was it like at their house?"

I explained the events of the day as best I could. I again became emotional over the entire situation.

"I wonder why Beverly did it, if she really did do it?" Mary Louise asked. "For the money?"

"Who's to say? I still don't understand why Ed was paying her all those years. And I don't know why he would make her trustee of the kids' money. I mean, if they were his children out of wedlock, why not just leave them the money and designate the parents as trustees? It makes no sense."

"Well, it looks like she's on the run. Maybe it will all settle out in the wash, Jim Bob. You never really know why anyone does anything, do you?"

"I guess not." I paused. "I will never forget Nolan Fischer. What a guy. A man among men. The whole thing blows me away."

"So, do you think Beverly used his truck while they were at the game and put her old license plate on the truck so it couldn't be traced?"

"I guess so, M.L. But what a shitty thing to do to Molly and a nice guy like Nolan. I mean, to run over a kid in your sister's truck? What kind of person is she, anyway?"

"Well, not very much of a human being in my mind, especially if she killed Stevie, and somehow killed Johnny Fischer and Ed Wilson. She would qualify for bitch-of-the-year in my book if she, in fact, accomplished all that."

Mary Louise never cursed or said anything bad about anybody. The comment was highly unusual, but justified.

"What are we doing for dinner?"

"I don't know. Where are you taking me? You're still on vacation, aren't you, big boy?"

"Yep. How about a burger at Beck's Prime and a movie?"

"Oh, how delightful, young man. What shall we see?"

"Well, I know how you love Al Pacino, right?"

"Yes. Quite."

"Well, then I would propose Beck's Prime cuisine, followed by

'Carlito's Way' at the Spectrum Cinema."

"It's a date. Do I look all right?"

In a low-cut sundress and sandals with little coins flopping all around, I thought she would qualify for Mrs. America.

"No, my dear. You look smashing. Let me clean up and change clothes. How about checking the movie times?"

"You got it."

Dinner was good, the movie was great. We had to catch the last showing at 9:30, since we piddled around so long at dinner. By the time we got home, it was after midnight. We fell fast asleep almost immediately.

On Saturday, I did something I never do. I played golf. It was a charity event for the March of Dimes, something that my darling wife had recruited me to do. I played with a great group of guys, and with a handicap of over 20, my score was respectable. Mary Louise had a tennis tournament that day, so we had planned to meet back at the house about five o'clock and go to dinner at Maxim's.

Maxim's held a special place in both our hearts, since I had taken her there when I proposed. I always reminded her of the fact that I was a lowly medical student at the time and had a part-time job starting IVs at the hospital, and another being a platelet donor at the Cancer Institute. I had used all my earnings from an entire month to afford dinner. But it was all worth it. She made my life worth something, to me, to her, to J.J., and hopefully, to my patients over the past twenty years.

I parked my car in the garage and came into the sun room through the patio. I put the key in the door lock, but nothing happened. I realized that the door was unlocked, which was forbidden around our house. There was too much crime in Houston not to lock the doors, even on short trips in and out of the house. It was a little after five. Although it was spring, Daylight Savings Time was not in effect, so it was a little dark. There were no lights on in the house, and I became nervous.

"Mary Louise, I'm home. Where are you?"

"Upstairs."

"I can't believe you left the back door unlocked," I yelled as I went up the stairs. "You know better than..."

As I walked into our bedroom, I saw that Mary Louise was tied up in one of the two chairs that we sat in at night to watch TV. I felt a presence to my left, but when I turned, something hit me over the top of the head. I must have lost consciousness for a minute, because the next thing I remember was being pulled into the chair next to Mary Louise. My hands were forced behind me, and a tight, rough substance was wrapped around my wrists.

"You think you're pretty smart, don't you, fuckhead!" screamed the assailant as she slapped me across the face with a gloved hand. Beverly Richard was dressed in black leather, with gloves and boots. Her hair was under a cap of some sort, which resembled the kind worn by Harley-Davidson riders.

"I had it made, you sorry sack of shit, until you came along and ruined it for me. Well, we'll see who's going to be fucked in the end. We'll just see." She hit me again.

"What are you going to do, Beverly?" Mary Louise asked. She seemed far too calm. I was near hysteria.

"I'm going to burn it down. The house, with you two in it. It'll look like an accident. You, Doctor Brady," she said with a slur, "and your stupid closet smoking. Like nobody knows. If you were a real man, you'd either quit or smoke in public. Oh, but no! You're an image kind of guy! The kind I despise, just like that fucking Wilson!"

I tried to collect my thoughts, which was difficult with an obvious madwoman waving a revolver at me. Fortunately, Mary Louise had her wits about her and she continued talking.

"You know, Beverly, the police know about everything. You can't get away with it. They know about the truck belonging to Nolan Fischer and about the license plate that says '7UP ICE.' One of the pathologists at the hospital picked up the muscle paralyzer in Ed's system that shouldn't have been there. I think they have you. Pete Huntley has traced the trust money to you. Why don't you just give it up?"

"Shut up, you bitch!" And with that, she got up from where she was sitting on our bed, and slapped Mary Louise so hard that I thought her neck was broken.

"Mary Louise!" I cried as I struggled to get out of my bindings. It was not possible. I slumped and felt that it was the end.

Beverly sat back down on the bed and stared at the carpeted floor with her boot prints all over it.

"Beverly?" I said as I mustered my courage. "Since I'm going to die anyway, would you mind telling me why you did this? I've been looking into it for three weeks, and I just don't get it. Would you show me that one courtesy before you fry me? And maybe consider letting Mary Louise go? She's done you no harm."

"Ha! She knows as much as you do, Brady. Forget it! But, I'll tell you a little story, if your Waco brain can handle it." She got up and paced.

"Once upon a time, there was a young girl from Lafayette, Louisiana, who came to the big city of Houston to work at the big University Hospital. She worked in the Orthopedics Department in surgery and came to meet, and know, the great, big, bad wolf, Dr. Wilson. I was the girl, ladies and gentlemen. I was starry-eyed and impressed by this powerful man who eventually got into my pants. He bought me presents, took me to nice places, and made me feel special. I could be a bitch in the OR, because Eddie was my man! Sure, he had a wife, but it was a marriage of convenience. A marriage of society and propriety! She would hardly ever fuck him, and never went down on him, so I was his girl! And nobody could fuck with me.

"But then, along comes another sweet and innocent thing. A frail little thing, but oh, so beautiful. My sister. She finished nursing school and came to live with me in the big, fancy apartment that the big, bad wolf had rented for me. And she goes to work in surgery, too.

And then, one day, when big, bad Eddie, gets, maybe, a little tired of me, he starts to hit on little, frail Mollie. I start to wonder about old Eddie and start listening to all the scuttlebutt about him being Mr. Fuck-Around-With-The-Nurses. Mollie keeps telling me he's coming on to her, and I tell her to be cool. It will pass. You see, Mollie was a looker. She's got O.I., see, 'cause it runs in our family, but as she got older, her bones got stronger. I didn't want her to be a nurse. Told her it was risky, with picking up and moving patients and all that shit we have to do for you asshole doctors. But she wouldn't listen. She did it anyway. Said she wanted to give something back to the world.

"So, one night, I'm working a late case in surgery, since I'm on call. Molly went home at three-fifteen, like always. I told her to take the car--we used to ride to work together--and I would call her when I was finished, and she could come to pick me up. So, I finished about eight, called her, and no answer. I finally took a cab home, and guess what I found? My sister, on the bed, bleeding from her vagina, both arms broke, both hips broken, her extremities all going in different directions.

"I called 911, told everybody she had been assaulted by a mugger, and got her the best care money could by. But it wasn't enough. She was ruined. Physically and emotionally. Ed Wilson had raped her. He was drunk, didn't know she had OI, and when he forced his way into the apartment and had his way with her, he broke every bone in her body that he touched or laid on. See, he had a key, since he rented the place for me, and the lousy son-of-a-bitch knew I was on call and would be at work when he came a callin.' He just had to have that girl, any old way the big, bad wolf could.

"So after I got Mollie patched up, we went home to Lafayette. She was crippled and pregnant. I wanted her to have an abortion, but Mom and Dad, good Catholics that they were, wouldn't hear of it. And neither would Mollie. Abortion was a mortal sin, damning you to hell forever. Having a child from a rape, that was forgivable, even if she was an unwed mother."

"So, this damaged, crippled child of twenty-two has twin boys. At first, we thought they were normal. But then, little Johnny gets a broken hip when he was a month old just having his diaper changed. The other boy was stronger. We thought maybe he was okay."

She left the room looking exhausted, and we heard her walk down the stairs. She was unloading ten years of misery onto us. Not that there was any prospect that we would be let go. I heard the refrigerator door close. She returned with a beer.

"So, a crippled mother with two kids, one for sure crippled like her...that was to be the life of my sister. She had no money, no job, no insurance. I got the idea to adopt out the normal-looking kid. Since he was a twin, I figured he must have OI to some degree, but why not sell him while he still looked healthy?"

"How could you talk your own sister into selling her own child, a child who was possibly normal?" Mary Louise asked.

"Shut up!" She stood up, and started to slap her, but changed her mind.

"Because I got balls, lady. I got balls! ! I called that asshole, Wilson, who by then was scared to death of me. He was afraid I'd ruin his reputation, or his rich bitch wife's precious reputation. I told him that Mollie had twins, that one was good, and one was bad, and that he was to find a home for the good one, pronto, or I would see to it that his ass would fry. Actually, that was pretty smart of me, because he was a lot more useful alive and well than he was in jail or divorced. So he came through. I got $50,000 from the buyer--oh, sorry, the adopting parents. Excuse my rude and disrespectful behavior, you pompous motherfucking do-gooders!"

She was becoming a little manic, and I was again worried, not that I had ever stopped worrying any time during the past however long it had been.

"So, that started that scam. Wilson's lawyer, Henderson, sent me the money, and I gave some to Molly. Then that stupid schmuck Fischer started coming around when we were back in Lafayette, eventually married the crippled sister, and adopted the crippled kid. Mr. Good-guy. They moved to Port Arthur and left me in Lafayette at home. So, I got to thinkin', I got some big thing hangin' over old Eddie's head, so I convinced him to get me hired back at the hospital and advance my unqualified ass into administration, which he does so willingly if I'll just keep my little trap shut about him and his wandering pecker. He buys me this big, old townhouse, sends me money every month, I move up the ladder to V.P., and all is well. I send Mollie enough money to take care of the kid, Ol' Nolie provides for her and dotes on her and Johnny, and all is just peachy keen.

"And then, that old fuck Wilson calls me up and tells me last year that he's got the big 'C' and that he's tracked down both of the twins, and he's gonna leave them some dough when he dies. And is that okay with me, since he doesn't want his precious little reputation tarnished even in death, mind you. So I say, no, it isn't, and I'll get back to you. So I hire that nerd-ass nephew of mine to find the whereabouts of the other boy, and then I have leverage. I know who Stephen Huntley is.

"So, Wilson and I get together, and I tell him how to structure the deal, so that when he croaks, and I got no more sugar daddy to rely on, then I have my alternatives."

"You mean, Beverly, that as trustee, you could...kill your own nephews if you had to? For money?" Shut up, Mary Louise, I wanted to say.

"A woman's got to do what a woman's got to do."

"Did you kill Ed?" Mary Louise, she's going to kill you, I thought!

"That was the best part. He was lying there, all wide awake after his surgery when I walked into his room with my little syringe of medicine. I told him what it was as I pushed it into the IV. He tried to ring for the nurse, but it worked too fast. I enjoyed watching him become paralyzed, not able to breathe. I know that for a minute or so, he was conscious, but couldn't move a muscle. As for runnin' down the

Huntley kid in Nolan's truck, tough shit. I watched the house for months to find the right time to do it."

"What about Johnny? How could you do that?" Mary Louise asked. I was surprised Beverly hadn't gone into a rage, and blown both of us away with all these questions.

"He was miserable, and so was Mollie. She needed a life, and I gave it to her. He was dead anyway...But now, for the grand finale." She pulled a syringe out of her jacket pocket, pulled off the cap, and squirted a little out the end.

"By the time they sort through this house, and your charred bodies, there won't be any trace of anything in your worthless carcasses except a few bones. It's been nice, but I must be going. This will hold you both still while you fry."

As she leaned over to inject my thigh with the needle, I looked over at Mary Louise.

"I'm sorry about all this. I love you. I always will."

As the needle poked through my shorts, a shot rang out, and Beverly Richard fell bleeding into my lap. Susan Beeson stepped the rest of the way out of the closet, came over, pushed the obviously dead intruder onto the floor and untied us. Mary Louise and I embraced each other, then Susan.

"Good job, Mary Louise," Susan said. "Just like we planned it." And they gave each other the high five.

CHAPTER 48

POETIC JUSTICE

T he house was a mass of confusion for a while with emergency personnel from the Houston Fire Department, staff from the county coroner's office, and at least a squadron of police officers. Seeking solace from the crowd, I found myself in the kitchen with Mary Louise, Susan Beeson, and Stan Lombardo, Chief of Police.

"You all right, Brady?" Stan had asked.

"I guess so, Stan. Was all this some sort of set-up?" I asked as I tried to make coffee.

"Sort of. Something Susan here thought of, and Mary Louise agreed to."

"She could have been killed. We both could have, Stan."

"True. Anything's possible, but unlikely with my daughter here as bodyguard." He patted her on the back. There had been a lot of back-patting in my life in the last few weeks.

"I don't understand something, Stan. Why did Beverly come here? And how did you know she would? Why would she think Mary Louise and I would know enough to bother with us? It makes no sense to me."

Susan answered. "Well, I think it started a long time ago, probably last year, when she used Setec to find the whereabouts of the child she had made arrangements to sell. In the letter Brad sent her, he mentioned that he had tried to keep his business partner, J.J. Brady out of it, but was unable to. I'm sure she figured out that he was your son. If she hadn't known then, she knew it after your picture was in the paper and after the TV interview. In fact, after she killed both Stevie and her nephew, Johnny, I wouldn't be surprised if she arranged the trip to Port Arthur for her and Brad just so she could come by your house and see you face to face. I think maybe she thought she could see suspicion in your eyes, if you had any. But at that point, I don't think you really suspected her, and if you did, she probably charmed you with her clothes, jewelry, car, and role as the loving aunt and sister. Not to mention that story about her gambling.

"However, what she didn't know was that on Thursday, when Gene and I met you and Mary Louise at the house and heard how Wilson had written her into the trust as trustee, and how she stood to make five million if both boys died, I had a feeling she was the culprit. So, Dad got a judge friend to allow us to tap her and the Fischer's phones.

"The only significant call we picked up was on Friday afternoon. And if my calculations are correct, Mollie Fischer was on the phone to Beverly while you and I were standing in the yard talking to Nolan Fischer. Mollie told her a Dr. Brady was there with a woman from the Houston Police Department. I think she put two and two together, and decided that you had figured something out. She couldn't risk it, so she came after you."

"Well, I wonder how long she had been stalking the house. She could have hit us anytime, even before that if she thought that Mary Louise and I knew enough," I said.

"We had it covered, Doc," Stan said. "Susan insisted I put plain-clothes men around your house starting Thursday night after she and Gene left."

"What about Mary Louise? How did this conspiracy come about?"

248

Susan spoke up again. "I called your wife Friday morning and told her that if we went to Port Arthur and if Molly Fischer called her sister after we were there, it was my guess that Beverly would soon come after you two. It was a hunch. Police work. That's what we do, Doc."

"How did she get in? And how were we allegedly being protected after that conversation you tapped into on Friday?" I was irritated, having recovered from the shock of being tied up and having a gun waved in my face.

"Well, you fell asleep on the way home. I called Dad and told him what we had learned at the Fischer house, and, since he was at that time manning the wiretap recorder, he dispatched two more plainclothes people to your neighborhood. I then called Mary Louise and filled her in on my plan. She agreed to cooperate."

"You know, Susan, we went to a movie and dinner Friday night. She could have followed us..."

"We had you covered. All the way."

"You're kidding?"

"Nope."

I looked at Mary Louise. "And you knew all this?"

"Yes, dear, I did. I'm sorry I kept it from you, but Susan and I thought it would be best that way." She put her arm around my waist and squeezed. At least she didn't pat me.

"But what about Saturday? Was all that planned? The golf tournament and everything?"

"No, that was a lucky break. That was planned months ago. What wasn't planned was for Mary Louise to forego her tennis tournament. She and I spent the day together, planning what to do in the event Beverly showed up. It was a hunch, again, but I just had a feeling that she would somehow try to get to you today. I happened to be right." Susan was proud of herself, and I was beginning to let my anger fade. A little.

"Okay, I understand so far. But what about transportation?

There was no car, or motorcycle, that I noticed. How did she get in?"

"Remember I told you in the car coming back from Port Arthur that the officers had gone to Beverly's house and that her motorcycle was gone?" Susan asked me that question like I was in the third grade.

"Yes, ma'am."

She laughed. "Sorry, Doc. Well, we had men stationed in all the public areas on Westheimer, and all along the adjacent streets, on the lookout for a motorcycle. Guess where she parked?"

"No idea, Susan."

"In the Avalon Shopping Center, in front of Buffalo Hardware, at Westheimer and Kirby. She went into the hardware store, then into the Groove, the audio-video place, and then walked north on Kirby, crossed the street, and headed east on Avalon to your house. Our men picked her up immediately from the license plate on her bike. Followed her right to the house, without her knowing, of course."

"Aha! ! But we always keep the driveway's electric gate closed and the patio door locked. What did she do, walk up to the front door and knock?"

Mary Louise took over. "No, sweetie. I left the gate open and the back door unlocked. Susan and her men observed her every step of the way."

"Well, once she got into the house, how did you two geniuses know she wouldn't kill you both from the start?" I tried to act a little smarter, though unsuccessfully.

"She never knew I was in the closet, Doc. No reason to even suspect we were on to her. Mary Louise played like she was asleep in the chair, and Beverly came up the stairs and confronted her."

"Well, I think it was all too risky. Anything could have gone wrong."

"But it didn't, did it?" Chief Lombardo boomed in his oh-so-Italian accent. "It all worked, just like my baby planned," he said as he hugged Susan.

"Dad!"

"Oh. Sorry." It was nice to see that he, on occasion, acted like a father.

About that time, there was a commotion at the front door. One of the uniformed officers came in and said that my attorney was there, demanding to speak to me.

"My attorney? What's his name."

"Huntley," he said. "But there are a whole bunch of TV and newspaper people out there, and it's all we can do to keep them out of the yard, much less the house!"

"Let him in. He's my next-door neighbor," I said.

Pete struggled in, wanting to know everything that had happened. I introduced him to Susan and Stan, while Mary Louise hugged him and then fixed him a cup of coffee. I let Susan fill him in. It was the right thing to do, since it was his child who had been killed at the start of the entire ordeal.

He was silent for a moment, digesting what she had told him.

"Interesting," he said. "That explains this." He handed an envelope to Susan. She passed it to her father, then to Mary Louise and I.

"One of my partners, who heads up the Trust Department, called me yesterday morning. He had heard through the country club connection that Ed Wilson had died. He gave me an envelope that was to be opened only if, for whatever reason, the two beneficiaries of the trust had not survived Wilson's death. I opened it this morning."

It was the final hurrah, the last piece of the puzzle that had stumped me. It had been made out by Henderson and signed by Wilson in June, 1993, right before the attorney had died. It stated simply that if there was any evidence of foul play surrounding the deaths of Wilson or the children, the trust money would not go to Beverly Richard, but rather, to the parents of the children involved. Beverly had been screwed from the beginning, and she hadn't had a clue. Poetic justice had been served.

When all the debris had been cleared and our house had been

freed of guests, and I had assured myself that the two police officers that Stan had stationed in the front yard were keeping away unwanted visitors, I took a shower. I then started a bubble bath for Mary Louise, and while the water was running, went downstairs to the bar and opened a bottle of her favorite champagne, Verve Cliquot. I brought it up the stairs on a silver tray holding two crystal champagne glasses.

She was in the tub. "What's the occasion?"

"Our survival."

"Oh. Good thought."

I poured us each a glass.

"Here's to you," I said.

"And to you, young man." She paused. "Are you going to watch me take a bath?"

"No place I'd rather be, lady." We sipped for a moment.

"So what do you think will happen to Molly Fischer, Jim Bob?"

"I doubt she really had much to do with any of it, except to call her sister and tell her that Susan and I were at her house asking about events that occurred ten years earlier. I think she's suffered enough, don't you?"

"Probably. It's all just too much for me to imagine. To think that a woman like Beverly would kill three people, including two children, her own nephews, for money."

"The criminal mind is a hard thing to figure."

"I guess." She paused. "You don't think Brad played any part it this, do you? I would hate to think so."

"I seriously doubt it. It's ironic that it was his concern about the license plate change that brought it all home. If Beverly had only known. Of course, it's a good thing she didn't, or he and J.J. might have been in danger, too."

As we drank our champagne, I wished there weren't so many bubbles in the bath water. I couldn't see a thing below Mary Louise's neck.

"So, I have one day left on my so-called vacation. What do you want to do tomorrow?"

"Well, it's Easter Sunday."

"Really? I guess I forgot."

"Yes. It comes every year, Jim Bob."

I was a little embarrassed, not being much of a churchgoer.

"Guess we should go, huh? Think the roof will cave in on me?"

"Sounds like the right thing to do. And I think the roof will hold up just fine."

As we sipped our champagne, I realized how truly thankful I was to have this woman as my partner. I figured it was a good time to go and pay my respects to the Great Matchmaker.

"By the way, Bennie Williams called today. Said the band was playing at the Satellite Lounge tonight and asked if you'd be interested in sitting in with them."

"What time do they start?"

"Ten. It's only 9:30. You can make it."

"I'd love to play, but I'd hate to leave you after all we've been through today."

"Jim Bob, I can't think of a better time for you to go and play some blues."

Neither could I.

Made in the USA
Monee, IL
02 December 2019